A GIANT
UNSEEN HAND

and other drama

Darren Baker

Published by Handshake Press

ISBN: 978-1-7392249-0-5

Contents

About the author
Darren Baker grew up in South Carolina. He served aboard a submarine before attending the University of Connecticut, where took his degree in Russian and German. He has lived in the Czech Republic since 1992.

A Giant Unseen Hand

Characters

Captain of a doomed flight
Co-pilot of the doomed flight
Barry, the flight attendant
Busybody, the captain's neighbor
Franta, Busybody's husband (non-speaking role)
Neighbor, the captain's other neighbor
Official of the European Union

Act I

Scene one
The scene shows what looks like an island with the sound of waves splashing ashore. Captain is sitting in her airline's uniform. Co-pilot is also wearing the uniform and is lying unconscious next to her. She grabs him by the arm and shakes him awake. He sits up startled.

Co-pilot What? What's wrong? Where are we?

Captain On an island.

Co-pilot How did we get here?

Captain You don't remember?

Co-pilot I must have blacked out. I remember going into the water and that's it.

Captain You're right "that's it". You were face down in the water. I had to pull you into the lifeboat by myself. We then drifted all night until we hit this island.

Co-pilot Did anybody else make it? Are we the only survivors?

Captain It looks like it.

Co-pilot So all the others went down with the plane?

Captain Probably. I kept calling out in case somebody else was in the water, but nobody answered.

Co-pilot That's terrible. A plane crashes and only the pilots survive? It won't look good for our career.

Captain Career? Are you forgetting who was on board? All those rich guys going to Tampa Bay to watch the final of the Stanley Cup. Half the Czech economy probably sank with them.

Co-pilot That's right, the final is tonight. I was really looking forward to being there.

Captain Ach, you men are pathetic. Tampa has one Czech guy playing for them and you act like it's our national team.

Co-pilot I'm not big on hockey, but I saw the menu for the VIP suite. Unbelievable. Champagne, caviar, truffles. Even the snails sound good.

Captain Don't talk like that. We have no food or water, we're stranded who knows where.

Co-pilot But there are probably search planes looking for us right now. We can't be that far from where we crashed.

Captain You don't understand. We are in the Bermuda Triangle. We could be anywhere or nowhere. Who knows what we'll find on this island.

Co-pilot I hope we find something to eat. I didn't have any dinner before we left.

Captain (*She starts fidgeting*) Is that all you can think about right now?

Co-pilot What's the matter?

Captain I have a problem.

Co-pilot Other than being stuck on an island with no food or drink?

Captain Yes!

Co-pilot What is it?

Captain I have been a pilot all my life. It's the only career I ever wanted. I love flying and seeing places all over the world. The money has also been good as you know from what those VIPs paid for chartering this flight.

Co-pilot Yeah, one of them tipped me 500 crowns for carrying his golf clubs on board.

Captain He did? Why didn't Barry do it?

Co-pilot You mean our American flight attendant? All he did was play with his phone the whole time. Why did the airline hire somebody so useless?

Captain They didn't. He worked for one of the companies owned by the VIPs. He said he was from Tampa, so they took him along to act as a flight attendant and tour guide.

Co-pilot He was totally useless. I had to load most of the luggage by myself.

Captain (*Snaps at him*) Well, you're here and he isn't, so be happy!

Co-pilot Fine. What about the rest of your story?

Captain So flying has been good but not for my back. It started hurting more and more until finally I decided to quit, but they made me captain. I decided to stick it out for a few more years but the pain got worse. Finally the doctor prescribed painkillers for me. They were perfect. The pain went away and I could keep on flying.

Co-pilot So what's the problem?

Captain The problem is I couldn't stop taking them, even when I wasn't in pain. I found out later that these pills are opioids, something like morphine. They make you addicted.

Co-pilot Addicted? And you're flying planes!

Captain It's not like marijuana or cocaine!

Co-pilot No, just heroin.

Captain Look, they were by prescription. They're legal. That's why I never failed any drug tests.

Co-pilot At least it explains what you were doing up there.

Captain What do you mean?

Co-pilot I remember you were acting all weird before the crash. You took the plane out of autopilot for no reason, started making all these strange turns, going up and down.

Captain That's because we entered the Bermuda Triangle! I had the feeling some giant unseen hand had taken control of the plane.

Co-pilot I can't wait to hear you tell the crash investigators that.

Captain (*She raises her fist*) I've had enough of your sarcasm and lack of understanding! (*She suddenly curls up in pain*) Shit!

Co-pilot What's wrong? I didn't hit you.

Captain No, you idiot! It's the withdrawal symptoms. They're making my whole body ache. It feels worse than any back pain I ever had.

Co-pilot Is there something I can do?

Captain Hold my hand. (*She takes his hand but starts to crush it. He jerks it back.*)

Co-pilot Ow! You have brute strength. You know what, I think what you need is water. I'm going to go look for some. I'll be right back.

Captain Don't leave me now! I really need you to be here with me. Oh, this feels horrible!

Co-pilot Really, what you need is some water. I'll be right back. (*He leaves*)

Captain Don't leave me! You bastard! (*She pulls a small flask from out of her pants pocket and takes a swig from it*)

Scene two
Just as in scene one, Captain is sitting upright and Co-pilot is next to her asleep. She grabs him by the arm and pushes him awake.

Co-pilot What? What's wrong? Are you conscious?

Captain (*Sarcastically*) Apparently so. I'm tired like hell, but I don't feel the pain anymore.

Co-pilot That was terrible to watch and hear. You were screaming, delirious, crawling up and down the beach. But it looks like you're all right now. Great, huh?

Captain (*Looks at him with exhausted eyes*) What do you mean 'great'?

Co-pilot I mean you have the worst behind you. You're clean now, ready to start a new life. You might not have had that chance if we didn't crash.

Captain (*Still sarcastically*) Oh yes, this is much better.

Co-pilot Really, it's not so bad here. I've found all these coconuts and something else you're not going to believe.

Captain (*Pointing at the coconuts next to him*) Is there something in them to drink? I'm dying of thirst! (*She grabs one and starts to drink from it*)

Co-pilot Sure, but...

Captain Ach, it's full of coconut milk!

Co-pilot (*Grabs a coconut*) Here, take this one. I filled it with rainwater. (*She grabs it in and drinks all the water from it*)

Captain Got any more? (*He hands her another coconut and another*) Where did you get the water?

Co-pilot It's been raining for the past two days.

Captain What about food?

Co-pilot As you can see, there's pretty much only coconut here (*He hands her an open coconut filled with something*)

Captain I don't care, I'm starving. (*She grabs it and starts eating from it with her hands*) It doesn't taste like just coconut.

Co-pilot That's because I added some extra ingredients that I found. Some crab (*she nods okay*), some clams (*less okay*) and something that looks like bird droppings.

Captain (*She looks at him in horror*) Bird droppings? Why would you put that in there?

Co-pilot Because there's protein and vitamins in it. That's why manure makes good fertilizer. Besides, it's bitter and balances out the sweetness of the coconut.

Captain (*Looks at him like she is going to be sick*) If somebody told me that the first thing they ate after coming off drugs is bird droppings, I would call them a liar. (*She rushes to the back of the stage and retches*)

Co-pilot It's not that bad. I spent a whole morning trying to get the flavor just right.

Captain (*She comes back*) It's not that. I think I have another problem.

Co-pilot What?

Captain I'm pregnant.

Co-pilot What? Jesus! Drugs and pregnancy. Are you sure you're fit to fly?

Captain Hey, buddy, if it wasn't for me, you'd be at the bottom of the ocean right now with crabs eating you instead of vice versa.

Co-pilot You're right, I'm sorry. I owe you my life. But you sound like you didn't know you were pregnant when we took off.

Captain It's because I didn't, but I was hoping I was.

Co-pilot Excuse me?

Captain I told you before. I had sacrificed everything to be a pilot, including children and a normal family life. Well, here I am getting on in years and figured this would be my last chance. I would have a kid, go on maternity leave and use that time to get my back and addiction in order.

Co-pilot And... are you married?

Captain No, are you implying that I should be?

Co-pilot No, just... I mean...

Captain I know what you mean. Look, I'm a captain flying for an exclusive airline. When I get to my destination, I check into the hotel, go to the hotel bar, and end up having sex with an employee who works in the back of the plane. That's what all pilots do.

Co-pilot I don't do that.

Captain Maybe that's why you're not a captain.

Co-pilot But how would that even work on this flight? The only employee in the back is that useless American and we never arrived at the destination for you to have sex with him.

Captain Actually he and I already met. I flew the VIPs to another hockey match last month, to Boston with a different co-pilot, and they threw a party in the hotel the night before. They offered me a huge amount of money if I showed up in my captain's uniform and did a strip show for them.

Co-pilot How much money?

Captain Fifty thousand dollars.

Co-pilot Fifty thousand dollars! I only got 500 for the golf clubs and those things were heavy.

Captain One of the perks of being a captain. Barry was also at this party making drinks for the guys.

Co-pilot Who?

Captain Barry, the flight attendant. He escorted me home afterwards, I invited him up for coffee, and the next thing you know we were in bed together. Now it's sad to think that the father of my child is being eaten by crabs.

Co-pilot Then have I got news for you! Remember how I told you that I found something else on this island besides coconuts?

Captain Yes.

Co-pilot Well, it's this Barry guy.

Captain Barry! What do you mean? He's here? Where is he?

Co-pilot On the other side of the island. I was out exploring and looking for food when I saw something moving by the water's edge. I got closer and found out it was him.

Captain My God, he's alive! But why isn't he here, why is he still over there?

Co-pilot I led him over here, but it was right at the time you were going through the worst of your withdrawal. You were crawling on the beach, screaming like an injured sea lion.(*Pointing to the back of the stage*) He stepped out of the jungle there, saw you and said (*enter Barry*)

Barry I can't handle this.

Co-pilot He then turned (*Barry leaves*) and went back to the other side of the island.

Captain What? That bastard sees that I'm in trouble and just leaves? (*She stands, Co-pilot stands with her*) I'm not going to let him get away with this. He knocks me up and thinks he's going to abandon me here!

Co-pilot I don't think he knows you're pregnant.

Captain Well, he's going to know now! (*She starts to march towards the back of the stage, Co-pilot blocks her*)

Co-pilot I don't think that's a good idea. It's going to be tough to survive until help arrives. We can't start a war here. Let me go and talk to him about this.

Captain Forget it! I'm the captain and you're the crew. You guys work for me, I don't care if our plane is at the bottom of the ocean! (*She starts to push by him, but then checks herself*) Oh, shit! (*She runs to the back of the stage to retch again*).

Co-pilot I think it's better if I go talk to him about it. (*He leaves*)

Captain Don't you leave. You bastard! Aeh!

Scene three
Just like the other scenes, Captain, who's now heavily pregnant, is sitting upright and Co-pilot is next to her asleep. She grabs him by the arm and pushes him awake.

Co-pilot What? What is it? Is it time?

Captain No, but I've been doing some thinking.

Co-pilot (*Sitting up*) Again? (*Waiting*) What now?

Captain I don't think Barry deserves to be the father of my child. In all these months we've been on the island, he hasn't once come over here, hasn't tried to make me comfortable in my condition, hasn't brought me any gifts.

Co-pilot Gifts?

Captain Yeah, gifts. He can make something artistic out of coconuts or bring me a plant. That jungle is full of them.

Co-pilot Maybe he's just not a sensitive guy.

Captain Or maybe he's just an asshole, and I don't want an asshole to be the father of my child.

Co-pilot Aren't you a bit late for making that decision?

Captain Of course I can't change the fact that my baby has the genes of an asshole, but I'm not going to let him be raised by one. I therefore won't let Barry have any contact with him or her.

Co-pilot I don't think that will be any problem if you don't take him or her to the other side of the island. The guy absolutely refuses to come over here.

Captain I know, like it's some sort of territorial thing to him. That coming over here is beneath him. Can you believe that? Here we are pilots, people who defy the laws of gravity, and this guy, who's a completely uneducated loser, looks down on us.

Co-pilot That's because he's an American. Looking down on people is what they do.

Captain Well, screw him. If he thinks he's going to screw me and then enjoy the benefits without putting any work into it, he can think again.

Co-pilot Well, it's like I said, unless we get rescued, I don't think it will make much of a difference.

Captain That's what I'm telling you. This is a small island. Sooner or later, the isolation is going to get to him. Loneliness will start to eat him up inside and force him to crawl over here for companionship.

Co-pilot You mean to have sex with you?

Captain That's right, but he can forget it. I want nothing more to do with him.

Co-pilot So your plan is to be a single mother on a desert island?

Captain Not exactly, because I have you. I want you to be the father of my child.

Co-pilot Does that mean...?

Captain You will have to earn the sex first, buddy.

Co-pilot Don't worry. I wasn't planning to leave after the baby comes. It's tough enough just for the two of us to survive.

Captain But I'm not just talking about on the island. Even when we get off, I want you to be the father.

Co-pilot I'm flattered, but you don't know that much about me in real life. We only met just before the flight.

Captain I know enough about you. When you applied for the job, the airline asked me to review the personnel file they put together about you.

Co-pilot And what did you find out?

Captain I know that you're my age, you love flying, you're completely dependable, maybe you're gay...

Co-pilot Whoa. They put maybe I'm gay. Why, because I've never been married or have children?

Captain No, because they interviewed several flight attendants you worked with over the course of your career and not one of them said you ever made a pass at them or even flirted with them.

Co-pilot Hey, I never flirted or made passes at any of my male colleagues either. I'm strictly professional when it comes to work.

Captain Look, it's fine with me. I regret sleeping with so many crew members. Not that I didn't want to, but when you're a woman, people treat you differently. Especially other women.

Co-pilot Let's just make it clear for the record that I'm not gay. I've had girlfriends, but like you, my career always came first.

Captain That's why I told the company to hire you. They wanted some other guy who applied for the job because he looks like a movie star, but I told them to choose you. And that's what I'm doing now by choosing you over Barry to be the father of my child.

Co-pilot Thanks. So you're envisioning us getting off the island after the baby is born?

Captain I hope before. I don't want to give birth on the beach like an elephant seal.

Co-pilot If it comes to that, I promise to be with you. There's just one thing you should know about me that I never mentioned in my job interview.

Captain What's that?

Co-pilot My only weakness is needles and blood. I can't stand to look at either.

Captain (*Suspiciously*) Why are you telling me this now?

Co-pilot Because I can't be by you when the birth happens. I might puke.

Captain Typical! Just when you think you've finally found a man you can depend on, he turns and runs.

Co-pilot I won't run. I just can't be there, you know, witnessing it.

Captain I don't want you there as a witness. I want you to hold my hand or do something for me if I need it.

Co-pilot Well, I can stand behind a tree and sort of close my eyes if I have to come close.

Captain Forget it! I want you right next to me.

Co-pilot Really, I will be just behind the tree.

Captain (*Eyes go wide, takes a deep breath, contractions are starting*) Oh no, you see what you caused? I had a contraction. I'm going into labor now!

Co-pilot What? (*Turns to leave*)

Captain Don't you dare go anywhere! Get over here!

Co-pilot Sorry, I just can't. You know what, I'll go get Barry.

Captain What! Are you crazy? I told you I don't want that asshole here. Get over here!

Co-pilot It's for the best. I'll be right back. (*He leaves*)

Captain Don't you leave me you bastard! Aeh!

Scene four
Just like the other scenes, Captain is sitting upright holding a baby in jungle leaves and Co-pilot is next to her asleep. She grabs him by the arm and pushes him awake.

Co-pilot What? What is it? Is the baby all right?

Captain Yes, but I heard something.

Co-pilot Like what?

Captain Like woo-woo-woo-woo.

Co-pilot Maybe your giant unseen hand is back.

Captain You know, I'm getting tired of all your sarcasm.

Co-pilot And I'm getting tired of you waking me up for every little bullshit.

Captain Bullshit? You know what, I've been doing some thinking.

Co-pilot Oh God, not again. About what?

Captain About the way you abandoned me to give birth alone. I've decided you're not fit to be the father of my child, either.

Co-pilot I didn't abandon you. I went to get the actual father to be with you.

Captain And did he come?

Co-pilot Almost.

Captain What do you mean almost?

Co-pilot He followed me here but it was just as the baby was being born. (*Pointing to the back of the stage*) He stepped out of the jungle there, saw you screaming in pain and said (*enter Barry*)

Barry I can't handle this.

Co-pilot He then turned (*Barry leaves*) and went back to the other side of the island.

Captain I can't believe this! And where were you?

Co-pilot I told you, behind a tree. You didn't hear me telling you the whole time not to worry, that it'll be all right?

Captain Ach, you're as big a chickenshit as he is!

Co-pilot (*Sitting up*) You know, I'm tired of you treating me like this. Now I realize that you saved my life, but I have done nothing but make your life on this island as comfortable as possible even though I wasn't responsible for your drug problem or getting you pregnant.

Captain Oh, you're tired, are you? Well, excuse me, I'll let you go back to sleep.

Co-pilot Thank you! (*He lays back down*)

Captain God, what luck I have. Getting stranded on a desert island with two men and each is a bigger pussy than the other.

Co-pilot (*Standing up*) That's it! I'm out of here! (*He starts walking to the back of the stage*)

Captain Where are you going?

Co-pilot To the other side of the island.

Captain What? You're leaving me for him? I knew it!

Co-pilot Knew what? Go on, say it!

Captain There's nothing to say.

Co-pilot Well, I've got news for you. He ain't even there.

Captain What do mean?

Co-pilot He's gone. Disappeared.

Captain What? Aliens abducted Barry?

Co-pilot Aliens?

Captain This is the Bermuda Triangle!

Co-pilot So why didn't the aliens give us a lift to Prague?

Captain (*She throws a coconut at him*) You're so smart, where else can he be?

Co-pilot (*Points to the ocean*) There! Out there.

Captain The ocean?

Co-pilot Yes! I found what looks like pieces of sticks that he must have used to make a raft.

Captain You saw no sign of him at all?

Co-pilot No, but I did see a dorsal fin out in the water.

Captain Dorsal fin? You mean...

Co-pilot Yes. Jaws.

Captain My Barry? Eaten by sharks?

Co-pilot Not the same thing as being eaten by crabs, but close enough.

Captain You're a heartless bastard! Talking about the father of my child that way.

Co-pilot Hey, remember you made me the father of your child.

Captain Do you think I would ever let you raise her? Forget it.

Co-pilot That's it! (*He turns to leave*) I'm out of here!

Captain Oh, abandoning me again. Well, forget it. No matter where you go I will… (*She stands to follow him, then stops and screams as Co-pilot walks back cautiously and two figures dressed in containment clothing approach. She hides behind Co-pilot's back.*) I told you there were aliens around here. (*Stepping from behind Co-pilot*) Do, do you come in peace? (*The taller of the masked individuals sweeps the air with a contraption that makes a sci-fi sound*) Oh my God, it's a space weapon! (*She runs back behind Co-pilot, the masked individuals confer*) What are they saying?

Co-pilot How the hell should I know? This is your specialty. (*The shorter individual takes off her hood and mask*)

Captain Oh my God. Is that you?

Co-pilot You know her?

Captain Yes, she's my neighbor. What are you doing here?

Busybody I came here to bring you home.

Captain Home? But how? How did you know I was here? How did you even get here?

Busybody By helicopter. The pilot landed it way over there.

Captain (*She hits Co-pilot in the arm*) You see, I told you I heard something. (*Pointing to Co-pilot*) He didn't believe me when I told him there was a helicopter.

Co-pilot You didn't say anything about a helicopter. Just woo-woo-woo-woo-woo and a giant unseen hand and all that other garbage.

Busybody I can see you two have been on an island too long. It's time to get you off of here.

Captain Yes, but how did you find us?

Busybody It seems there were three of you on this island. A castaway was picked up on a raft who said he had survived a plane crash in this area.

Captain Oh my God, you found Barry? He's alive! Oh thank God. (*Co-pilot snarls at her*)

Busybody Yes, he came to my home to collect the keys to your house.

Captain Keys? To my house? Why?

Busybody He produced an e-will in which you left everything you own to him. Is that true? (*Co-pilot snarls at her again*)

Captain Well, yes. I figured it was a joke, because he was going on the same flight as me. If I die, he dies.

Co-pilot What a great sense of humor you have!

Captain But it doesn't matter because I'm alive.

Busybody That wasn't his story. He said you two sank with the plane and the VIPs on board. He's the only survivor.

Co-pilot Typical.

Captain That scumbag!

Busybody I thought there was something fishy about it all, so I got the families of the VIPs to rent a satellite to zoom in to see if we couldn't find other survivors. We found this island and saw two figures moving about. So we went to him and he admitted you were still alive.

Captain I hope he's arrested and awaiting trial.

Busybody Actually, he's still in your house, but he's not free to go outside.

Co-pilot He's under house arrest?

Busybody No, he's under quarantine. You see, shortly after your plane disappeared, a terrible pandemic broke out all over the world. It's a new virus that has already killed millions of people.

Co-pilot My God. Where did it come from?

Busybody Science still doesn't know, but they have narrowed the origin down to an unknown animal.

Co-pilot Like a unicorn?

Busybody All I can tell you is the virus is nothing like we've seen before, but there's now a vaccine for it and once we get the whole world injected, everything will go back to normal.

Captain So why are you wearing all that protective clothing? The virus obviously isn't here.

Busybody I know, that's what we were checking for with our special detector here. But the rules say we have to wear protection any place where there are unvaccinated people.

Captain (*Pointing to Busybody's partner*) Why doesn't your partner take off his hood?

Busybody You know him. It's Franta, the doctor who lives on our street.

Captain That's Franta? Hi, Franta. (*He waves at her*)

Co-pilot Why doesn't he take off his hood?

Busybody The rules say one of us must be completely contained until you have been tested and vaccinated. Are you ready?

Co-pilot Ready for what?

Busybody To test and vaccinate you.

Co-pilot What's the point if we obviously don't have the virus.

Busybody Sorry, but those are the rules.

Captain Quit making trouble and let's just get out of here. (*Franta steps forward, tips Captain's head back, and inserts an extremely long swab up her nose. He pulls it out, measures it with his contraption, looks at it and nods at Busybody.*)

Busybody Oh dear, your test shows you're positive.

Captain Really? (*Hitting Co-pilot*) You see, I told you I'm a positive person!

Busybody No, positive means you have the virus!

Captain What? How's that possible? I've been stuck on this hellhole for a whole year!

Busybody (*Looking at Franta*) Yeah, Franta, how is that possible? (*A worried Franta adjusts his machine, measure again, and shakes his head*) Okay, you're negative. Next. (*Franta goes up to Co-pilot*)

Co-pilot What's the point if you've already switched your contraption to negative? (*Franta performs the same test on him. It's also negative.*)

Busybody Good, now the vaccination. (*Franta takes out a syringe*)

Co-pilot Wait a minute. You said this pandemic broke out a year ago. You're telling us they've already developed a vaccine for it?

Busybody Several vaccines. But all of them seem to be working.

Co-pilot Seem to be working?

Busybody Yeah. You can still get ill, but not so bad.

Co-pilot I thought vaccines were meant to prevent disease.

Busybody Look, this is all new. What do you want?

Co-pilot (*Sarcastically*) Oh, I don't know. Maybe just the full story.

Busybody What do you care if it gets you off this island?

Co-pilot Maybe because the last time I was in civilization, the drugmakers were dumping opioids on the market. They got caught and had to pay billions. For all I know, they're dumping these vaccines on the market to recoup those billions and make more billions on top of them.

Busybody (*Looking at Captain*) Is he always this difficult?

Captain You don't know the half of it.

Busybody The helicopter's waiting. Do you want to leave this island or not?

Captain I sure do. Give me the shot, I'm getting out of here! (*Franta gives her the shot*) There. I'm still alive, ain't I? (*She suddenly starts gagging and going into convulsions*)

Co-pilot (*To Busybody*) Do something!

Busybody (*Hitting Franta*) Franta, do something! (*He looks left, looks right, looks left again, completely at a loss*)

Captain (*Jumping up laughing*) Hah, just joking.

Busybody Joking? You about gave me a heart attack!

Co-pilot You call that funny?

Captain Come on, lighten up. We're going home!

Busybody (*To Co-pilot*) What about you? The helicopter is waiting.

Co-pilot What if I decide I don't want the vaccine?

Busybody It's not your choice. The mandate says anyone who wants a normal life needs to be vaccinated. This island doesn't look very normal, so if you want to get off, take the jab.

Co-pilot That sounds like extortion.

Busybody No, it's coercion. Big difference.

Captain Do it, goddammit!

Busybody Look, it's a perfect storm of vaccination. It's safe. (*Co-pilot looks unconvinced*) It's effective. (*Still unconvinced*) It's free.

Co-pilot Fine, but I'm doing it under protest. (*He closes his eyes*)

Captain That's the real problem here. He's afraid of needles. (*Franta approaches Co-pilot and injects him*)

Busybody Good. We're going to go now, but we'll be back in a month.

Captain What, we've had our shot. We're going with you.

Busybody Oh, I guess I should have told you. This vaccine requires two doses. You get one shot, have to wait one month for it to start working, then you get the second shot.

Captain We have to stay here another month. I have a baby here!

Busybody A baby? You had a baby? It looks like you two have been doing more than just fighting on this island.

Captain I have no more milk. We're giving her coconut milk, but that can't be healthy.

Busybody That is serious. I guess what we can do is take you off the island, put you in quarantine, and administer your second shot there. Where is this baby? (*Captain goes to the side and pulls out the baby bundled up in leaves*) Boy or girl?

Captain Girl.

Busybody Oh, she's so sweet.

Captain (*Looking at Co-pilot*) Yes, she's the only one on this island who doesn't complain.

Busybody That's perfect, because we have to give her the shot too.

Captain What?

Co-pilot Even a baby?

Busybody Of course. Every person gets a vaccination. The only way we can beat this pandemic is by turning our planet into a giant bubble where every human being is breathing the same antibodies.

Co-pilot You're saying you have vaccinated the whole world?

Busybody Not yet. There are some dissenters like you still refusing to comply. No matter how many times you tell them that they are a menace to public safety, they keep crying that they have rights. But don't worry. We have plans for them.

Co-pilot Extortion or coercion?

Busybody Both.

Captain But are you sure the vaccination is safe for a baby?

Busybody Well...just to be on the safe side, let's give her only half a dose. (*Franta nods his head. He pulls out a needle, squirts out half the contents towards the audience, then jabs the baby with it. She starts crying like hell*).
Captain Oh, I'm sorry, sweetheart, but we're doing it for your own benefit.

Busybody Does she always cry that loud?

Captain No, never. Not even when we give her coconut milk.

Busybody Terrible. Let's get out of here before it drives me nuts. (*Busybody and Franta leave, Captain and Co-pilot take one more look around them, then at each other, and leave the stage. There's a pause, followed by the sound of the helicopter taking off. Busybody re-enters in her underwear and runs to the front of the stage.*) I'm free, I'm free!! (*Franta re-enters, still fully dressed in PPE and carrying his medical case*) Franta, we're free at last. Take off that shitty costume and fuck me here on the beach! (*Franta slowly removes his helmet, revealing the head of a greenish lizard/frog-like creature. He lunges for her with arms wide open. Busybody screams as she evades his grasp. She runs to the back of the stage and circles back to the front, waving her arms to alert the helicopter.*) Help! Help! (*Hot on her trail, the creature comes up behind her and drags her away.*)

Act II

Scene one
The stage is made to look like a meeting room with a table and four chairs. Official enters holding a plastic cup of coffee with a lid on it followed by Neighbor. She sits down, Neighbor starts to talk, but she puts up a hand to stop her while she takes off the lid, adds sugar to the coffee, and takes a sip.

Official There, that's better. Now what's the problem?

Neighbor (*Sitting down*) They can't find a babysitter.

Official Who can't find a babysitter?

Neighbor The other two members of the committee. The rules say for an emergency session we all have to be here.

Official Are these two married?

Neighbor No, but they have this baby together that nobody wants to babysit.

Official Why not?

Neighbor Because she cries all the time, day and night, endless crying. I know it, because I live next door.

Official Don't they understand the gravity of this situation? The reason why I'm here?

Neighbor To be honest, it wasn't really that clear in the conference call.

Official Well, let me make it clear to you now. You live on the worst street in the European Union. I'm not just talking about the Czech Republic; I'm talking about the whole European Union. Your street has failed the top two priorities of the Global Crisis Management Policy.

Neighbor That part is clear. We have had some problems. But we are not clear on who you are and why you're here.

Official I'm the Czech representative to the European Union's Street Committees Commission. I have come here to figure out what's wrong.

Neighbor We know what's wrong, we just don't know how to fix it.

Official You can start by having a street committee that knows how to meet on time.

Neighbor I'm afraid we're not your typical street committee. Are you aware of the status of the two people we're waiting for?

Official You mean besides that they're late?

Neighbor They're the two pilots who crashed while flying a planeload of VIPs to watch a hockey match in America. That was a year and a half ago, just before the start of the pandemic. They survived and spent a year on a desert island before they were rescued.

Official Everyone knows this story. That crash wiped out the richest people in this country. It's why we're still in a recession.

Neighbor The later part of the story is that the black box from the plane showed that the captain of the flight did these crazy moves that caused the crash. When they asked her about them, she said she was trying to avoid, and I quote, some "giant unseen hand."

Official Was she on drugs or something?

Neighbor The transportation safety board decided that she was and took away her pilot's license away. They also took away the co-pilot's license because he didn't report her.

Official How could he report her if he too was stranded on the island?

Neighbor That's what he kept saying to defend himself, but the rules make no exception.

Official And rules shouldn't make exceptions, else they're not rules.

Neighbor So the captain needed a new job, and since she lives on the street, and no one wants to be on the committee, she joined it.

Official I remember reading that the captain had a baby while on the island. Maybe the crash was caused by the two of them having sex in the cockpit?

Neighbor No, she was having sex with the flight attendant. He also survived the crash.

Official What? She was screwing the flight attendant in the cockpit and the co-pilot was there?

Neighbor That would make a better story, but apparently it happened a month before the flight. She ended up pregnant, but the flight attendant decided not to stay for the birth and left the island on a raft.

Official Sounds like something my third husband would do. (*Enter Captain and Co-pilot wearing masks. They take them off*)

Captain Sorry, we're late. We had trouble finding a babysitter. Have we already started?

Official No, because we're waiting for you.

Captain You must be the official, the lady we were talking to on the conference call. Nice to meet you in person.

Official Please have a seat. (*They sit down*) As everybody knows, your street has been judged the worst in the EU in meeting the targets of global warming and the pandemic. Let's see if we can't fix things, shall we?

Captain All right. With global warming, every house on the street has installed solar panels except one, but we just can't get the owners to cooperate.

Official Why not? The EU is footing the entire bill, for installation and recycling.

Captain I'm afraid they're a special case. They're the two people who were sent to take us off the island. They're my neighbors, a married couple.

Official (*To Neighbor*) I thought you're the neighbor.

Neighbor I'm the other neighbor.

Official Why were these two sent?

Neighbor Because he's a doctor and she's a bit of a busybody.

Captain The thing is, as we were walking to the helicopter, she suddenly took off her mask, ripped off her protective clothing and ran into the jungle screaming, "I'm free, I'm free."

Co-pilot And he ran after her.

Official Why didn't you wait for him to catch her?

Co-pilot Because he turned to us and did this. (*He flips her his middle* *finger. Captain slaps it down.*) Then he disappeared with her.

Official You're telling me they flipped out? From what? Not the pandemic, surely.

Co-pilot We don't know.

Captain Yes, we do. The island is in the Bermuda Triangle.

Official Ach, you sound like those wackos opposing industrial-scale vaccination. Look, just appropriate their house as an emergency measure and install the panels.

Neighbor There's a special rule that says when you're giving vaccines in the field and end up doing something crazy, you're free from all liability. We can't do anything against them until they regain their senses and come home.

Official How do you know they're even alive? Maybe they went for a swim and got eaten by sharks.

Captain Because every month we get a shopping list from them.

Official A what?

Captain A shopping list. They send us a list of all the supplies they want and we send them to them.

Official What! That's crazy.

Neighbor The rules say we have to support them until they recover.

Co-pilot And you should see his shopping list. Champagne, caviar, truffles. That's why we're running a negative budget.

Official I don't believe this. Using the pandemic to live the good life!

Co-pilot Go figure.

Captain What do we do about it?

Official How the hell should I know? Brussels has more than 5,000 training courses, but not a single one for this scenario. Let me think about it. Go on with the next crisis.

Captain The next crisis is the pandemic. Again, the problem is one holdout, someone who refuses to get vaccinated.

Official Who is this menace to society? (*The other three look at each other*)

Captain/Co-pilot/Neighbor Barry.

Official Who?

Captain/Co-pilot/Neighbor Barry! The flight attendant.

Official But I read he was picked up off a life raft. They would've vaccinated him before bringing him ashore.

Neighbor He told the people who rescued him that he had already been vaccinated, only they neglected to ask him which one. It was only after he started squatting here did we check and find out he doesn't have a vaccination passport.

Official Squatting where?

Captain In my house!

Official Your house? All three of you are living in the same house together?

Captain Yes, but just like on the island. We're in the front of the house and he's in the back. He refuses to get vaccinated until I sign over the whole house to him.

Official He's practicing extortion in the middle of a pandemic?

Co-pilot Who isn't?

Official Excuse me?

Neighbor Don't mind him. He's a dissenter.

Official A dissenter on your street committee? No wonder you have problems.

Co-pilot What's wrong with questioning your government?

Official What's wrong with it is that we're in an emergency situation. Public safety is at risk. Our planet is at risk. Science would have saved us by now were it not for you dissenters spreading misinformation and disinformation.

Co-pilot And the government and drugmakers are only spreading truthful, reliable information. Is that it?

Official Of course. They care about people.

Co-pilot (*Looking at Captain*) All right, you win. I believe in the Bermuda Triangle.

Official So what are we going to do about this Frank?

Neighbor Franta.

Captain Barry!

Neighbor Whoever. I was hoping it wouldn't come to this, but I suggest we institute code 111.

Official I'm thinking the same thing. Who will be the jabber?

Neighbor It will have to be you. He knows all three of us.

Official Fine. But we need a backup plan in case it doesn't work. Be ready to institute code 222.

Neighbor That's pretty drastic.

Official Do you have everything you need for it? (*Co-pilot stands up and goes to the locker at the back of the stage. He opens it up to reveal two marksman rifles inside. He takes one out.*) What's the second rifle for?

Neighbor We have had a problem with pigeons roosting on the solar panels of our street. All their bird droppings have robbed us of solar energy. So we shoot at them to scare them away.

Official Wait a minute. (*She starts scrolling through her phone*) Does that have something to do with what I saw here in your negative budget? The millions you spend every year on buying new solar panels?

Neighbor I'm afraid so. Somebody here doesn't know how to shoot straight. (*They look at Co-pilot*)

Captain I think he does it deliberately. He likes bird droppings.

Official (*Looking at Co-pilot*) Can we trust you to hit this Frank...

Neighbor Franta.

Captain Barry!

Official ...hit this troublemaker and not a solar panel?

Co-pilot Don't worry. (*Looking at Captain*) I've had Barry in my sights for a long time.

Official Hopefully we won't have to go that far. (*Stands*) Otherwise we may have to go even further.

Neighbor (*Stands*) You mean...

Official Yes. Code 333. (*Official exits with Neighbor following her*)

Captain (*To Co-pilot*) Load the vaccine now so you don't forget it here.

(*Exits*)

Co-pilot (*To himself*) Always taking me for an idiot. (*He pulls a dart out of his pocket, then looks confused as he tries several ways to insert the dart into the barrel of the gun*)

Scene two
The scene shows what looks like the door to a house on the right. Official, Captain, Co-pilot and Neighbor, who's holding a package, enter from the left. Co-pilot is carrying a marksman rifle with a scope on it. All are wearing masks. The cries of a baby can be heard.

Official Is that the baby?

Captain Yes. I told you we couldn't find a babysitter, so Barry is watching her.

Official You mean the father?

Co-pilot I'm the father!

Neighbor Look, people, let's get this over with, all right? (*She prepares the syringe and hands it to Official*)

Official (*To Captain and Neighbor*) You two be ready on both sides of the door in case things get rough. (*To Co-pilot*) You go take your position over there. Remember, aim for his shoulder. Hitting him in the head or the heart won't do any good. It's got to be the shoulder. And don't pull the trigger unless I tell you to. Are we ready?

Captain Be careful. He's more belligerent than ever.

Neighbor Who can blame him with that all crying in there?

Captain Hey, my baby was fine until she got vaccinated!

Neighbor Oh right, blame it on the vaccine.

Official Quiet or you'll give us away. (*Captain and Neighbor hide on each side of the door. Official hides the syringe behind her back and knocks. Nothing. She knocks again. Nothing. She bangs on the door. Barry angrily opens it and storms out.*)

Barry What the fuck do you want?!

Official (*Takes a step back in shock, puts her free hand on her heart*) Oh dear! (*Breathless*) Help me, sir, I think I'm having a heart attack.

Barry (*Pause*) I can't handle that. (*Turns and walks inside. The furious Official raises the syringe.*)

Official Then handle this! (*She runs in after him.*)

Barry (*From inside*) What the...! (*A struggle ensues.*)

Official Get in here. I need your help!! (*Captain and Neighbor gesture to each other to go inside, then run into each other before entering, where the struggle continues. Suddenly Captain flies out the door as if Barry threw her out, followed by Neighbor and Official.*) That's it, Code 222! (*Nothing happens*)

Neighbor Code 222! (*Nothing*)

Captain Code 222! (*Still nothing. Barry appears in the doorway with a water machine gun*)

Barry Handle this! (*He starts squirting the three of them*)

Captain/Official/Neighbor Fire!

Barry (*Looking confused*) I am firing.

Co-pilot (*Jumping out from his hiding place*) Hah! Smile, Barry! (*Aiming his rifle*)

Barry Oh, fuck. (*Walks backward into his house. Co-pilot fires. Barry falls dead. The women look stunned.*)

Neighbor My God, was that a real bullet? (*Goes inside to inspect Barry*)

Official (*To Co-pilot*) What the hell was that? I said code 222, not 333!

Captain (*To Co-pilot*) You idiot! You grabbed the wrong gun. (*Neighbor emerges*) Is he...?

Neighbor Yeah, dead. Shot right between the eyes.

Captain Oh, Barry! (*Runs into the house*)

Official (*To Co-pilot*) That makes you an idiot twice over. I told you to aim for the shoulder!

Neighbor Oh my God, what will we do? This is terrible.

Official Maybe terrible, but you fixed your problem. There's no more unvaccinated people on your street. No more alive, anyway. You can remove your masks. (*She removes hers, the others follow suit*)

Neighbor Yeah, but how do we explain this?

Official Nothing to explain. Under the Emergency Authorization Act, no one is liable for any vaccine administration that goes wrong if, and this is the key part, it's done with planning and professionalism.

Neighbor What!? (*Pointing at Barry*) You call this planning and professionalism?

Official I've seen worse. The only thing is, the rule says we must be out in the field. Inside his house could be a problem.

Captain It's my house!

Official Whoever's house it is, it's still iffy. We need for him to be more on the outside. Grab his legs and drag him to at least across the doorstep. (*Captain and Neighbor grab him by one leg each and drag him until his legs are visible on stage. Captain looks at Co-pilot doing nothing to help*).

Captain I remember a time when you used to be a gentleman.

Co-pilot I doubt that.

Official All right. (*Pointing at Barry*) Let me handle this with the authorities. (*Scrolling through her phone*) For now, I am extending the Emergency Authorization Act for your street committee by one week. That's how much time you've got to fix your other problem. Good luck, let me know how it turns out. (*Exits*)

Neighbor I can't believe what I just saw. An EU official who gets things done. I will go order the helicopter. (*Exits*)

Co-pilot Helicopter? What's going on here?

Captain Oh, God, you're dense. How many bullets do you still have in that gun?

Co-pilot A full magazine minus one.

Captain That should do it. Come on. We're going back to the island.

Co-pilot To the island? (*Indicates shooting*) You mean Busybody and Franta too?

Captain Why not? We're on a roll. Come on. (*He follows her and she stops him short*) What are you doing? Go get the child!

Co-pilot Oh, yes. (*Stepping over Barry*) Sorry, Barry. Covid's a bitch.

Scene three
Back to the island, where Busybody is sitting on the beach with Franta sleeping next to her. He is covered head to toe in PPE and still wearing his helmet. She shakes him awake.

Busybody Franta, I've been thinking. (*He sits up and shakes his head*) We've tried coconut milk, crab juice and bird droppings, but nothing has helped your skin problem. I know you don't want to go swimming because you're afraid the sharks will think you're a fish and eat you, but spending a long time submerged in saltwater might restore your old face. (*He shakes his head*) Well, I'm getting sick of looking at you with and without your helmet on. Either you fix that fishy face of yours or I'm out of here! (*A shot rings out and Busybody falls down dead. Franta turns, a second shot rings out and he falls dead too. Neighbor enters wearing beachwear and walks up to their bodies.*)

Neighbor Damn, that dumbass co-pilot's aim really is getting better. (*Looking around*) I can see why these two morons wanted to stay here. This place is beautiful. Maybe I'll stay for a while, have those other two morons back there send me champagne and caviar every month. (*The cry of a baby is heard in the distance.*) I can't believe they brought that goddamn baby along for a hit job. (*A shot rings out and she falls dead. Captain and Co-Pilot enter. He's holding the gun, she's carrying the baby in a frontal textile carrier. She walks up to Neighbor's body, he to Franta's and looks under his visor.*)

Captain Bitch about my baby, will you?

Co-pilot Hah, I knew it! Look here! (*He points to Franta's face under the visor*)

Captain Ugh! That's not the Franta I knew.

Co-pilot I told you. He was either CIA or an alien. Probably both.

Captain (*Looking around*) I never thought I would say this, but it feels good to be back here. (*Pause*) You know what? I've been thinking....

Co-pilot (*He looks at her in horror.*) I can't handle that! (*He runs off.*)

Captain Get back here, you bastard! (*She runs after him!*)

Coconuts

Characters

Matt Nolasco, *marooned on a desert island while on a business trip*
Roland Garfield, *the president of the company Matt works for*
Jill Garfield, *Matt's former fiancée, now Roland's wife*
Craig Meeting, *Matt's co-worker and best friend*
Janice, *an employee from human resources*
Page, *a popular daytime talk show host*
Stewardess

Scene one – The beach of a desert isle
The stage is barren. At the right center stands a scarecrow, consisting of a cross made out of two sticks, clothed in a tattered shirt and crowned with a coconut with eerie-looking eyes and a mouth. A faded medal hangs from around the crossbar. Matt, with long hair and a beard, enters wearing tattered pants and shirt and dragging a sack of coconuts. He looks at the audience.

Matt A brisk breeze and calm seas ensures our passage home with ease. (*He looks at the scarecrow*) What? These? Please! (*Pause*) I'd just as soon not wear them at all, but I've got to get used to such things again. (*Introspectively*) Got to get used to a lot of things again. (*Pause*) Nope, there's no going back. The raft is ready, the winds are right. Tomorrow we say goodbye to this place forever. (*Pause*) But the truth is I'm a little afraid to go back. (*Worrisome*) Afraid to find out about Jill. Did she get married, have children? Is she still waiting for me after five years? (*Looking at the scarecrow*) What's that? (*Chuckles*) You amaze me, your optimism. That's the one thing I'm going to miss about this miserable little island. You and the others. You were always here for me, always sympathetic and understanding. I'll never find anyone like you guys back there. (*Pause*) Even Jill. For all our love, we could bicker endlessly about nothing. Like that fight at the airport before I left. God, what were we even doing bringing up our pasts at a time like that? Personally, I think her secret was worse than mine. (*Pause, looking at the scarecrow*) What's that? I'm not complaining. I'm just telling you like it was. (*Pause*) Look, I don't want to get into it now, okay? Forget it. (*Pause*) I said forget it, all right? (*Pause*) Goddammit, shut up! (*Grabs the head and smashes it with a stone*) There! Get cute with me, will you? (*Rummages through the sack, pulls out another coconut and installs it on the stick*). Let's see, where was I? Oh yes, going home. I guess everybody's going to want to hear me tell my story of survival. I'll have to describe over and over again how to make rope or rip into a fish. (*Pause*) What's that? No, I'm not going to tell them that. That stuff's personal. (*Pause*) Honesty's got nothing to do with it. (*Pause, then pointing a finger at the coconut*) Are you getting cute with me? (*Pause*) Exactly, else you'll end up in little pieces too. (*Pause*) Let's see, where was I? Oh yes, telling my story. Of course, some goofball will start waxing poetically about living on an island, away from the stress and noise of civilization. Why would I risk my neck to leave paradise for humanity? Well, the only way I can answer that is by telling them to try it themselves. Live on this hole for five years and tell me how you like it. Or I could just tell them the truth. Tell them how I miss taking a hot shower, reading a book, sleeping in a comfortable bed, and eating real food. (*Pause*) But that's just about the living. To see my family again, to see Jill again, that's the real reason we're getting on that raft tomorrow and trying it again. Because we miss them. Because we want to go home. (*Pause*) What's that? (*Pause, then pointing a finger at the coconut*) I'm not going to tell you again.

Scene two – The home of Roland and Jill Garfield
Roland, wearing a suit, is sitting at a table facing the audience, drinking coffee and going over paperwork. Jill enters from the right wearing a bathrobe. She sits down.

Roland You might want to get dressed. Meeting is coming over this morning.

Jill Craig is coming here? What for?

Roland We received some new guidelines this morning and I want to go over them before the board meeting this afternoon.

Jill Can't you do that at the office?

Roland No, I can't give the appearance that I actually prepare for these meetings.

Jill Yes, appearance is very important, Roland.

Roland So...maybe you could get dressed then. Looking at you in that bathrobe is distracting

Jill Yeah? More distracting than this? (*She gets up and goes around the table to face Roland with her back to the audience. She opens her robe and flashes him.*)

Roland For God's sake, Jill, I don't have time for this. (*Knock at the door, she covers up.*) That's Meeting. (*Assembling his papers*) Will you get the door?

Jill Have Craig see me like this? Forget it. (*She exits right*)

Roland Perfect. (*Stands up, exits left, re-enters with Craig behind him holding a folder*) Let's do it like this, Meeting: You go over the guidelines point-by-point and I'll add what I think. Got it? (*Sits down*)

Craig Yes, sir. Shall I sit?

Roland Suit yourself.

Craig (*Hesitates, decides not to sit*) Okay. (*Opening the folder and reading*) First: Establish terms of operational performance conducive to highly variable customer demands and implement them in sectors undergoing transformation into strategically viable and ultimately desirable vigorous and dynamic units.

Roland (*Resoundingly*) Done.

Craig Two: Address issues pertaining to holistic views and perspectives relevant to the attainment of an effective and effectual interface for deploying and demolishing persuasively developed arguments and facilitating alternative approaches and procedures.

Roland Done. (*Jill's phone starts ringing*) Forget it. Go on.

Craig Three: Build a highly efficient... (*disturbed by the ringing*) ...infrastructure...indestructible for the purposes of...

Roland Dammit! Jill, your phone! (*Still ringing*) Go on.

Craig ...indestructible for the purposes of...

Roland You already said that.

Craig Yes, sir. Is Mrs. Garfield not at home?

Roland What do you care?

Craig Nothing, sir. So...indestructible for the purposes of...

Roland I said you already said that. (*The ringing stops*)

Craig Sorry, sir, it was very distracting.

Roland Let me ask you something, Meeting: You've known Jill longer than I have. Was she always this miserable?

Craig Miserable, sir?

Roland Yeah, she acts like she's never happy.

Craig I don't think so.

Roland (*Sighing*) Well, she seems adrift these days. Just like when I first met her, at the funeral of that employee of ours who went down in the Pacific.

Craig Yes, sir. She was engaged to marry him.

Roland I know, Meeting. I ended up marrying her myself. Remember?

Craig Yes, sir. I didn't mean to imply...

Roland What?

Craig That there was anything wrong with you marrying her.

Roland Why should there be? Besides me leaving a wife and four children for her.

Craig Yes, sir.

Roland Look, Meeting. I also know you were his best friend. You don't have to hide the fact that you think it was all inappropriate.

Craig Thank you, sir.

Roland So you do think it was inappropriate?

Craig I think it was a terrible time for everyone. I'm just glad Jill didn't end up alone and miserable in the world.

Roland But I just told you she is miserable.

Craig Pardon me for saying so, but Matt was a tough act to follow.

Roland Who?

Craig Matt Nolasco. Her fiancé? My friend?

Roland Did they really get along as famously as she likes to portray it?

Craig You mean Matt and Jill?

Roland Yes, who the hell you think we're talking about here?

Craig Well, yes. They were going to get married. I was going to be the best man.

Roland Do you know if they were planning to have kids?

Craig Kids?

Roland Yes, children! Damn, Meeting, you better be brighter than this come the board meeting this afternoon. (*The phone rings again*) Goddammit! Jill! (*Hesitates*) What's the use? (*Goes to pick up the phone*) Yes? (*Pause*) One moment. Jill! Telephone! (*Puts the phone down and returns to his seat*) You see what I'm getting at here, Meeting? She knows I have to prepare for an important meeting today, and yet she can't manage to answer her own phone. (*Jill comes in, all dressed and nicely made up*)

Jill What's that, darling?

Roland Your phone's been ringing all morning.

Jill Oh, I didn't notice. Hello, Craig.

Craig Hello, Jill.

Roland Please, answer the phone so we can get some work done here.

Jill Who is it?

Roland What am I, your secretary? (*Jill goes to pick up the phone*) Now, Meeting, let's get back to that fourth point.

Craig I believe we're still on the third point, sir.

Roland Whatever.

Jill (*Picking up the phone*) Hello?

Roland Start from the beginning. "Build a highly efficient..."

Craig (*Absentmindedly*) Ah, yes, "a highly efficient..." (*Looking at his paper*) ah, "efficient...infrastructure..."

Roland Yes?

Craig "...infrastructure...indestructible for the purposes of..." (*Jill suddenly collapses and falls to the floor*) Good lord. (*Rushes to her side*)

Roland What happened?

Craig I don't know, sir. She just fainted.

Roland God, I hope she's not pregnant.

Craig Pregnant?

Roland That's the last thing I need now.

Craig Maybe she got some bad news over the phone.

Roland What now! (*Goes to pick up the phone*) Hello, who is this? (*Pause*) This is Roland Garfield, Jill's husband. (*Pause*) What's that? (*Pause, growing alarm*) What? (*Pause*) When? (*Pause*) Are they sure? (*Pause*) No, no, don't do anything till I get there. (*Pause*) Right. (*Puts down the phone, looks like he's in shock*) You're not going to believe this. That guy we're just talking about, the one who went down with the plane? (*Pause*) He's back.

Scene three – The cabin of a private jet
The stage now looks like the inside of a corporate jet, showing two seats separated by a small aisle. Matt enters from the left, followed by Craig.

Matt (*Agitated*) I don't know why you just won't tell me.

Craig (*Flustered*) I will, just as soon as we get off the ground.

Matt Come on, Craig, just tell me. I'm already expecting the worse.

Craig Matt, there's going to be 5,000 people waiting. We can't be late. Take a seat. We're going to take off.

Matt But all you got to do is say yes or no. How's that going to make us late?

Craig Matt, it's complicated. You see...the fact is...I hate to fly! Okay?

Matt What's that got to do with Jill?

Craig I want to tell you everything but let's just get off the ground first. God, these things make me nervous.

Matt Okay, okay, take it easy. When did you develop this fear of flying?

Craig Right after your plane went down.

Matt That's understandable. (*The sound of takeoff rumbling can be heard*)

Craig (*Ultra nervously*) Here we go.

Matt Hang in there, Craig. I'm here. (*Craig grabs him by the hand. The rumbling slowly tails off.*) That's it. Piece of cake.

Craig (*Slowly regaining his composure*) Yeah. Till the landing.

Matt So what's the deal?

Craig (*Taking a deep breath*) Okay, the deal is...she got married.

Matt (*Pretending to take it in stride*) Yeah, sure. I knew it. I mean...I was gone for five years.

Craig No, Matt, you were dead for five years. Life had to go on without you.

Matt And apparently it did. (*Pause*) Is she happy?

Craig I think so.

Matt Kids?

Craig No.

Matt When did she get married?

Craig Not long after you disappeared.

Matt What? What'd she do, meet somebody at my funeral?

Craig In a manner of speaking...yes.

Matt What?!

Craig Okay, Matt, here's the other part of the deal. Jill married...Roland Garfield.

Matt What!? She...she married the president of the company?

Craig I'm afraid so.

Matt Jesus, how did that happen? And...wasn't he already married?

Craig Again, I'm afraid so. You see, we had this memorial service for you. After the speech, Roland went up to hug Jill and...

Matt I don't believe this. That bastard uses my funeral to pick up my fiancée?

Craig Look, Matt, it was all in innocence. It just...got less innocent as time went on.

Matt Less innocent, my ass! (*The stewardess enters from the rear*)

Stewardess Would you gentlemen like a drink?

Matt Yeah, whisky for me.

Craig Nothing for me, thanks.

Stewardess Would you like ice with it?

Matt No, just give me the bottle. (*The stewardess pulls out a mini bottle of whiskey from her pocket and hands it to him*)

Stewardess Here you are.

Matt Thanks. (*The stewardess leaves, he opens the bottle and downs half of it*)

Craig Whoa, you better take it easy there, buddy. We have a show to do today.

Matt Screw their show!

Craig Look, Matt, you're a celebrity now. There's going to be loads of women for you. What do you want with only one?

Matt Did it ever occur to you that maybe I love this woman? That maybe my love for her kept me going these five years?

Craig Of course, and I'm not trying to play that down. It's just this is one hell of an awkward situation for everyone.

Matt Well, sorry if my coming back from the dead is putting a dent in you people's lives.

Craig Don't be like that, Matt. We're genuinely happy you're alive and back with us.

Matt So will she be at the celebration?

Craig I don't know. Roland and the board have been huddled up all week long scripting the event. Have her there, not have her there. (*The stewardess enters again*)

Stewardess Another drink, Mr. Nolasco?

Matt You read my mind. (*The stewardess pulls out another mini bottle from her pocket and hands it to him*)

Stewardess Could I ask you for a favor? Could you sign this for me? (*She hands him a magazine*)

Matt With pleasure. (*He looks at the magazine*) Ugh! What a horrible picture of me! I look like some lunatic.

Craig That's what you looked like when they picked you up off that raft.

Matt But I don't want the world to see me like this. I look scary. (*To the stewardess*) Don't I?

Stewardess Not at all. I think you look like a caveman.

Matt Caveman? And that's good? (*He opens the bottle and starts drinking from it*)

Stewardess Oh yes. Women are really into cavemen now. They prefer guys who are strong and hairy.

Matt (*Feels his face*) I guess I shaved too soon.

Stewardess Not at all. Civilized men are also very nice. I personally like both.

Matt In that case... (*He autographs the magazine cover and hands it to her*) Here you are.

Stewardess Thank you so much. By the way, Mr. Nolasco, I'm going to the beach with some girlfriends tonight and you're welcome to join us.

Matt You mean sleep on the beach, like I've been doing for the past five years?

Stewardess Sure, it'll be fun.

Matt Thanks, I'll let you know. (*She smiles and turns to leave*) Please, one more bottle so we don't keep bothering you.

Stewardess (*Handing him another bottle from her pocket*) It's no bother at all. Here you are. (*She leaves*)

Craig You see what I mean? The girls are going to be all over you. You're all the world is talking about these days.

Matt So everyone was just waiting for somebody like me to drift into their lives.

Craig Yeah, it's good timing. One of the most popular shows on TV right now is about a guy like you who ends up on an island after his boat sinks. There he has to fend for himself by spearing fish and storing rainwater in coconut shells.

Matt That sounds about right. People want to watch that every week?

Craig Of course not. What they like is how he fights off boredom with fantasies. One week he gets ambushed by a grizzly bear, another he's sleeping with super models, fighting ninjas, having tea with the queen...

Matt Tea with the queen? He sounds like a lunatic.

Craig Sure, and now people are excited because they can hear about the real thing from you.

Matt Jesus, you leave the world for five years and look what happens. Maybe I should tell the pilot to turn this thing around and take me back to my island.

Craig Should I ask him if it's possible?

Matt Craig, I was joking. I didn't risk sharks on the open sea just to go back there. I had enough of that joint, let me tell you. Besides, I have to see Jill again no matter what. I have to.

Craig I understand.

Matt So will she be there?

Craig Honestly, Matt, I don't know. I'm as much flying into the unknown as you are.

Matt Yeah, and the only thing you can guarantee me is a nutty world awaiting me. (*He pretends to be looking out the window*)

Craig That's about the look of it. (*Pause*) But if you don't mind me asking, Matt. What's that scarecrow-looking thing doing back there with all the coconuts? (*Matt turns and looks at him.*)

Scene four – An airport lounge
Chairs line the back of the stage. Janice is sitting one of them. She stands when Roland enters, followed by Craig.

Roland Disgraceful! Disgraceful!

Janice What happened? I'm sitting here waiting and waiting for him to come out of the plane but nothing happened.

Roland That's right, nothing! Apparently the man of the hour was too drunk to get off the plane!

Janice Drunk?

Roland Yes! Meeting here let him empty the bar on the way here. My bar!

Craig I'm sorry, sir. When Matt heard the news about Jill, he asked for one drink after another. I couldn't deny him after all he's been through.

Roland It was your duty to deny him. Now the newspapers are going to have a field day speculating over what became of him. Wait a minute: Where's Jill?

Janice I'm afraid we've had another incident.

Roland What now?

Janice She was understandably nervous waiting for the plane door to open. The wait finally became too much and she collapsed. She's all right, but she sprained her neck. We're hiding her from the media now.

Roland Perfect, just perfect. I spend the whole week planning this welcome home ceremony and the two principle characters cop out on me.

Craig Maybe this could work to our advantage. We just tell everyone we arranged a secret meeting between these two, to give them some peace and quiet for their reunion.

Janice The only problem with that is it assumes the press is full of idiots.

Craig Excuse me, but who are you anyway?

Roland Meeting, meet Janice. She works in human resources. I asked her to assist me here because her specialty is human relations.

Janice I also worked in the media before coming to the company and was only pointing out that your plan will work if we assume the press is full of idiots. I can tell you that it is.

Roland Great. We release a statement that the company decided to give him a private moment with his former fiancée, and that her husband, the company president, has nobly stood aside so these two could have that moment. Sound good?

Janice Perfect.

Craig So will they actually get that moment?

Roland Of course. They might even get lots more if everything works out between them.

Craig Sir?

Roland I guess you might as well know, Meeting. My marriage to Jill is on the rocks.

Craig You're getting a divorce?

Roland I hope so. That will pave the way for Nolasco and Jill to get back together again as they were meant to be. A happy ending for all concerned. Right, Janice?

Janice Yes, there's a new study out that shows people are really into happy endings these days. It's all the rage.

Craig And who'll break the news to Matt and Jill?

Roland No need. When these two finally meet, they'll fall into each other's arms and that'll be it. Right, Janice?

Janice Right. A reunion with a long-lost lover topped the list of happy endings most people dream of. Mr. Nolasco and Mrs. Garfield will be living the dream.

Craig There could be a problem, though. It seems Matt didn't come back from that island alone.

Roland Who'd he come with?

Craig Well, to pass the time away, he constructed this scarecrow-looking figure who he regularly talked to. At first I thought nothing unusual about it. In that situation, we would all need a Friday of sorts to keep us from losing our minds.

Roland Friday? Today's Tuesday.

Craig I mean Robinson Crusoe, sir. He meets a native on the island who eventually becomes his companion.

Roland Oh, yeah. Long time since I saw that film. But what's that got to do with Friday?

Craig What I mean, sir, is Matt took this scarecrow-looking figure back with him on the raft. And, well, I once actually caught him talking to it.

Roland What are you suggesting, that he's completely flipped?

Craig Not at all, sir. It's just…he developed a bond with this…thing, and whoever enters his life at this point will probably have to reckon living with the scarecrow too.

Janice You know what? I have a friend who's the mental affairs correspondent for IV news. He could give us some insight into a case like this. (*Takes a cell phone out to make a call*)

Roland Does it look like the typical scarecrow you see out in the fields? Some of those are pretty creepy.

Craig This one looks creepy too. It has a hairy coconut head with stones embedded into it for its eyes and mouth. Plus, he's got a bag full of these coconuts.

Roland Well, that's Jill's problem now, not ours.

Craig But what if she decides she doesn't want to compete with a scarecrow for his affections?

Roland Affections? You mean attention, I hope.

Craig Yes, sir. Sorry.

Roland Look, the script calls for these two getting back together again. The scarecrow will have to go.

Craig But what if Jill doesn't want to follow the script? What then?

Roland Then we drop the bombshell. Janice?

Janice Right. (*Hanging up the phone*) Well, apparently having an imaginary friend under isolated circumstances is a totally normal thing.

Roland We've moved beyond that, Janice. The issue now is what if Jill decides not to cooperate.

Janice Oh, well, that's easy. Apparently Mrs. Garfield has been having an affair. Either she cooperates or we spill the beans.

Roland You could've put it a bit more nicely at the salary I'm paying you.

Craig You have proof?

Janice Absolutely. Our new behavioral analysis software. We ran Mrs. Garfield's variables through it and the result was clear: monkey business.

Roland That means Jill follows the script and leaves me for Nolasco or I divorce her on the grounds of adultery.

Craig But that would also mean Jill has to leave the other man too.

Roland That's his problem, not mine.

Craig Sir, this is such a crazy situation and Jill...Jill is probably more confused by it than anyone. I...I would just let nature take its course.

Roland That's why I'm president of the company and you're not. We don't leave things to nature, Meeting. We take nature by the balls and squeeze. Hard when we have to. Right, Janice?

Janice Most definitely.

Craig So what do we do now?

Roland Good question. Janice, what do we do now?

Janice Mr. Meeting here releases a statement that Mr. Nolasco and Mrs. Garfield are spending time alone together. He then arranges for them to get that time alone.

Roland What about us?

Janice We go to lunch.

Roland Excellent work. Exemplary. Meeting, you don't need to eat, right?

Craig I guess not, sir.

Roland Good. See you back here in an hour. Come on, Janice. (*He leaves, Janice follows.*)

Scene five – Airport lounge, five years earlier
Chairs again line the back of the stage. Jill and Matt are sitting looking at each other. He's holding a gift-wrapped present.

Matt Shall I open it now?

Jill Of course.

Matt (*He opens it and pulls out a medallion hanging on a chain*) What is it?

Jill It's a St. Christopher's medal. He's the patron saint for safe travel. It's like a good luck charm for all your flying.

Matt But, Jill, I hate to wear rings, chains and all other types of jewelry.

Jill I know. But I want to make sure you come back to me safe and sound.

Matt All right, I'll wear it, but on one condition:

Jill What? (*He hands her a ring box*) For me? What is it?

Matt Open it up and see. (*She nervously opens it.*)

Jill Oh, Matt, I don't know what to say.

Matt Just you'll marry me when I get back.

Jill But, Matt, it's not as easy as that. I mean...I want to get married and have children and all, but I'm not ready to be home with a baby while you're always on the road somewhere.

Matt I've been thinking about that too. What if I give up my job and stay at home? You could go right back to work when you're ready.

Jill But I want to enjoy motherhood. I want to breastfeed my children, not pump the milk out and keep it in the refrigerator. And besides, you like your job.

Matt Yeah, but I'm tired of the travel. I'm tired of taking my shoes off at the airport. And besides, they're working on a program where we fire people online. I can do it from home.

Jill But this is such a big step. There's something I have to tell if we're really going to do this.

Matt What?

Jill (*Taking him by the hands*) Matt. The truth is...I've been married before.

Matt What? When? With whom?

Jill It was a long time ago. I was just out of college and I married this guy I was dating at the time. I was stupid. It didn't even last a year.

Matt So you're divorced, right.

Jill Probably.

Matt Probably?!

Jill The thing is he was sent to prison for stealing from the bank where he worked. He asked me not to divorce him, saying the only way he could survive prison was knowing I would be waiting for him when he got out. So stupid me, I waited. (*Pause*)

Matt And?!

Jill So he got out and ran off with another woman. He sent me a letter from Las Vegas telling me he would get a divorce there.

Matt So you're divorced?

Jill Well...I never got any letter, so I don't know for sure. I've wanted to tell you about it for some time, but I was just too embarrassed to.

Matt I'm glad you did, because there's something I have to tell you about my former life.

Jill Oh no, I hope I didn't open the floodgates here.

Matt Actually, I can only tell you what I know, but this is it: I may be a father.

Jill What?!

Matt You see, I was going out with this girl and one day she told me she was pregnant. We didn't know each other well enough to start a family so I naturally assumed we weren't going to. Then one day she disappeared and that was the last I heard from her.

Jill Where did she go?

Matt I don't know.

Jill How can you not know?

Matt Because I don't. She just took off.

Jill And did you go looking for her?

Matt Yes. A little.

Jill A little? You could have a child somewhere in this world?

Matt Look, Jill, it was a casual relationship. She just told me she was pregnant, that's all. I never saw any tests, never went with her to any doctor.

Jill But still, there's a chance. And the one thing I never wanted to be in this world is an evil stepmother.

Matt You're not an evil stepmother. Just a woman who may or may not be divorced.

Jill That's not fair, Matt. I opened up my secret past to you.

Matt And I opened up mine to you. We're even.

Jill Even? My ex-husband will never be a part of our lives. But your child...

Matt I don't know if I have a child! Just as I don't know if your ex is really an ex. (*A horn sounds*) Great, that's the boarding call. Fine way to leave now. (*He stands and picks up his bag*) Look, Jill, let's pick this up when I get back.

Jill So go then. If you feel it's necessary to go like this, then go.

Matt What can I do?

Jill Take your ring back for starters. (*She stands up and puts the ring box on her chair.*)

Matt Jill, this is childish. Look. (*He takes the St. Christopher's medal out of the box and puts it around his neck. He picks up the ring box and gets on his knee.*) Jill, darling. (*The horn sounds again.*) Shi, that's the final call. (*He stands up and puts the ring box back on the chair.*) Look, we'll do this properly and romantically just as soon as I get back.

Jill So I should pen your proposal in my calendar? Maybe hire a TV crew to film it for the world? Forget it! (*She storms off.*)

Matt Jill. Jill! Goddammit! (*He picks up his suitcase and runs for the exit. Once the coast is clear, Jill sneaks back, picks up the ring box and leaves.*)

Scene six – airport lounge today
Craig is standing at the right side of the stage, his left hand cupped to his ear as if he's eavesdropping in on a conversation. Roland and Janice enter from the left, Craig straightens up and pretends nothing is

happening.

Roland Meeting, what are you doing?

Craig Nothing.

Roland Nothing? It looks like you're eavesdropping in on their private moment.

Janice Definitely.

Craig No, it's just that...

Roland Just nothing. You're doing exactly what you should be doing. So what are they talking about?

Craig Well, I'm not sure. It all sounds so confusing.

Janice What do you mean?

Roland Janice, I'll ask the questions. Meeting, what do you mean?

Craig I don't know. I hear them saying something about a divorce and a child.

Roland (*Beaming*) Then that's it! Janice, you're a genius. (*Hugs her*)

Janice The software doesn't lie.

Roland So, Meeting: How big were the sparks?

Craig Sparks?

Roland Yes, when they saw each other again.

Craig She was already waiting in the room when he walked in.

Roland Have you heard any silence in there, like they were...?

Craig No, Mr. Garfield. (*Roland moves past Craig and cups his hand to eavesdrop*)

Roland I don't hear a thing. They must be... (*Matt emerges from the right with a white towel wrapped around his head, followed by Jill with a neck brace on*) Oh, hello, you must be Matt. I'm very glad to meet you. I'm Roland Garfield, president of the company.

Matt Yes, sir. We met before. I used to work in retrenchment.

Roland Retrenchment?

Matt Yes, sir. Chopping heads?

Roland I know what retrenchment is. I just don't remember you being there. What was your biggest job?

Matt Probably the Labor Day massacre at Coca-Cola.

Roland That was you? Great job you did there. Five hundred heads in five days, wasn't it?

Matt Five-hundred-fifty.

Roland Exemplary work. But of course it doesn't compare to your story of survival. You've been an inspiration to us all.

Jill Oh, God, Roland, give the man a break.

Roland Nice to see you, darling. I heard you've had another spill.

Jill Yes, I did, and as usual my husband wasn't there to catch me.

Roland I'm supposed to be responsible for that as well?

Janice People, please. Mr. Nolasco here is going to have to make an appearance before the press sometime today.

Roland You're right, and this young man deserves better than to watch an old married couple squabbling his first few minutes back home.

Jill Old?

Matt I'm sure he didn't mean anything by it, Jill.

Roland Now, Matt, I know you've been through a lot, but the fact is you were on the company payroll all the years you spent on that island and I'm going to make sure you get all your back pay. In return, however, I expect a little more professionalism from you. This getting drunk right before a company-sponsored event is totally unacceptable.

Jill You are unbelievable, Roland. Matt endured five years of hell because of a business trip and you have the nerve to lecture him about professionalism?

Janice People, I'm afraid I have to remind you of the priorities facing us.

Jill Who is this woman anyway?

Janice I'm Janice. I work in human resources.

Roland That's neither here nor there. Look, darling, I can understand your loyalty to Nolasco here. After all, he was your fiancé when he disappeared.

Jill That's got nothing to do with it. I just think he deserves to be shown sympathy and respect right now.

Roland Fine, but it may interest you to know that I'm fully prepared to give him everything he came back for.

Jill What, his back pay?

Roland No, his former fiancée.

Jill What?!

Roland That's right. You two were going to get married when that plane crashed. The only thing that stopped you was his supposedly being dead. Well, we can clearly see that he isn't. So you might as well go through with the wedding after all.

Jill You're forgetting one little problem, dear. I'm already married. To you!

Roland Yes, but it's only fair that Matt here should get his old life back after his ordeal. This is what you two want, right?

Jill What makes you think that?

Roland I don't know. I... (*Confused, looks to Craig, then to Janice, gets no response*)

Matt Mr. Garfield, I appreciate your concern. For five years I tried to get off that island just to see Jill again. Well, I did. And now...now it's time to move on.

Jill Yes, and I feel the same way. Matt was the love of my life, but that ship has sailed.

Roland What the hell? This is nothing like we prepared in the script! Janice, explain.

Janice Obviously these two need some coaching.

Jill Coach yourself, Janice. (*Janice looks at her PDA*)

Roland Enough of this: The whole world out there is expecting more than this depressing tale you're offering. I'm willing to be the gentleman and step aside. The least you two can do is play along until the world has moved on.

Jill Forget it. I'm happy Matt is back but that's as far as it goes.

Roland Well, we're getting divorced anyway, just in case you two change your mind.

Jill Divorced? On what grounds?

Roland Janice, if you please?

Janice (*Looking up from her PDA*) Mrs. Garfield, we have information that you have been having an affair. (*Goes back to looking at her PDA*)

Jill What information?

Roland I asked Janice to run your behavior variables through some special software we have and the results all point to you and monkey business.

Jill Monkey business? What about you and that woman from Purchasing?

Matt Purchasing? Even I remember that affair.

Roland That's right. I was sleeping with her when we got married. But you started up with somebody afterwards. Much worse if you ask me.

Jill Unless your software has a name for this monkey I supposedly have, there's nothing to talk about.

Roland I don't need any...

Janice (*Looking at her PDA*) Mr. Garfield, I have just received and installed a software update. Incredibly, it now gives us the name of that monkey.

Roland Janice, I'll say it again. You're a genius. So let's have it.

Janice I think it would be better for Mrs. Garfield to go along with the script and nobody needs to know a thing.

Roland (*Moment's reflection*) Yes, that is the best way. How about it, my dear?

Jill Screw you.

Janice Mrs. Garfield? One last chance?

Jill Screw you big time, bitch!

Janice Very well. The name of that monkey is...

Craig All right, all right, it's me, for god's sake!

Janice You? I was going to say...but what the hell, this is even better.

Roland What better? Your software update is for shit. Meeting, what's the meaning of this?

Matt Yeah, Craig, what's going on?

Craig I'm sorry, Matt. It's just that Jill was in such a vulnerable state at the time. She looked so...sad. My heart went out to her.

Roland What are you apologizing to him for? I'm her husband!

Matt But you're my best friend.

Craig I know, Matt. I'm sorry.

Matt And Jill, I don't get you. Pawning the engagement ring I gave you, marrying my boss, sleeping with my best friend? This is how you honor my memory?

Jill I'm sorry, Matt, but I was feeling vulnerable. Roland came along offering me home and security. It's when he wouldn't or couldn't offer me a child that things went to hell.

Roland I told you a hundred times! I've already got enough children.

Jill So I turned to Craig here to help me.

Matt You mean you got together just to have a child?.

Craig That's all it was, Matt. Believe me, I didn't try to enjoy her sexually.

Roland I don't believe what I'm hearing. You're fired, Meeting!

Matt So, are you two in love, or what?

Jill/Craig (*Looking at each other, somewhat unsure*) Well, yeah.

Matt Why didn't you tell me this on the flight?

Craig Come on, Matt. How could I tell you something like that so easily? Believe me, I've been in anguish about this since I found out you were alive.

Jill Me too.

Roland Not that anyone here cares, but me too!

Janice I care, Mr. Garfield.

Roland Oh, shut up, Janice.

(*Long silence*)

Matt Well, it's like we said earlier. It's time to move on. I wish you two much happiness together.

Jill Thank you, Matt. You'll always have a special place in my heart.

Craig Thanks, buddy. I'm so glad you're home again.

Matt Mr. Garfield?

Roland What? Am I still relevant here?

Matt I think it's time for me to move on in my career as well. Please make sure I get my five years' back pay.

Roland Jesus Christ, does anyone have any good news for me?

Janice All this is good news. The scenario is the fiancée marries the boss but is sleeping with the best friend. It's incredible publicity for the firm.

Roland (*Moment's reflection*) Yes, that's not a bad scenario. Meeting, can I trust you to sell this saga to the media? Including your despicable role in it?

Craig But you just fired me, sir.

Roland (*Sarcastically*) And now I'm re-hiring you! Are you on it or not?

Craig No problem if your wife comes home with me tonight?

Roland Don't press your luck. But yes, she's all yours.

Jill I'm not yours to give away, Roland.

Roland You know what I mean. Let's just get this show back on the road. I'm going out there to make a statement; the rest of you follow me when I give the cue. Got that? (*No response from anyone*) Janice!

Janice Sir?

Roland Got that?

Janice Yes, sir.

Roland Good, let's go. (*Starts to leave, gestures to Janice's PDA.*) Let's have the name of that other monkey. (*They exit.*)

Scene seven – The stage of Page's talk show
Two chairs are positioned at ninety-degree angles in the center of the stage. Page enters from the left, to the piped in sounds of clapping and cheering, and stands in front of the audience.

Page I don't have to tell you all what an incredible show we have for you here today. You know it and I know you know it! (*Clapping and cheering*) Imagine, you're on a plane over the ocean and you're caught in the middle of a thunderstorm. It looks like you're going to crash. And you know what? You do. (*"Oooh" from the audience*) Somehow you survive that crash, but now you find yourself stranded on an island. Every day you expect a rescue party to come and take you home. And you know what? It never does. (*"Ohhh"*) Today, folks, we're going to talk to that real life survivor, and later we're going to bring out two people who formed a triangle with him on his return. But for now, please welcome, Matt Nolasco! (*Matt enters from the left to the sound of clapping, carrying the scarecrow in one hand and sack of coconuts in the other. He greets Page and sits down with the scarecrow on his lap.*) Who you got there?

Matt Well, as you can imagine, it can get pretty lonesome on an island after a while. So I made this companion here to keep me company.

Page Does he have a name? Or should I say she? (*Audience laughter*)

Matt It's not really a he or a she and there were just too many of them to give them all names.

Page How many of these "companions" did you have with you there?

Matt I don't know. I lost track. Dozens, maybe hundreds.

Page Hundreds? So you basically built yourself an army of companions on the island.

Matt What army? (*Pointing to the body of the scarecrow*) There was just this bamboo frame. I simply switched coconut heads whenever I wanted to talk to someone new.

Page So it was just you and one companion at any given time. There were no threesomes on that island. (*Audience laughter*)

Matt No, the last thing I needed there was more complications.

Page So how were all these coconuts different from one another?

Matt They just were. Like the one you see here. He's the "gentleman" because our conversation always emphasized politeness and elegance.

Page That's good, because I emphasize the same on my show and I may just have a few questions for him later on. Maybe corroborate your story. (*She laughs, the audience laughs, Matt looks uncomfortable*)

Matt But he knows better than to cross me. The minute he does, off he goes and I put another one up in his place.

Page And what happens to him after that?

Matt Nothing. He's just a goner.

Page Dear me, I'm glad I'm not married to you. (*The audience laughs*) So what other kinds of companions did you have with you there?

Matt (*Reaches into the sack and pulls out a coconut*) Well, this one here has a great sense of humor. (*Pulls out another one*) This one is sarcastic as hell. (*Another one*) And this one: he's super aggressive. You don't want to mess with him.

Page Honey, I've been doing this show for twenty years. I ain't had a guest yet who could rattle me. (*Audience laughter*) But enough about the coconuts. Let's talk about the island. How would you describe it for our audience here?

Matt You mean honestly?

Page Of course. That's what this show is all about. Honesty.

Matt So can I say this? (*Whispers something in her ear, she appears quite troubled*)

Page I don't think the gentleman here would approve of that word.

Matt Piss on him.

Page Matt!

Matt Look, the only reason why he's out here is because your producers kept rushing me, kept telling me, "Let's go, let's go." I didn't have time to carefully think about which one to bring on your show. He was the first head to come out of the sack.

Page Still, I don't think that word is appropriate for a daytime audience.

Matt So what about "hellhole"? Can I use that word?

Page It sounds like you didn't like that place very much. What about all those sunsets you got to watch over the water?

Matt Yeah, sure, they're beautiful. But then comes the long bleak darkness of night, followed by another long dismal day full of thirst, hunger and despair.

Page So if it wasn't that great, why did you wait five years to leave?

Matt That's how long it took me to build a raft. It ain't easy with your bare hands, you know.

Page But weren't you frightened of going out all alone on a raft in the middle of the ocean?

Matt Not with the kind of job I do.

Page What job is that?

Matt I'm a retrenchment specialist.

Page Which means?

Matt You would probably understand it better if I used the layman's term for it: the chopping block.

Page Chopping block? Good lord, were you an executioner?

Matt Not exactly. My job was firing people. I chop heads for senior management. I was on my way to chop a few heads overseas when my plane went down.

Page So you were not the kind of guy people wanted to see walk in through the door every day. (*Audience laughter*)

Matt You got it. I was feared. I would walk into an office and the workers there would start praying, "Please, please, don't let it be me."

Page So what you're saying is, since you're not afraid to destroy someone's livelihood, you're not afraid of anything?

Matt That's right. A baby crab crawling by? Chop. An innocent fish swimming by. Chop.

Page Sure, baby crab, little fish. But what about a shark?

Matt Hah, a shark. I once fought one for ten minutes over a fish. The shark won, but he never came back.

Page I think it's time for a commercial break. Stay right there, folks, we'll be back to hear Matt talk about fear and the plane crash. (*The audience claps, lights dim on the stage, a commercial is played out. The audience claps and lights come back on the stage.*) We're back here with Matt Nolasco, who survived a plane crash in the middle of the ocean and then five years alone on an island. Now, Matt, you were saying you were never once scared the whole time out there. Not during the plane crash?

Matt I can't remember it.

Page What about after the crash?

Matt I can't remember that, either. I did get scared once by this whale eyeballing me. But then he winked and everything was all right. (*"Ahhh" from the audience*)

Page I know the feeling. I too had a whale wink at me! Amazing experience.

Matt But yours was trained to wink. Mine did it naturally. (*"Oooh" from the audience*)

Page Are you belittling my amazing experience? That's not very polite of you. Your gentleman there must be thinking "rude, rude, rude" right now.

Matt Well, let's find out. (*Looking at the scarecrow*)

Page Don't tell me you're going to start talking to that thing.

Matt (*To the scarecrow*) I know it's her show but now she's starting to become a pain in the ass.

Page Hey, are you talking about me?

Matt (*To Page*) Yes, but don't worry. He agrees with you. He thinks I'm being rude.

Page I never thought I would say it but the coconut is right. (*The audience claps*)

Matt He may be right, but he also knows the penalty for crossing me. (*Matt grabs the coconut head off the stick, drops it to the floors and smashes it with his foot. Page reels in shock.*)

Page Are you crazy acting like a maniac like that?! Look at what you did to the gentleman.

Matt He deserved it for getting cute with me. (*Looking into the sack*) Let's see, who shall we invite to sit here and listen to all these goofy questions. I know, you can butt heads with Mr. Super Aggressive for a while. (*He takes a coconut from the sack and installs it on the stick*)

Page Are you trying to scare me? Let me tell you something, mister. This is one shark you don't want to wrangle with. (*The audience laughs*)

Matt (*Looking at the scarecrow, then at Page*) He says your show is dumb.

Page (*Sarcastically*) Oh, is that the best you can do?

Matt   He says it represents all that's bad about civilization. Sloppy fashion, sloppy diet, sloppy implants.

Page   Sloppy? Now you listen to me...

Matt   He says people like you belong to the OB generation: obese and obnoxious. (*"Oooh" from the audience*)

Page   Now I've got news for you and your hairy little friend there. You talk about doing something good for civilization? Look at you. All you do is go around chopping heads.

Matt   Hm, maybe if I chop the right head. (*He pulls a medieval axe out of the sack and menacingly points it at her. Page freezes with horror in her seat.*)

Page   Now, Matt, there's no need to bring an axe into this. We're just talking, that's all.

Matt   Yeah, well I'm tired of all the talking. What do you say, people? Is it time to chop? (*A "chop, chop, chop..." can slowly be heard coming from the audience*)

Page   But I thought you people loved me.

Matt   Welcome to the island, lady.

Page   Mr. and Mrs. Garfield, get out here and save me from this lunatic! (*Jill and Roland enter*)

Jill   Matt, what are you doing?

Roland   Nolasco, what did I tell you about unprofessional conduct? Put that axe down!

Matt   Somebody has to teach this big mouth a lesson. Besides, I don't work for you anymore.

Roland   But I want you to come back. Today we got this huge order.

Chopping over five hundred heads. Another bloodbath, and I need someone like you for it.

Matt Five hundred heads?

Roland Yeah, and what's more it's on Hawaii. It'll be like you going back to your island.

Matt Island?

Roland Sure, only you'll have a five-star hotel, open bar, limousine service. No more crabs and coconuts. What do you say?

Jill And that's not all, Matt. Craig and I are no longer together. We went to the doctor the other day and found out he's sterile. So if you want, we can get back together again and try to have that family we planned so long ago.

Page This is actually turning out to be a pretty good ending.

Matt (*Threateningly*) Quiet, mouth lady!

Roland How about it, Nolasco? You and Jill together again, on Hawaii enjoying good food and drink and sunshine and chopping heads. What more could you ask for?

Matt Jill, is this what you really want?

Jill Yes, Matt. Like I told you at the airport. You're the love of my life.

Matt And you're mine.

Jill But please, just you and me. No coconuts.

Matt (*Pause*) All right. (*The audience out in cheer*) What now (*To Jill*)?

Jill Give the lady the axe and the coconuts and come with us.

Matt (*Pointing to the scarecrow*) Including...?

Jill Yes, darling.

Matt (*Long pause, then to Page*) I'm sorry for being so rude on your show. The gentleman was right. But please, promise me you'll take good care of them.

Page All but Mr. Super Aggressive. How dare he talk about my implants like that.

Matt Fair enough. (*Matt hands her the axe and sack*)

Roland Great, come along then, Matt. We need to talk about this new chopping block. (*The three head for the exit*)

Jill And our wedding day. Roland and I filed the divorce papers yesterday.

Matt And what about your first divorce?

Roland First divorce? (*They exit*)

Page (*Holding the axe in one hand, one coconut in the other*) Well, folks, it's been a long time since we had a wild show like this one. But it's over now, and if I were to describe it for future generations, all I would say is it was about a nut. And I don't mean coconut! (*The audience starts whooping and hollering, she starts laughing and clapping. Curtain.*)

No Ship in Sight

Characters

Robert, the fifth officer of a ship that could well be the Titanic
Agatha, a wealthy widow
Bertha and **Beryl**, her sexually frustrated nieces
Daniel, **Henry**, and **Stan**, friends on a stag voyage
Stoker, a hairy beast of a man
Death, portrayed as a woman in white

Act I

Scene one – The stage is set up to look like a quayside, with the image of a large passenger liner covering the back
Robert is there in uniform, standing near a carry-on bag, smiling and greeting the arriving guests. Daniel, Henry and Stan enter from the right.

Robert Good day, gentleman. Will you be travelling in steerage for the voyage to New York?

Daniel Steerage? Hah, second class and nothing less. (*Handing their tickets to Robert*)

Robert Yes.

Daniel They say second class aboard this ship is almost like first class aboard any other.

Robert True, but the first class here has got everything imaginable. Turkish baths, lounges, cafes and restaurants, even a grand staircase.

Henry What does second class have?

Robert Second class is not too shabby either. It has a smoke room for gentlemen and library for the ladies.

Henry No grand staircase?

Stan I can live without the staircase, but I don't need a smoking room.

Robert Of course some extra amenities can always be arranged on an individual basis.

Stan Amenities?

Robert Sure. I can get you into the Turkish baths, if you like. For a small fee, naturally.

Henry You mean a bribe?

Robert No, a small fee. A bribe is for bigger things. Like playing captain on the bridge.

Henry And the captain knows it?

Robert Let's say it doesn't concern him.

Daniel None of that will be necessary. We're heading to New York because Stan here is getting married. This trip is his bon voyage from freedom. We want to take him around all the brothels in Manhattan.

Stan Really, fellows. I could be happy in Paris for a week. The brothels there are supposed to be a better class anyway than in New York.

Daniel But more expensive. The sailor here can tell you that.

Robert New York is a bargain compared to Paris but you have to forgo things there like perfume, clean sheets, clean girls for that matter. Also, whores in New York don't try to hide the fact that they're bored with their jobs. They figure you're just there for your own pleasure and so count the spiders on the ceiling waiting for you to finish. But in Paris, all the girls dream of stardom. Every customer is their audience.

Daniel We know all about that. But we only got so much money for this trip and decided that more is better than better.

Robert As I was saying about amenities, gentlemen. I could arrange something for you now.

Daniel You've got a brothel here on the ship? In second class?

Robert Of course not. But there will probably be at least a thousand lonely ladies on board and you can't imagine the primal forces exerted by nature on their bodies.

Henry What primal forces?

Robert The gentle rocking motion of the ship beneath their feet, the wind through their hair, their eyes feasting on a glorious sunset across the horizon. It's the most incredible aphrodisiac you can find.

Daniel You mean you can set us up right here on the ship?

Robert All yours, gentlemen, for a fee.

Daniel What kind of fee are we talking about?

Robert Very accommodating, I assure you. All you're paying for is my time and the use of my facilities. Cheaper and safer than anything you're going to find in New York. Now if you'll excuse me, other passengers are arriving. (*He moves toward the right exit, where Agatha and her two nieces, all of them wearing frilly dresses and big hats, enter. The three gentlemen step to the side and observe.*) Ah, good day, ladies. Boarding for the trip to New York?

Agatha Yes. I'm Agatha Magness and these are my nieces, Bertha and Beryl. (*Handing their tickets to him*)

Robert How do you do, ladies. (*They nod to him*) First time at sea?

Agatha Yes, I'm taking my nieces to New York to give them the chance to see the world before they get married. (*The nieces find her standard* *response tiresome*)

Robert Well, you couldn't have picked a finer vessel to sail on, especially in first class. The décor inside is incredible, absolutely exquisite.

Agatha So we've heard. (*Stepping back and looking at the ship*) It does indeed look grand. I've also heard the guest list is quite remarkable.

Robert It certainly is. Sailing with you in first class is Samuel Michael Ellison, the wealthy dry goods merchant; Hildegard Stuckermayer, the current star of the German stage, and Julian Westbrook, who owns the largest grapefruit plantation in the world. The list goes on and on.

Agatha Please do go on, because I haven't heard of any of these people.

Bertha Come on, auntie. You eat grapefruit, don't you?

Agatha (*Exasperated*) Does that mean I should know the name of the person who grows it?

Robert You probably wouldn't recognize their names. They are very respectable people, not the kind you find in the daily newspapers.

Agatha (*Aggrieved*) My dear, sir, are you suggesting that I read that trash?

Robert I didn't think there was anyone in England who didn't.

Bertha He's right, auntie.

Agatha Hold your tongue! (*To Robert*) Now about that roster of passengers in first class. You were saying...

Robert All in good time, madam. For now, the ship is departing. Kindly board with your nieces and I'll be happy to show you around first class once we're underway. You'll find your private suite, number 13, on the bridge deck.

Agatha Number 13? But that's bad luck.

Beryl It's only bad luck if the day is Friday too, auntie.

Agatha Just the same, I would prefer not to take any chances. Is it possible to switch to another suite?

Robert I'm afraid not, madam. Your neighbors on the bridge deck have already checked into their suites.

Agatha And who might they be?

Robert (*Impatiently looking at his list*) You're in a corner suite, so your only immediate neighbor is Julian Westbrook.

Agatha Who?

Bertha The grapefruit grower, auntie!

Agatha Oh, dear. Not quite the start I was hoping for. Well, come along, girls.

Robert Madam, what about your luggage?

Agatha Yes, have it brought up to our suite.

Robert It has to be checked in at the main terminal first.

Agatha Don't you have people to take care of that sort of thing?

Robert Not on the quayside, madam. Of course, I could ask these three gentlemen here to lend a hand.

Agatha Who are they? All I know about them is they've been standing there and staring at us this whole time.

Robert They're your fellow passengers, madam. Travelling in second class.

Agatha In that case, they're more than welcome to lend a hand.

Robert (*Summoning Dan, Henry, and Stan to approach*) Would you gentlemen be so kind and carry the luggage of these lovely ladies to the main terminal around the corner? (*They appear confused. With his back turned to the women, Robert gestures to the men that this is only the first step.*)

Daniel Oh, gladly! (*Tipping his hat to the ladies, followed by the other two*) My name's Daniel and these are my friends Henry and Stan. Glad to make your acquaintance.

Agatha (*Hurriedly*) Yes, yes, likewise, I'm sure. (*Leading them offstage*) Now be careful with the trunk. It contains some priceless porcelain.

Bertha (*To Robert*) Are those three gentlemen travelling alone?

Robert Yes. They were about to board this magnificent ship, about to depart on its maiden voyage, when they caught sight of another pair of beautiful maidens. (*The girls giggle*) You are maidens, aren't you?

Beryl (*Shocked*) What a question to ask? Sailor or no sailor, you should be ashamed of yourself.

Robert There's nothing to be ashamed of, I assure you. The wide expanse of the open sea often has a strange, mysterious effect on women that leaves them swooning on deck. They want nothing more than for a man to come along and sweep them off their feet.

Bertha Whatever man might come along for us will have to get through auntie first. She's determined to watch us like a hawk.

Robert Perhaps I can get Mr. Westbrook to keep her company for a while. (*They laugh*)

Bertha Yes, he can join her for breakfast (*with Beryl*) and bring the grapefruit. (*They laugh some more, Agatha enters*)

Agatha What's so amusing? Are you girls making another joke at my expense?

Beryl No, ma'am. We were laughing at Mr. Westbrook and his grapefruit.

Agatha Oh, well that's okay. Only have the decency and politeness not to do it in front of him when we're on board.

Beryl Yes, ma'am.

Agatha Bertha?

Bertha Yes.

Agatha Good, (*looking off to the right*) now let's finally...aeh!! There's a great hairy beast approaching!

Robert Pay him no heed, madam. He's one of the stokers on this ship. Arriving quite late, I might add. (*He bends over and pulls a whip out of the bag. The stoker enters from the right exit.*) You there! What are you doing arriving this late? You were supposed to be here at least an hour ago. (*The stoker barely gets a grunt out when Robert lashes him with the whip. The women look terrified, the stoker flinches in pain.*) Get down below decks now! Now, you hear me! (*He lashes the stoker again, who disappears exit left*)

Agatha Dear lord!

Robert Don't be alarmed, ladies. The stokers will not be allowed to wander from their hole during the duration of the trip. I assure you, you will be safe.

Agatha I should hope so. Just the sight of him could easily put me in a watery grave.

Beryl But how can you beat a fellow human being like that? It's inhumane.

Robert I agree but unfortunately it's the only way to keep them in line. The stokers have their own special entrance. That way they don't frighten unsuspecting passengers.

Agatha Yes, Robert. You apply that whip all you need to until we get to New York.

Beryl Well, I still think it's barbaric.

Agatha Ach, you girls do need to learn something of the world. Let's get aboard. (*Agatha disappears through the left exit, followed by Bertha and Beryl*)

Robert Have a pleasant journey. I'm sure we'll be in touch again soon. (*Bertha looks coquettishly at him over her shoulder. Beryl frowns at her, then at him. They exit.*)

Scene two – The deck of the ship underway
Agatha, Bertha, and Beryl are lying on three lounge chairs at the back center of the stage, snoozing beneath large hats. Daniel, Henry, and Stan enter from the left and stop when they see them.

Daniel There they are, right where Robert said we'd find them.

Henry All right, we found them. Now what?

Daniel We're supposed to wait for Robert to get here. Till then, we keep walking by, tipping our hats each time.

Stan Can you tell who's who under those hats?

Daniel The one on the left is obviously the aunt. We just have to worry about the two sisters.

Henry Sisters? I thought he said they were cousins.

Daniel Practically the same for our purposes.

Stan Hey, watch out, they're stirring. (*Bertha raises her hat and sees the three gentlemen. They tip their hats to her, she nods back. They slowly walk off, exiting at the right. Bertha shakes her cousin awake.*)

Beryl (*Lifting her hat*) What is it?

Bertha Those three men from the quayside, the ones who carried our luggage, were just here.

Beryl So?

Bertha So they tipped their hats to me. I think they're interested in meeting.

Beryl And we'll meet them. Tonight at dinner. Auntie invited them to our table.

Bertha I mean meet them under other circumstances.

Beryl Are you talking about...?

Bertha Yes. Everything Robert said about the ocean having some kind of effect on us I feel it now. Don't you?

Beryl I'm not sure. But it doesn't matter. Auntie is never going to let us out of her sight during this voyage.

Bertha Robert says he can fix things for us.

Beryl Of all the nerve! Is he offering to be our pimp?

Bertha He's not a pimp if no money changes hands. (*The three men re-enter, tipping their hats to the girls as they walk by and exit at the right*) Besides, what's wrong with finding a husband from among them? Robert says one is about to get married but the other two are available.

Beryl Then we wouldn't want to rendezvous too early anyway. They may take us for sluts and never marry us.

Bertha Oh, Beryl, you're so naïve. Do you still think you have to be a virgin to get married?

Beryl It helps.

Bertha (*Laughing*) You are naïve. (*The three men enter from the right, sauntering by and tipping their hats, then exiting at the left*)

Beryl I don't know. We know nothing about these three, just that one of them is getting married and we don't even know which one.

Bertha That makes it more exciting. It's like playing roulette. Which one would you choose if you could? (*Pointing to offstage*) Let's call that one 6, that one 12, and that one 22.

Beryl 22.

Bertha Me too. He's tall, looks strong and yet has a sensitive look. He's a man you can respect and mother at the same time. (*Robert enters from the right*)

Robert Ah, having a nice chat, ladies. Today is a perfect day to be on the sea. The sun and breeze are just right, that whiff of brine through the nostrils is enough...

Bertha Thank you, Robert, we quite get the picture.

Robert Are we all set for our tour below decks?

Bertha If we must. It's auntie's idea.

Robert (*Extending his arm to the left exit*) I've asked these three gentlemen to accompany us if that's all right with you. (*The three gentlemen enter, again tipping their hats. Bertha and Beryl sit up in their chairs*)

Bertha It's all right with us but you'll have to ask auntie. (*She shakes her aunt*) Auntie. Auntie! Auntie, wake up! (*Agatha arouses and removes her big hat*)

Agatha What?! What's the matter? Is the ship sinking?

Robert Hardly, madam. This ship has been dubbed unsinkable.

Bertha Auntie, Robert says it's time for the tour.

Agatha Tour?

Robert Yes, madam, the one I promised you below decks. I have time to give you a private tour.

Agatha A private tour? Just for us?

Robert Yes, madam, although I've asked these gentlemen to accompany us.

Agatha (*Looking at the three men*) Them? What for? I've already invited them to dinner.

Robert Yes, madam, but we'll be descending into some dark spaces where crewmembers like stokers work. It would do well to have three men with us just in case.

Agatha You mean it could be dangerous? Maybe it would be better to wait for the public tour.

Robert I'm afraid the public tour is all booked up until New York. Mr. Westbrook tried to get into it but had to be turned away.

Agatha Yes, but if we need bodyguards, I don't know.

Bertha Oh, please, auntie, it will be all right. We want to see the ship, don't we, Beryl?

Beryl I guess.

Agatha All right, but just this once.

Robert (*Summoning the three*) Gentlemen, if you'll join us. (*They approach*)

Daniel, **Henry**, and **Stan** Good day, ladies.

Agatha Gentlemen. First the quayside, now the tour, and tonight dinner. There's over 2,000 passengers on this ship and yet you're the only three I can seem to meet. I still don't even know what Mr. Westbrook looks like.

Daniel Neither do we, ma'am.

Agatha I should say not. You're in second class and he's in first.

Henry And who, may I ask, is this Mr. Westbrook?

Agatha Grapefruit merchant, gentlemen.

Henry Oh, him.

Agatha You've heard of him?

Henry Sure. We eat grapefruit.

Robert Right this way if you please. (*Gesturing them to exit right*)

Scene three – Below decks in a hot, steamy, noisy part of the ship
Robert is leading the party of six through the engine room spaces to the boiler room. He and Agatha are at the left side of the stage, Bertha and Beryl are in the middle, and the three friends are at the right.

Agatha Good lord, it's like we have descended into the depths of hell!

Robert This is the most demanding part of the tour, madam. The engine room and boiler room. It's all fresh air and light after this.

Agatha I should hope so. It won't do with me perspiring like this. Is it always this hot down here?

Robert Hotter, madam, when we're doing full speed.

Agatha Well, I think I have seen enough. I could faint down here under these conditions.

Robert Come along, the rest of you. Squeeze in here for a closer look.

Agatha Don't you find it strange that those three men haven't asked a single question this entire tour? I thought men were supposed to be interested in machines.

Robert I believe they're clerks, madam. Not engineering types.

Agatha But they are men, aren't they? I know little boys who have shown more interest in machines.

Robert Yes, madam. Now if you'll all look down there (*pointing to the audience*), you'll see what we call the stokehole. This is where our stokers shovel coal into the boilers, putting fuel to the fire, which in turn heats up the water, thereby creating steam, and that steam we use to drive enormous pistons which exert their force on that equally enormous crankshaft down there, and it drives the propellers which in turn drive this ship. And that's all there is to it. Any questions? (*Agatha looks at the three men as if expecting a response*)

Agatha I knew it. Nothing. No interest. Why did they even come on this tour?

Bertha Problem, auntie? (*Robert moves over to the cluster of men*)

Agatha Yes, those three men show no interest in this ship at all. Why did they come on the tour when they can be topside in the breeze and sunlight?

Bertha Maybe they already know it all.

Agatha Hah! Robert says they're clerks, but there's something disturbing about any man who doesn't ask questions when surrounded by machinery.

Bertha So go talk to them. They're probably waiting for your invitation to speak.

Agatha You think so?

Bertha Positive. Go on. Beryl and I will wait here and do the observing.

Agatha All right, but keep a lookout. Those hairy beasts are just below.

Bertha Right, auntie. (*Agatha joins the cluster of men*)

Beryl Do you see how profusely auntie is sweating?

Bertha She's starting to suspect the intentions of our three admirers. We're going to have to make a move fast.

Beryl What move? I didn't agree to any move.

Bertha All this heat and steam and you don't feel any special desire?

Beryl Like what?

Bertha Oh, come on, Beryl. The flesh underneath my corset is so hot and sticky I would sleep with one of those stokers now.

Beryl Those hairy beasts? That's disgusting.

Bertha They're men, aren't they? Look, we haven't got much time. Will you or won't you?

Beryl With a stoker!

Bertha No, with one of two of our three gentlemen!

Beryl No, I won't do it! Don't bring it up again!

Bertha Fine, you had your chance. I'm taking 22. (*She moves towards the cluster*)

Beryl Bertha!

Robert Now the ship itself is made of iron. As the weight of the ship pushes down on the water, the water pushes back with an equal force, and that's what keeps us afloat. Of course, if water were to get into the ship, it would negate that upward pressure and we would all sink and drown. That's why we maintain watertight integrity. As long as we have integrity, this ship is unsinkable. Any questions?

Agatha Perhaps the gentlemen care to ask one?

Robert Gentlemen?

Daniel What's on the menu for dinner?

Agatha Good lord, and these three are joining us!

Robert Lamb in mint sauce, roast duckling, sirloin of beef, and chateau potatoes.

Henry And for dessert?

Agatha Mercenaries!

Robert Waldorf pudding and French ice cream. And there's more good news. The captain will be sitting at your table tonight.

Agatha The captain? Tonight? Can't it be another night?

Daniel I would love to meet the captain.

Henry Me too.

Agatha I'm sure you would. But there's protocol to follow, gentlemen.

Robert I will look into it, madam. Now, I will give you a couple of moments to observe and think about all this magnificent machinery before you. So please kindly commence contemplating.

Agatha You mean just stand here? I prefer to contemplate in the privacy of my suite.

Robert Believe me, madam, you'll enjoy it much more here.

Agatha But it's so noisy and steamy in here!

Robert The perfect conditions. And after this, I shall lead you through steerage on our way topside.

Agatha What! I can't have the people in third class staring at me now after this sauna. My hair, my makeup!

Robert But, madam, steerage is a rite of passage for all first class travelers.

Agatha That's absurd. I didn't read about it in the brochure.

Robert Trust me, madam, they all do it. Your neighbor Mr. Westbrook was down there just last night.

Agatha Then I guess we're going to steerage. As usual, the grapefruit merchant decides.

Robert Good, now then, if you'll kindly contemplate. (*During the lull, Robert moves amidst the party, whispering to the men and Bertha as he goes. Bertha in turn whispers to Beryl, who each time shakes her off. Bertha shrugs and indicates to Robert that she'll be the one, and he then communicates this to the gentlemen. She points at number 22, who turns out to be Stan. All the men nod, whereupon Daniel slips Robert some money and Robert him a key. With the deal confirmed, Bertha puts her hand up to her forehead and pretends to grow faint.*)

Agatha Are you all right, my dear?

Bertha I don't feel well, auntie. I feel faint.

Agatha I shouldn't wonder standing down here in this heat. It's time we went up.

Robert But, madam, the rite of passage?

Agatha We'll have to do it some other time. My niece isn't well.

Robert Surely one of these gentlemen can escort her to the deck for some fresh air.

Stan I can do it. I've already been in steerage.

Agatha But my niece hardly knows this man.

Daniel Rest assured, madam, that Stan here is a most reliable chap.

Bertha (*Pretending to grow fainter*) I really have to go up now, auntie. I'll be all right. See you later in our suite. (*Stan follows her out the left exit*)

Agatha Oh, dear. I don't know about any of this.

Beryl She'll be fine, auntie. Let's just get this bloody tour over with.

Agatha You mean you're not having a good time?

Beryl Good time? I'm totally wet and sticky under my dress and there's oil in my hair.

Agatha Ach, there's just no pleasing you girls!

Robert Has everybody had enough contemplation?

Agatha Yes. Let's get this blasted tour over with.

Robert I'm sorry, madam, are you not having a good time?

Scene four – The first class dining room
Agatha, Bertha, and Beryl are sitting at a circular table, all done up for the evening.

Agatha Are you sure you're feeling up to dinner tonight, my dear?

Bertha Completely, auntie. I'm starving.

Agatha I can't say the same about my appetite. I would be in my bed right now if the captain weren't dining with us tonight. (*Robert enters*)

Robert Ah, good evening, ladies. Nice to see you looking so charming tonight.

Agatha I should wonder after that exhausting tour. It took me an hour to do my makeup and hair.

Robert Time well spent. And now, madam, if you follow me, I'll be happy to introduce you to Mr. Westbrook.

Agatha What? He's here now in the dining room? Why doesn't he come over and introduce himself like a gentleman?

Robert He's painfully shy, madam. But he asked to meet you. He said, "Robert, my good man, who is that delightful creature in the private suite next to mine."

Agatha Did he actually call me a creature? I've heard far more delicate ways of addressing a lady.

Robert He meant it in all sincerity, madam. Now if you please...

Agatha But the captain is coming.

Robert Not for another 20 minutes, madam. We have received reports that there are icebergs in the area. He feels it's his duty to remain on the bridge until the danger has passed.

Agatha Oh, very well. (*She rises*) I'll be right back, girls. (*She leaves with Robert*)

Beryl Auntie is finally gone. So tell me, what was it like with number 22?

Bertha All I'll say is you really missed your chance. We were in perfect rhythm with the rocking and rolling of the ship.

Beryl Oh, I wanted to go. I...I need more time.

Bertha We have no such time with auntie always around. But Robert has assured me he will keep her occupied so you can have your chance too.

Beryl Where did you go?

Bertha Robert's cabin.

Beryl (*Angrily*) Then he is a pimp!

Bertha Who cares as long as you get a little privacy? I'm anxious to go back.

Beryl Again? Then you are a slut!

Bertha Only here on the ship. Just imagine, Beryl. You're lying there breathing in all that salty air as your body takes one manly thrust after another.

Beryl Stop it or I shall die of jealousy.

Bertha And when it's over, you gaze out over the ocean sparkling underneath the sun and you think nothing can get better than this moment.

Beryl All right, I'll do it! Can I also go with 22? I mean, he is yours.

Bertha If I'm going to be a slut, I might as well play the whole field. You go with 22, I'll make plans for number 12.

Beryl I didn't mean to call you that. Forgive me?

Bertha Nothing to forgive. But if you decide to become one too, I want to hear all the details. (*The three gentlemen appear*)

Daniel Ladies. Good evening.

Henry and **Stan** Good evening. (*The ladies nod*)

Bertha Please, have a seat.

Daniel Don't mind if we do. (*They sit*) Is your aunt not joining us tonight?

Bertha She's meeting some other passenger at the moment. She'll be along shortly.

Daniel Good. It'll give us the chance to become better acquainted.

Bertha How so?

Daniel Well, I for one don't even know your names.

Bertha I'm Bertha. And this is my cousin Beryl.

Daniel And I'm...

Bertha Number six. (*She and Beryl break out laughing*).

Daniel I beg your pardon?

Bertha I'm sorry. My cousin and I are playing a little game. Trying to guess... what hat size the other passengers have? We guessed you're a size six.

Daniel To tell you the truth, I don't even know what hat size I have. You fellows know yours? (*Henry and Stan shake their heads*) You ladies care to guess?

Bertha Rather not. (*The girls start laughing again. Their aunt approaches.*)

Agatha What's so funny here? (*The men stand up*) Still joking about Mr. Westbrook?

Beryl No, auntie.

Agatha Well, do so. Boring man. He did nothing but talk about his vile grapefruit. Ach, I could gladly have done without that acquaintance. So, I see you gentlemen managed to make it here before the captain did.

Henry Right on time.

Agatha What right on time? You're 15 minutes late. I don't mind inviting passengers in second class to dine with me but I will not be taken advantage of. When I say eight o'clock, I mean eight o'clock. Is that understood?

Henry If it means we're going to get another invitation, yes.

Agatha Another invitation? Look here, gentlemen: I paid a lot of money to travel in style with my nieces and yet you three are the only ones I have intercourse with on this ship. (*Bertha and Beryl suppress laughter*) What's so funny now?

Bertha Sorry, auntie. We were just thinking of Mr. Westbrook.

Agatha Oh, I wish you two would grow up. (*Robert enters*)

Robert Good evening again, everyone. Everything satisfactory?

Agatha My nieces could learn a thing or two about table manners.

Robert Well, they won't be so necessary tonight. I'm afraid I have some bad news. The warnings about icebergs continue, so the captain must remain on the bridge for the rest of the evening.

Agatha You mean he's not coming?

Robert I'm sorry to say, madam, but no. But he has asked a member of his wardroom to sit in for him. Yours truly. (*He sits down between Agatha and Daniel*)

Agatha You? What about the first officer, or the second officer?

Robert All busy, madam. But the fifth officer, as always, is at your service.

Agatha Yes, I gathered that.

Robert And how did your meeting with Mr. Westbrook go?

Agatha Frightful experience. Such a vainglorious man, constantly playing with his moustache, eyes always trying to catch the attention of other people.

Robert Well, madam, it was quite an honour for him to have you sit at his table. He wanted everyone in first class to notice.

Agatha So why hasn't anyone else in first class asked me to join them? I'm sitting here for all to see.

Robert All in due time, madam, all in due time. For now, tell me more about your husband. He must've been a bold and adventurous man.

Agatha That he was. (*As she continues to relate, Daniel whispers something into Robert's ear, Robert uses his tapping fingers on the table to signal the two girls across from him, and Bertha looks at Beryl, who closes her eyes to signal back. Robert gently elbows Daniel, who then slips him some money in return for the key, which Daniel passes along to Henry. Meanwhile Death enters and starts flitting around the table. No one but Stan seems to notice. He starts looking around, oblivious to Henry's attempts to give him the key.*) On the wall in our main study is the skin of a jaguar he strangled with his bare hands. He even once captured an anaconda but it managed to escape before he could give it to the zoo. (*Chuckles. Death has latched on to Stan and focuses her wild maneuvers on him. He starts to grow more uncomfortable but the others don't notice it until he takes to swatting at the air.*) But of course it wasn't all play for him. He had to constantly shuffle between his diamond mines to make sure the workers weren't stealing from him. Of course they were. That's why he had to use his whip on them. (*Notices Stan swatting*) Good lord, young man. What are you swatting at?

Stan Don't the rest of you sense something in the air? Like flies everywhere?

Robert There are no flies aboard this ship. We're in the middle of the ocean.

Agatha I was afraid of this. Invite people to first class and the first thing they do is help themselves to the bar.

Daniel He hasn't had anything to drink. He may be feeling a bit seasick, that's all.

Agatha What's that got to do with him swatting the air?

Daniel I think all he needs is some fresh air. Right? Stan? (*Stan doesn't respond*) Maybe I will accompany him up, just to make sure he gets there all right. Pardon us. (*He leads Stan up from the table and out of the dining hall*)

Agatha Strange, this reminds me of when my husband came upon a nest of termites in Africa. (*Bertha nudges Beryl, but she refuses to budge. She thought that Stan was merely putting on an act to excuse himself from the table, which was all right with her, but not Daniel accompanying him. She's now under the impression she is being set up for a threesome. Beryl now taps a signal to Robert to indicate she has changed her mind and would prefer to go off with Henry. Robert quickly taps on the now empty chair next to him to signal to Henry that Beryl is all his.*) There were millions of them and he said it was much worse than dealing with ants because their jaws are bigger. Of course, the big difference was the sheer persistence of these termites. My poor husband was covered in whelps for days on end after that.

Beryl Auntie, I'm afraid I'm not feeling well either. I have to go up for some air too.

Agatha What? Is everybody coming down with something? I might suspect food poisoning but we haven't eaten anything yet.

Robert I'm sure this young gentleman here will be honored to escort her to the deck while I go see what's keeping dinner. (*Henry and Robert rise. Henry goes around to Beryl to assist her in getting up.*)

Henry It'll be an honor.

Beryl I'll be fine, auntie. You eat without me.

Henry Madam, mademoiselle. (*Beryl exits, followed by Henry*)

Agatha Eat what?

Robert Yes, I'll go take care of that now. (*He exits*)

Bertha Pardon me, auntie. I have to go to the ladies' room. (*She rises and exits*)

Agatha Wonderful. First no captain, now nobody period. And no food. Lord knows what else is in store for this cruise.

Act II

Scene one – The luxurious private suite of Agatha and her nieces
Beryl is sitting alone as Bertha enters.

Bertha Already here? What happened?

Beryl Are you alone? Auntie didn't follow you?

Bertha No, she's still at the table with Robert, telling him all those ghastly stories about uncle. So, which one did you take: 6, 12, or 22?

Beryl None.

Bertha What?

Beryl Yes, and we went to Robert's cabin. We had some small talk, then we got close, did some kissing and suddenly I was overcome by the urge you were talking about.

Bertha Good. Go on.

Beryl So I got all undressed and so did he and...

Bertha Wait a minute! You got *all* undressed?

Beryl Sure.

Bertha Your top too?

Beryl Of course.

Bertha Of course? Darling, you're not supposed to do that!

Beryl Do what?

Bertha Take your top off. Show a man your breasts. That you save for your husband. Most single men have never even seen a woman's breasts before and when they do the effect is powerful.

Beryl Oh dear. That's when it happened.

Bertha What happened?

Beryl Well, when Henry came to me...

Bertha Who?

Beryl Henry. Number 12.

Bertha Ah yes.

Beryl When he came to me, he went straight for my breasts. Started fondling them and slobbering all over them like an animal. And then, well, he was early. (*Bertha starts laughing*) It's not funny!

Bertha I'm sorry, Beryl, I shouldn't have laughed. (*Going up to her*) I'm sure your next boy will be more of a man.

Beryl I hope so. To tell you the truth, I've been having some dirty little thoughts about one man in particular here.

Bertha Who? Mr. Westbrook?

Beryl No.

Bertha Robert?

Beryl Please...but he is a member of the crew.

Bertha The captain?

Beryl No! The stoker.

Bertha (*Laughing in shock*) You can't be serious! The man's an animal, a beast.

Beryl I can't help it. Something exciting came over me when Henry was gnawing and pawing at my breasts. It will be even more exciting if I put them into the hands of a real man.

Bertha He's an ogre!

Beryl I don't care. I want to be ravished. I will ask Robert if it's possible.

Bertha Robert?! You can't expect him to do that. He would be putting his job on the line.

Beryl He already has with us.

Bertha How so? All he did was let us use his cabin. But this is like asking him to play pimp for you.

Beryl Why not? He did it for those three gentlemen.

Bertha (*Flustered*) I beg your pardon?

Beryl Really, Bertha! You didn't see money changing hands between those men and Robert?

Bertha Money? They paid him to set something up with us?

Beryl Of course.

Bertha Dear me! I feel like a whore.

Beryl Slut, Bertha. You're only a whore if you get some of the money.

Bertha And where do you propose to get any money to pay Robert?

Beryl I'll pay him nothing. If he refuses me, I will threaten to inform his superiors that he is operating a brothel here on the ship.

Bertha I don't like this, Beryl. Primitive men can be unstable when they get their emotions aroused.

Beryl I'll have Robert stand by with his whip just in case.

Bertha You're going to let Robert watch? Beryl, what's got into you?

Beryl Not watch. Just be close at hand.

Bertha And you think he won't try to peek? He's a sailor, Beryl! (*The door opens at the left exit, in walks Agatha*)

Agatha Hello, girls. Talking about sailors before bedtime?

Bertha Yes, auntie.

Agatha Then you should have stayed with me and Robert at the table. He's a sailor well worth knowing.

Bertha I got the feeling you were getting tired of him being around all the time.

Agatha That was before I realized that as an officer and gentleman, he is only doing his duty in looking after us. And tonight, I can even say he was a worthy replacement for the captain at our table.

Bertha My, auntie, it almost sounds as if you're swooning over him.

Agatha People my age don't swoon anymore. We're just grateful to have the attentions of a gentleman. I'll even let you girls in on a secret. (*All three draw closer*) He's asked me to accompany him to the bow tomorrow.

Beryl The bow? But, auntie, that's where couples go to be romantic.

Bertha Or stand there like a crucified Jesus shouting like baboons.

Agatha I know all that. I read the brochure too.

Beryl So why does he want to take you there?

Agatha I have no idea. But don't worry. After the bow, I'll give you girls my undivided attention again.

Bertha and **Beryl** Of course, auntie.

Agatha There. Now if you'll excuse me, I'm off to bed. Good night, dears. (*She rises*)

Bertha Good night, auntie.

Beryl Good night, auntie. (*Agatha exits by entering her room on the right and closing the door.*)

Bertha I guess there go your plans to meet the stoker.

Beryl Why?

Bertha Why?! The only time you will be free of auntie is when she has Robert in her grasp. He won't be able to go with you.

Beryl Then you will have to help.

Bertha You want me to stand there with the whip and watch you make love to the stoker?

Beryl No, keep auntie busy so Robert will be free for me.

Agatha (*Voice offstage*) What on earth are you two talking about in there?

Beryl Uh, about Robert's whip, auntie.

Bertha Yes, we finally understand why he needs to use it sometimes.

Agatha Well, thank god for that. Good night.

Scene two – The second class room of Daniel, Henry, and Stan
There are two bunk beds on each side. Daniel is sitting on the lower left bunk, Stan is lying on the lower right one. Death is on the upper right bunk leaning over the edge and harassing Stan with gestures of her arms and hands. Stan remains transfixed by her movements, occasionally swatting at the air in a vain attempt to ward them off. Henry enters from the left, Daniel rises.

Daniel There you are. We've got a real problem with Stan here.

Henry He's still swatting at the air? I thought that was all an act to leave with the other girl.

Daniel I thought so too. But there's something really bothering him.

Henry What?

Daniel I don't know. Stan? What's wrong?

Stan (*Exasperated*) Can't you feel it? Something evil in the air?

Daniel No, Stan. There's only air and us in here.

Stan Yes, us! That us is more than just us right now. There's something else.

Henry What, Stan?

Stan I don't know. But it's after us, whatever it is. After all of us. This ship is doomed.

Henry He's starting to scare me.

Daniel I was too at first. Now I just find it tiresome. (*Stan screams*)

Henry Jesus!

Daniel Maybe we should take him to see the ship's doctor.

Henry At this hour? And what's he going to do with him anyway? Lock him up in the brig until we get to New York is all he can do.

Daniel At least he can tell us what the problem is. All we really know right now is he's losing his mind.

Henry It sounds like syphilis.

Daniel Syphilis?

Henry Yes, it eats away at the cell membrane in the brain. That's what causes people to go crazy before they die.

Daniel Oh my god! Stan is going to die? But he's getting married this summer!

Henry Syphilis shows no mercy to anyone.

Daniel But...but I'm almost positive that Stan never had relations with a woman before. The whole purpose of this trip was to let him try other women before marriage.

Henry Like I said, syphilis shows no mercy.

Daniel Fine, but my question is where did he get it from?

Henry Do you think Stan ever snuck away to a brothel?

Daniel No. He would've told us if he had. Near as I can figure, the only one he could have caught it from is that girl, Bertha.

Henry But they had sex today. Syphilis doesn't spread through the body that quickly.

Daniel Maybe it's some kind of super syphilis. Once it gets in you, it takes over.

Henry Then why is Bertha all right?

Daniel I don't know. She probably has stronger immunity. How do you feel?

Henry Me? Fine. Why?

Daniel You were with that other girl. For all we know, they both have it. It was easier than we expected to get them into bed.

Henry I have no need to worry.

Daniel Why? Didn't you have sex with her?

Henry Sure. But she...she was a virgin.

Daniel A virgin? You lucky devil! How was it?

Henry Fine, I said.

Daniel Did she scream?

Henry Scream?

Daniel Yes. Stan was telling us Bertha screamed.

Henry Nah. I was very gentle. But that's not all.

Daniel What else?

Henry I got to see her totally naked.

Daniel What?! Get out of here!

Henry I swear it.

Daniel I don't believe your luck!

Henry I couldn't either. She took everything off.

Daniel How did they look?

Henry Her legs?

Daniel No!

Henry Oh, those. Beautiful.

Daniel Man, you're so lucky! Stan here said Bertha wouldn't let him touch hers. You hear that, Stan? You really missed out tonight. (*Stan is still preoccupied with his demons*) So are you going to try to hook up with her again?

Henry No. Once was enough. Besides, there are lots of girls on this ship.

Daniel Great, so I will call on her. I still haven't scored that far with a woman yet. I'm always worried when I finally do, I will get so excited that I lose it too early.

Henry (*Nervous*) I thought you were worried about catching syphilis?

Daniel You just said she was a virgin.

Henry Yes, but I think we should move on. I'm a little tired of always hanging around those three.

Daniel Fine. Let me get my squeeze and we'll root around for other opportunities. Robert is sure to have other prospects lined up for us. (*There's a knock at the door. Henry opens it at the left entrance to find Robert standing there.*)

Henry Speak of the devil. It's Robert. Come in. (*Robert enters. Death takes notice of him, leaps off the bed and scurries out the door before Henry closes it. Stan stops swatting at the air and grows calm.*)

Robert I'm glad to see I caught you gentlemen before you went to sleep. I have a small favor to ask.

Daniel Sure. What is it?

Robert Could I bunk with you tonight? I noticed on the passenger list that you booked an entire four-berth room, so I presume that you have one bunk free.

Henry That's true, but can we ask why you need it?

Robert As you probably guessed, you are not the only passengers I provide facilitation services for. One man, an elderly gentleman, asked to use my cabin for the entire night and I found it impossible to refuse him.

Henry You mean he paid you a lot of money?

Robert If you must know, yes.

Henry So what are you, Robert? The unofficial ship's pimp?

Robert I prefer to call it facilitation, but whatever the label, all sailors need to supplement their incomes before they become too old to go to sea anymore.

Daniel Don't you get a pension?

Robert Yes, but it's barely enough to cover the cost of ending your days in a rat-infested sailors' home with three bowls of oatmeal to eat. So we all spend our careers saving up a nice little kitty to tide us over during our twilight years.

Henry You mean you're all pimping?

Robert Of course not. Some plunder the ship's stores, some the machinery, and sell them on the black market. I prefer facilitation because I also like to make people happy. I trust you gentlemen are?

Daniel Actually, we've run into quite a scare with Stan here. He seems to have lost his mind and we're worried that the reason for it is syphilis.

Robert Syphilis? Good lord, if he gave syphilis to that girl, I could be ruined!

Daniel We think she gave it to him because he's never been with a girl before.

Robert That's ridiculous, gentlemen. You don't catch syphilis and then go crazy in a matter of hours.

Henry Then what else explains his erratic behavior? You saw him at the table tonight.

Robert I thought that was all part of the act to leave with the girl?

Daniel We did too, but now he's talking about the ship being doomed.

Stan (*In a cool and collected voice*) Don't worry, fellows. The danger has passed. Whatever it was is gone now. (*Daniel and Henry look at each other, Robert approaches Stan and bends low*)

Robert What danger? What is gone?

Stan I don't know. Some horrible, oppressive feeling that death was near.

Robert And now it's gone?

Stan I just said it was.

Daniel So you're all right now, Stan?

Stan I suppose. At any rate, I feel a whole lot better.

Robert Does this mean you're back in the game?

Stan I hope so. That Bertha was incredible.

Daniel *She* was incredible? You should have heard what Henry just said about the other girl. She was a virgin.

Robert Really?

Henry Really.

Stan Oh, no. She would have been the perfect training for my wedding night.

Daniel And not only that, Stan, but she gave her entire body to him, including her top.

Robert Really?

Henry Really.

Stan Oh, no. I couldn't even get that far with Bertha. Dear God, I just get over one torment, why are you putting me through another?

Scene three – The forward edge of the bow represented in front of the audience
Robert enters escorting Agatha by the arm.

Agatha Oh, look, it's free.

Robert Yes, I made sure of that.

Agatha How did you manage that?

Robert The fifth officer on a ship has more power than his rank might suggest. I told the crew to make sure the bow would be free for us.

Agatha Oh, Robert. You surprise me more and more.

Robert Well, madam, a promise is a promise.

Agatha Yes, but you don't seem to be like other men I know. Last night, when I was telling you those stories about my late husband, you sat there with such deep interest in your eyes. Most men would never tolerate that in a woman.

Robert I guess, madam, we can say it has to do with my life as a sailor. When you're out at sea, working around men, eating around men, even sleeping around men, you grow ever more lonesome for the sound of a woman's voice.

Agatha That sounds like you're saying you were just listening to my voice, not paying attention to what I was saying.

Robert On the contrary, madam, I heard every word. The jaguar, the termites, the anaconda. The story about the flesh-eating monkeys was particularly enthralling. But it was the sound of your voice that held me in such rapture.

Agatha Oh dear, you flatter me to no end.

Robert I assure you, it's not flattery, although I can think of no one else aboard this ship who deserves it more than you, including the captain.

Agatha I think now would be a good time to cast all formalities aside. Please, Robert, call me Agatha.

Robert With esteem (*taking her hand and kissing it*), Agatha.

Agatha (*Blushing*) You tell me something about yourself now, Robert.

Robert Well, Agatha, mine is a pitiful story. I grew up in poverty and squalor and was only able to escape it by joining the royal navy. I soon found out that was a hard life too, always at sea, always being beaten by your superiors, always being robbed in ports-of-call. Finally I got the chance to serve in the passenger fleet and become an officer. In another 15 years, I could easily make captain.

Agatha Captain? Of a ship like this?

Robert Of course. And when I am captain, I will make sure you, Agatha, dine at my table every night for all to see. I will even invite you to the bridge to take control of the ship if you please.

Agatha (*Blushing more*) Dear me. Not even my late husband could have managed a feat like that.

Robert But of course it all depends on if I survive.

Agatha (*Concerned*) Survive? Dear lord, Robert, what's wrong with you?

Robert Nothing physically, I assure you. It's just that I have given my life to the sea and that has demanded many sacrifices. First and foremost is a home life. To be able to leave your work and come home to a woman who loves you, it must be the greatest joy in the world and one most sailors will never be able to partake in.

Agatha Oh, Robert, that's so sad.

Robert I know, Agatha. But at least I am able to spend part of my lonely life in the company of a charming woman such as you.

Agatha Robert, I have a confession to make. For all the talk about my late husband, he was in fact an extremely boring man to be married to. Unloving too. Sure, he conquered the world, but he didn't even try to conquer my heart.

Robert If I may be so bold, did you know all this when you married him?

Agatha Of course. His children thought I was gold digging, and I suppose I was. I was working as a maid in his home when one night, while drunk, he grabbed me. I put up such a fight that he grabbed me again the next night, just so I would fight him. He said I reminded him of the jaguar and he loved it.

Robert Did you use your fingernails?

Agatha I most certainly did. But he enjoyed it so much that he soon decided he had to have me. Domesticate me were his words. So he married me, domesticated me, and then grew tired of me.

Robert Wretchedly unfair.

Agatha But it gets worse. As my husband grew old, he became bloated and feeble but still he insisted on having a hot, bubble bath every day. It was such a strain on my back to lift him in and out of the tub. I suppose someday I will have to marry a strong, robust man to do the same for me when I've become too old.

Robert I don't know that fellow but I already consider him lucky.

Agatha Do you, Robert? Do you consider any man who would want to be with me lucky? My nieces certainly don't think so.

Robert They're just children, Agatha. But if I may again be so bold...

Agatha Yes, Robert?

Robert Could I ask you to stand up here on the edge of the bow?

Agatha Dear lord, isn't that dangerous?

Robert Not with me behind you.

Agatha Oh, well, I suppose there's no one better on board I should trust than you. (*He assists her in stepping up*) Oh my! What a view!

Robert And now, Agatha, I would like you to extend your arms, stretch them completely out at your sides.

Agatha Like a crucified Jesus?

Robert No, like you're about to do a swan dive.

Agatha Swan dive? Into the water?

Robert Only pretending, Agatha, so you can feel the freedom of the swan; to let yourself go and not be afraid, to know I'm always behind you, ready to catch you if you fall, ready to lift you up whenever you need me.

Agatha Oh, Robert. Could you be that lucky man?

Robert I would very much like to be. (*As she turns her head over her shoulder to meet his eyes, Daniel enters, running up from behind.*)

Daniel Hey, Robert! We need your help. (*Robert and Agatha step down, pretending nothing is happening*)

Agatha Good lord, him again? Everywhere I go it's always one of you standing there. Are you stalking me?

Daniel No, ma'am, we have a serious problem with our friend. We think he's really gone out of his mind.

Robert But you said that last night and he appeared perfectly normal to me.

Daniel Maybe it was a relapse, because he's really lost it now. He's running around, swatting at the air, yelling at something or other to leave him alone. He's totally loony.

Agatha Are you talking about that young man at the dinner table last night? That was indeed most unbecoming.

Robert What would you like me to do about it? Take him to the ship's doctor.

Daniel We can't do that. They'll put him in a lunatic asylum when we get to New York. He's going to be married this summer.

Agatha Heavens! The poor girl.

Daniel If we can just get him to New York without alerting the authorities, we'll hop on the next ship back home and get him some professional care there. (*Stan enters running from Death hot on his* *heels, swatting at her and yelling, "Go away!" Henry is right behind her, as if trying to catch Stan.) See what I mean? (Daniel helps Henry pin down Stan and restrain him. Death hovers nearby still making faces at Stan.)*

Agatha Oh, this is most unseemly! Excuse me, gentlemen. (*She bolts for the exit*)

Robert Wait! (*Calling after her*) See you for dinner? (*No answer is heard*) You boys may well have cost me a comfortable retirement.

Daniel Sorry about that, but you've got to help us.

Robert What should I do? Knock him over the head? He's your friend, you do it!

Henry We would like you to lock him up in your cabin until we get to New York.

Robert You must be mad! You expect me to bunk with this halfwit?

Henry No, you'll bunk with us.

Robert But I have my facilitation service to think of. That affects you too, gentlemen.

Daniel The games are over, Robert. If the reason for his madness is syphilis, the problem could get back to you.

Robert Now I know you are mad if you think syphilis is behind this. It just doesn't happen that fast.

Henry Look, Robert, help us out here. We've been good business for you. We let you stay in our cabin last night free of charge.

Robert Oh, well, let's do it then. But we'll have to handcuff him around a pipe to keep him from trashing the place. And you gentlemen are to see to all his needs, including food and going to the toilet. Is that understood?

Daniel Of course. He's our friend.

Robert Your friend! And he's lucky he's your friend (*going to help them pick Stan up*), otherwise I would suggest we toss him overboard and be done with him. (*All three commence leading Stan away with Death still harassing him*)

Henry (*Snidely*) Another part of your facilitation services, Robert?

Robert That's right. (*The other two look at each other in disbelief*)

Scene four – A dark and steamy hold within the ship, just before the stokehole
Robert enters leading Beryl behind him.

Robert This is crazy. Crazy. Absolutely crazy. But in any case here we are. You wait here while I bring one of them up here.

Beryl Wait. Can I have the one we saw on the pier before we left?

Robert There are several dozen stokers down there and all of them look the same, I assure you. But do you even know what you're doing? Stokers are raw, uncouth savages. I know because I was one when I first went to sea.

Beryl You don't seem to have turned out too badly.

Robert That's because I had the good sense to work my way out of the hole. But some of these men will always be there. They were born for the hole. Some of them like it, are even proud of it

Beryl And that's the kind of man I'm after. A real brute who knows he's a brute, who doesn't try to pretend he's something he's not; who doesn't use suave speech and fine manners to cover up the fact that he's a lout.

Robert I beg your pardon, miss? Are you by chance referring to me?

Beryl There you go again, Robert. It's obvious that I am referring to you.

Why don't you just come out and take offence instead of pretending you're not sure?

Robert I needn't take offence. As I told you, I used to be a stoker too and my hide is as tough as it was in those days. But may I ask you why you think I'm a lout?

Beryl Because you are. I know all about the money those three gentlemen paid you to set them up with my cousin and me. That makes you a pimp. I also know about you hoping to marry my aunt and get a hold of her fortune. That makes you a gold digger. Put a pimp and gold digger together and what you get is a lout.

Robert You are observant, miss.

Beryl And because you're a lout, I'm turning to you to fulfil my fantasy. So now bring that stoker up here, then kindly remove yourself around that corner there and be ready with your whip.

Robert As you wish, miss. (*Robert exits left. Beryl stands there facing the audience, patting her hair and adjusting her garments as if wanting to look her best for a date who's about to arrive. A moment later Robert enters followed by the stoker. Beryl can't believe her eyes and nervously summons Robert to her with her hands. He approaches.*) You're good, Robert! That's one who was on the quayside when we were boarding.

Robert I'm not sure how you can tell. They're all sweaty, grimy and hairy.

Beryl Yes, he's perfect! (*Robert shakes his head, then goes back to the stoker. He exchanges some words with him, the stoker looks excited. Robert leads him to Beryl*)

Robert Here you are, miss. He understands what's required of him. I will now adjourn to the corner over here and await the outcome. (*Taking his whip out and admonishing the stoker*) Bear in mind that you are at the lady's services here. Failure to respect her desires will result in this whip coming down hard on your back. (*The stoker grunts and nods*) Very well. Miss, enjoy. (*Robert leaves through the right exit. The stoker stands* *there gawking at Beryl, who doesn't look directly at him. The stoker slowly takes off his shirt to reveal a supremely hairy chest and back. He still has the shirt around his neck when Beryl starts laughing hysterically.)*

Beryl Oh my. You really are hairy. (*The stoker stands there confused. Robert emerges from the shadows.*)

Robert Is there a problem?

Beryl No, I was just surprised what a gorilla he is.

Robert Would you prefer a man now?

Beryl No, I'm all right now.

Robert I'll be right over here. (*Robert extends a finger of warning at the stoker and then exits again. The stoker finishes removing his shirt and tosses it aside. Beryl breaks out laughing again.*)

Beryl I'm sorry. I just never imagined any man could look the way you do. (*The stoker becomes incensed, thinking he's been set up by a superior officer just to provide some amusement for a passenger in first class. He lunges for her but Robert appears just in time with his whip and beats him back. Beryl runs behind Robert's back for safety. Now the stoker is really angry and dashes out the left exit, presumably the stokehole.*) Dear lord, what a beast! He wanted to harm me.

Robert I tried to warn you this could be dangerous.

Beryl You were right, Robert. Please, take me out of here. (*Robert starts to turn but notices something in the stokehole. He goes up to the left exit and sees how the stoker – offstage of course – is shoveling heaps of coal into the boiler at a furious rate. Beryl goes up and stands behind him.*)

Robert What are you doing there? Are you mad? Stop that or you'll blow up the boiler. Do you hear me? Stop that at once or I will give you a lashing you'll never forget! Stop it, I say! (*Takes his whip and start lashing through the exit. He lashes again and again but to no effect.*)

Stop it, you fool! You'll blow us all up! (*Lashing again and again*) My God, the pressure in the boiler has reached the danger point! It's going to blow!

Beryl Can't you stop him?

Robert I'm trying! Stop it, damn you!! (*Lashing away*)

Beryl (*Yelling to the stokehole*) Good, sir! I'm sorry I laughed at you. I didn't mean it. Please, come up here and we'll try again.

Robert Good God, we've got to get out of here! Quickly! (*Robert runs for the right exit, followed by Beryl. A moment later a huge flash is seen, followed by an equally huge explosion, and smoke fills the stage.*)

Act III

Scene one – On the open deck of the ship at night
The sounds of pandemonium can be heard over chamber orchestra music. Agatha and Bertha enter, both wearing life vests.

Agatha Beryl! Beryl!

Bertha Beryl! Beryl!

Agatha Dear lord, where can she be? What did she tell you?

Bertha I told you she said she was just going for a walk topside to get some fresh air. That's all.

Agatha Well, we're topside and I don't see her anywhere. Beryl!

Bertha Maybe she went to our suite after the accident happened. She's probably waiting for us there now. I'll go and check.

Agatha (*Stopping her*) No, you won't. You stay right here. I'll go there and check. (*Agatha leaves out the left exit. Bertha is standing there shivering when Robert and Beryl run up from the right exit.*)

Bertha There you are! (*The girls hug. Robert looks around.*) Auntie was getting so afraid. She went to our suite to look for you.

Beryl You didn't tell her where I was, did you?

Bertha Of course not! So, did you…? (*Beryl shakes her head*) What? Even those beasts below aren't real men?

Beryl No, it was my fault. There's definitely something wrong with me.

Bertha Oh, Beryl. Don't worry. It'll happen someday.

Beryl If we survive. It's because of me the ship is going down.

Bertha What do you mean?

Beryl I got that stoker so worked up that he started putting in too much coal into the boiler. The whole thing then exploded.

Bertha Exploded? But auntie and I heard that the ship hit an iceberg.

Beryl Well, my explosion can't have helped. (*Daniel and Henry, both holding glasses in hand, enter from the left*)

Daniel Robert, is it true? The ship is going down?

Robert I'm afraid so.

Henry But how can that be? All it did was graze a bloody iceberg.

Robert What iceberg? There was an explosion in the engine room.

Henry No, we saw the iceberg, we felt the impact. I even got hit with chunks of ice falling off of it. One even landed in my drink here. (*Showing his glass*)

Robert I don't have time to argue about what's sinking the ship. You want to believe it's an iceberg, that's your business. Now if you'll excuse me, I have other business to attend to.

Daniel Wait! You've got to give us the key to your cabin. We've got to rescue Stan.

Robert Oh, you people have been more trouble than your worth. (*Handing them a set of keys*) Now be quick about it. (*Daniel and Henry exit*)

Bertha Robert, did they say they have to rescue Stan from your cabin? What's he doing in there?

Robert Apparently he's lost his mind or something. He's been acting like a total imbecile since last night.

Bertha Imbecile? What brought that on?

Robert I don't know. His friends say it's syphilis but that's ridiculous.

Bertha (*Shocked*) Syphilis?

Robert You'll excuse me, ladies, but I really have to see to the safety of the ship. (*Robert exits*)

Bertha (*Reeling*) Syphilis? (*She faints but is caught by Beryl, who lays her on the deck. Agatha enters wearing a chain around her neck with a big diamond at the end of it. She's overjoyed to see Beryl.*)

Agatha There you are, my dear. I was so worried. Where were you? And what's happened to Bertha?

Beryl She fainted, auntie. What's that you're wearing?

Agatha A gift from your step-uncle. (*Stuffs the diamond down her top*) Why did she faint?

Beryl I suppose all this pandemonium was too much for her.

Agatha Quite right. It's too much for me as well. But kindly tell me where you have been all this time? Bertha said you went up for some fresh air.

Beryl Yes, auntie.

Agatha And did you see this iceberg that supposedly hit us?

Beryl No.

Agatha Well, of course not. It's ludicrous to think that an iceberg can sink this ship. Unfathomable. (*A bell is heard ringing in a pattern. Robert enters.*)

Robert That's the signal to get into the lifeboats. There's only capacity for less than half the people on board but, Agatha, I'll make sure you and your nieces find a place on one of them.

Agatha Thank you, Robert.

Beryl He calls you Agatha now? (*Daniel and Henry enter, this time without their glasses. Bertha comes to and slowly gets up with Beryl's help.*)

Agatha Are you all right, my dear?

Bertha No, auntie, but I've got no choice.

Daniel Robert, none of these keys work. You have to give us another one.

Robert They must work. Those are the only keys to the cabin I've got.

Daniel The cabin we can open. It's the key to the handcuffs we need. (*Robert starts searching his pockets for more keys*)

Agatha What's this? You've locked him up?

Henry Had to, ma'am. He's gone completely out of his mind.

Agatha Dear, yes, I remember that fearsome display on the deck this afternoon.

Daniel He had a premonition that death was at hand and it looks like he was right.

Beryl It's terrible. (*Wailing*) I don't want to die a virgin!

Agatha Good lord, what a thing to say! Especially in front of these gentlemen. (*Daniel looks at Henry as if to ask, "What about this?"*)

Beryl I'm sorry, auntie. (*Putting her head on her aunt's shoulder*). It's just that I'm frightened.

Agatha (*Comforting*) There, there, child. I'm sure it's not as bad as all that. Is it Robert?

Robert (*Handing over other keys*) Here. Try these, and hurry up. (*Daniel takes them and leaves with Henry*) In the meantime, let's get you ladies into a boat. This way. (*He leads the women to the right exit.*)

Agatha What about the three men? It's true I've grown sick of their presence but it wouldn't do to leave them behind, particularly the imbecile. It's our moral duty to look after him.

Robert We'll wait as long as we dare, but it could be dangerous having any imbecile on board, and this one is complaining of demons tormenting him. He could capsize the boat trying to fight them off.

Agatha Demons? He really has lost his reason, hasn't he? What could bring something like that on, Robert?

Robert I don't know. His friends say syphilis.

Agatha Good lord! What a dreadful disease. Thank heavens you girls didn't get too close to him. (*Bertha and Beryl look forlornly at each other*)

Robert All the more reason not to be too worried about him. He should be getting married this summer and we don't want to spread the disease around. (*Bertha and Beryl look even more forlornly at each other*)

Agatha Still, we can't leave him behind in such condition.

Bertha Oh, yes, we can, auntie!

Agatha Bertha! How dare you talk like that? Your mother raised you better.

Robert I will see what's taking them. But, please, get on board a lifeboat now; before all the seats are taken.

Agatha Very well. Come along, girls. (*The women exit. Daniel and Henry enter from the left leading Stan, still tormented by Death hovering around him.*)

Daniel Got him, Robert. Here are you keys. (*He tosses them to Robert, who fails to respond in time. The keys go flying through the right exit.*)

Robert That's just great.

Henry I don't suppose you'll be needing them anymore.

Robert Don't be too sure. (*The bell tolls again, this time in a different pattern.*) Uh-oh, bad news, gentlemen. I'm afraid that last command from the captain says that only women and children are to go in the lifeboats. Sorry, you'll have to remain on board.

Daniel But at least take Stan here. You can see he's sick.

Robert I'd sooner take you two than him. He could sink the lifeboat in his condition.

Daniel We'll put the handcuffs back on him. (*Henry looks out the right exit*)

Robert Look, the order is women and children only. There are not enough lifeboats for everyone.

Henry Don't give us any of that! You've got plenty of room on that boat for all of us. (*Daniel goes up to the exit with Stan still in his grasp*)

Daniel Yeah, lots.

Robert Orders are orders, gentlemen. Take your friend back to my cabin if you want. In fact, it's all yours now. I have other responsibilities to take care of. Kindly stand back from the railing.

Henry Forget it. We're getting on that boat too.

Robert (*Pulling out a gun*) I wouldn't recommend that. Now I'll tell you one more time. Back away from the railing.

Daniel You're going to shoot us, Robert?

Robert If I must. (*He approaches them, they back away*) Until that bell tolls otherwise, you gentlemen will just have to go down with the ship. (*Starts leaving, with his gun still on the two men*)

Henry What about you? Not that you're much of a man, but what are you doing getting into the boat?

Robert Somebody needs to pilot it.

Henry Pilot what? We're adrift in the middle of the Atlantic!

Robert The rules state that a member of the crew has to be on board. For insurance reasons.

Henry Better to go down like a man here than sneak away like the coward you are.

Robert I'm glad to see you've come to your senses. Farewell. (*Robert exits*)

Daniel Let's go see if we can find a more reasonable officer to help us.

Henry We should first tie Stan to something so that he doesn't scare off whatever prospects we find. Let's cuff him to this pipe here. (*They cuff him to a pipe prop at the back of the stage*)

Daniel Wait a minute. I just threw the keys overboard. How are we going to get him out of here?

Henry (*Looking around, exits, comes back with an axe*) This will cut through that chain. Maybe it'll even help us find a place on a boat. (*One shot is heard, followed by screams, then another shot*) That doesn't bode well for our escape.

Daniel Do all these sailors carry guns?

Henry I don't know, but this axe doesn't have much of a chance against pistols.

Daniel So what now?

Henry (*Drops the axe*) I guess this is it, Dan. We're going to die.

Daniel Looks like it, Henry. Our dream of a lifetime has turned into a nightmare. Stan losing his mind and all of us losing our lives.

Henry And what a way to lose our lives. Shivering in the water, listening to the screams of others in the night while our bodies go painfully numb. First our hands and feet, then our testicles, and finally everything else.

Daniel Testicles too? At least the women won't have it so bad.

Henry Believe me, Dan, it's going to be bad. And the worst part is we'll eventually sink to the bottom where crabs will completely erase any trace of our existence.

Daniel Henry, you were always such a pessimist!

Scene two – On the lifeboat in the dark
Bertha and Beryl are sitting side by side at the left exit, Agatha is just in front of them, and Robert is sitting facing them.

Agatha Robert, would you mind telling me why we are already in the water and moving away from the boat? You said we would wait for those gentlemen.

Robert I'm afraid that last bell was the captain's order that only women and children are to go in the lifeboats. There's simply not enough room for everyone on board and so the men, unfortunately, must make the ultimate sacrifice.

Agatha What are you talking about? I see plenty of room in this lifeboat. (*Turning around and pointing*) There, there, and there. At least enough room for those three gentlemen, certainly enough for that ill one.

Robert The bell also signaled that the ship has entered the final stages of its death throes. It will start sinking now at an even faster rate, increasing the risk that the lifeboats near it might be sucked down with it.

Agatha We can see from this distance (*pointing to the audience*) that that is clearly not the case. There's plenty of the ship left above water. The electricity is still on. I can even hear the orchestra playing.

Robert (*Taking a close look*) Hm, you're quite right. It's just further indication that the captain hasn't had the best judgment since we left port.

Agatha Fine. Now you make the right call and go back to the ship.

Robert The problem there is that panic has surely set in among the remaining passengers. If we go back now, and they see us, they could all try and jump in, thereby swamping the boat. That would be the end of us all.

Agatha I would be willing to take that chance as opposed to knowing that I ran for safety while a stricken human being was in need.

Bertha Oh God, auntie, will you let it be? Better the man die here than spend the rest of his life in a lunatic asylum. It would be better for his fiancée too.

Agatha How can you be so heartless? If it must be, fine, but to not even try is beyond my comprehension,

Robert Then maybe this will better help you understand the situation. It's now after midnight, with no moon in the sky or a ship around for miles and miles. We are in the middle of the Atlantic Ocean, where the temperature of the water is below freezing point. The boat you are in is secure and under the command of an experienced officer. If you let that officer do his job, the chances of you people surviving until help arrives is quite good.

Agatha Of course, that's all clear to me, Robert, but...

Robert (*Yelling*) Then shut up and let me do my job!

Agatha Well! You will not take that tone of voice with me.

Bertha He just did, auntie. Sit down and be quiet.

Agatha Nor you, young lady. I'll take care of you later. Robert, I know the weight of responsibility is a terrible burden on your shoulders right now, but...

Robert But nothing, Aggie. We're not going back to the ship, plain and simple. You might as well sit down and enjoy the ride.

Agatha So that's it, huh? All that talk on the bow today was just a pretense. You're no more interested in the sound of my voice than you are in cries coming from the ship.

Robert You got it, Aggie.

Agatha Ooh, how I hate it when somebody calls me that!

Robert Then be still and nobody will.

Agatha Horrible! So you really were just after my money!

Robert I should hope so. I would hate to think I suffered through all your nonsense just for love.

Agatha You vile creature! Oh, you wait till we get to safety. I will report you immediately to the maritime commission.

Robert Be my guest. You won't be the first.

Agatha You mean they know what a despicable person you are and they still let you have intercourse with paying passengers?

Robert I not only have intercourse with them but arrange it for them as well. Isn't that right, girls?

Bertha Shut up! Shut up the both of you! (*Starts crying*)

Agatha What are you talking about?

Robert Oh, you don't know? For your information, those gentlemen you are so eager to go back and rescue paid me money during this voyage to use my cabin for the purpose of having intimate relations with your nieces here.

Agatha (*Floored, then turning around*) Is that true, girls?

Beryl Come on, auntie. You've just seen for yourself what a snake this man is. You're going to believe him?

Robert Then maybe she will believe you when you tell her about the explosion you caused in the engine room. All because you wanted to have sex with a stoker.

Agatha With a stoker? Dear god, I'm going to have a heart attack!

Beryl Don't listen to him, auntie. For all we know, he caused that explosion. He's just trying to pin it on somebody else. Make sure you tell the maritime commission about that too.

Robert Hah! You ladies don't frighten me. I've been sailing the seas since I was a kid, have seen more danger than you can imagine. I have survived it all and I'll be damned now if I don't survive this latest mishap all because of a bunch of chattering women. Now shut up and let me be the hero here!

Agatha Hero! Hah! My late husband would have laughed to be stuck in a boat with a pathetic creature like you. (*Standing up and turning around*) Ladies, this lifeboat is under the command of a person not worthy of the job. There are people in desperate need back there and we have more than enough room for them. I say we take control of this boat and go back. (*Loud voices of support can be heard*)

Robert And I say sit down and be quiet before there's going to be one less person aboard his boat.

Agatha You hear that, ladies. He's nothing but a wretched bully. I hereby declare a mutiny. Let's throw him overboard. (*Beryl stands up, Robert pulls out his gun*)

Robert I've had just about enough of you, Aggie. You take one step closer to me and I'll shoot. So help me god, I'll shoot you without batting an eye and dump you overboard.

Agatha Really? How many bullets have you got in that gun? Enough to kill us all? We're still going to get command of this boat one way or the other.

Robert (*Waving his gun*) They will get command, because you'll be dead.

Agatha You don't scare me. You don't scare any of us. Isn't that right, ladies? (*No voices of support can be heard*) Ladies? (*She turns around and finds a sullen Beryl sitting down*) So that's it, huh? Not a bit of courage to be found among any of you. I'm stuck in a boat full of weak, spineless, lily-livered...! (*Robert shoots his gun into the air. The women scream.*)

Robert I told you that's enough! Not another word. (*Agatha sits down and glumly looks towards the ship. After a moment of silence, he continues.*) Of course, we can always barter for their lives. Maybe that big diamond you've got around your neck.

Agatha What are you saying?

Beryl He's saying he'll turn back if you give him the diamond!

Agatha On my word! Have you no shame whatsoever?

Robert Not a bit. Do we have a deal?

Agatha No, and it's only because of principle, the immorality of it all.

Robert Oh, Aggie, you are more priceless than that stone. Look around you. Look at yourself. All of you here are in first class. Do you think it's just a coincidence that third class passengers are berthed in the lowest portion of the ship? You talk about morality!

Agatha I didn't build this ship.

Robert So who do you think did? Men whose wives ride only in first class! All of you got your wealth by exploiting the misery of others. All of you! And now you have the nerve to call my morals into question. If you had any decency, you would have given up your seats for those women in third class who never got a break in all their lives. They're the ones screaming back there. You want to go and rescue them?

Agatha Yes! I would if I could.

Robert Then hand over the diamond. As long as the orchestra is playing, there's still a chance to rescue people.

Agatha Oh, if only my late husband were here. He'd show you! (*Robert shoots the gun again in the air, more screams follow*)

Beryl Just give him the diamond, auntie! He's going to get it one way or the other. (*Agatha removes the necklace and tosses it at Robert*)

Agatha So long as I live...

Robert (*Starting to turn the boat around*) I know, you'll report me to the maritime commission. (*The orchestra stops playing, Robert stops* *rowing*)

Agatha Keep rowing! The orchestra is merely taking a break.

Scene three – The deck of the ship, the pandemonium is louder
Stan is still wailing, Daniel is swinging the ax at the deck of the ship.

Henry Daniel? What the hell are you doing?

Daniel (*Breathless*) Working up a sweat. If we raise our body temperature, we'll survive longer in the water.

Henry You mean take longer to die?

Daniel Will you stop with the pessimism, Henry. They're still sending up flares. They must know of some ship close by. It could be a matter of minutes between life and death when we go in the water.

Henry Sure, if we don't get sucked down by the ship first. It's over.

Daniel I would feel better about my chances if Stan were here and you were there tied up.

Henry I wish I were in Stan's place too. He doesn't know the horrible fate that awaits him.

Daniel It looks to me like his fate is horrible enough.

Henry That's what I mean. Going in the water will only be a salvation for him.

Daniel Henry, do yourself a favor and take a couple of swings of this ax. You'll feel better. Trust me. (*Henry grabs the ax and starts laying into the boat*) Well, I'm glad to see you haven't totally given up.

Henry I have. I'm just working out my anger on the ship. Getting sunk by an iceberg is pretty pathetic. (*Robert appears at the right exit.*)

Robert Planning to build yourselves a raft, gentlemen?

Henry You miserable slime! (*Charges him with the ax in the air*)

Robert (*Pulling his gun out and pointing at him*) I wouldn't get so hasty if I were you.

Henry What did you come back here for, Robert? To make sure we go down?

Robert You're hardly worth the attention. No, it seems you have a savior. (*Agatha appears*)

Daniel Ma'am? You told Robert to come back for us?

Agatha I had to pay him to make him come back.

Henry That figures.

Agatha I couldn't leave you and this poor sick man behind. But we have to hurry. The water has practically reached the deck. I was able to step directly on board.

Daniel But Stan? We cuffed him to this pipe after you left. We don't have the keys.

Robert I warned you they would be needed. There goes your mission of mercy, madam. Back in the boat.

Henry We can use the ax. Come on. (*They go to Stan, but he's writhing too much under the harassment of Death for Daniel to hold the chain link in place on the pipe.*)

Henry Hold him still!

Daniel I'm trying.

Agatha Hurry, gentleman.

Daniel Robert, come here and help me.

Robert I can't do that and hold the gun at the same time.

Henry Then put the gun away! We're all in this thing together now.

Robert I beg to differ. You had better take your swing because the lifeboat is leaving. Madam?

Agatha Do it!

Henry I can't. I might cut off a finger. Maybe his ring finger.

Daniel Come over here. You hold down one arm, I'll hold down the other. Ma'am, you'll have to swing the ax. (*Henry hands her the ax and joins Daniel behind Stan*)

Agatha Dear lord, I've never held one of these things in my life.

Daniel It's the only way, I'm afraid.

Agatha Wait a minute. (*She goes to the exit and calls out*) Bertha, Beryl, come here. (*Back to the men*) My nieces are stronger than me in any case. (*Bertha and Beryl enter*) Girls, we have an unfortunate situation here. We have to cut the chain that binds this poor fellow to the pipe. Those two gentlemen have to hold him still and Robert, no surprise, won't help. One of you will have to swing the ax.

Beryl Swing the ax?

Agatha Yes!

Beryl I'm sorry, auntie, but I have never swung an ax in my life. (*To the surprise of all, Bertha takes the ax from her aunt without saying a word, raises it high above her head, and lets it come down with full force. Stan shrieks.*)

Daniel Good lord, she chopped off his hand!

Agatha Bertha!

Beryl That wasn't very nice.

Bertha I never swung an ax either. (*Drops the ax*)

Daniel Here. Let's tourniquet his arm somehow.

Henry Girls, rip off a strip from your garments so we can use it as a tourniquet.

Bertha Not mine.

Beryl Oh, all right. (*She tries to rip a sleeve off but in vain*) I can't manage.

Daniel We need a knife. Anybody got a knife?

Henry Robert probably does.

Robert I do but this has gone far enough. Leave him. (*Waving his gun*) Into the boat, everybody.

Agatha We will not leave this man behind. Especially now that he's mutilated in addition to being insane.

Robert We're not taking that man with us. He'll die of either cold or loss of blood in no time anyway.

Henry (*Threatening*) And we say we are taking him with us. (*Robert shoots Stan, who falls to the deck lifeless. Death falls on top of him.*)

Robert There, that settles that argument.

Agatha Oh, you wicked, horrible... (*She rushes at him to claw at his face. As he turns to fight her off, Daniel picks up the ax and hits Robert on the back of the neck with the blunt end of it. Robert falls unconscious on top of Death. Daniel drops the ax, Henry picks up the gun and stashes it in his coat. Bertha and Beryl exit, Agatha starts to, then turns back* *and kneels next to Robert. She goes through his pockets, pulls out the chain and diamond and puts it around her neck.)* Just some unfinished business between me and that worm. *(She exits, Henry starts to follow her)*

Daniel Wait a minute. Shouldn't we retrieve something of Stan's to give to his fiancée for remembrance?

Henry Don't tell me you mean his hand.

Daniel No, some keepsake *(Henry goes through Stan's pockets)*

Agatha *(From off-stage)* Hurry, gentlemen.

Daniel Anything?

Henry Only this one-shilling piece.

Daniel That was his lucky coin. Take it. Come on! *(Stops short)* Farewell, Stan.

Henry Yeah, farewell. *(They exit. The pandemonium grows worse, sounds of the ship breaking apart can be heard. Robert slowly comes to and looks around. He stands up, rubbing his head.)*

Robert Oh, no. *(Searches through his pockets)* Oh, no! *(Goes to the exit)* Come back. I'm sorry. Look, you're going to need a sailor to find your way around the Atlantic.

Henry *(From afar)* That's okay, Robert. We'll take our chances.

Robert But...but...*(Looks around the deck, sees only the ax. He picks it up and heaves it out the exit.)* You think I'm beaten! Not by a long shot. We're going to meet up again, you wait and see! *(To himself)* I'll show them. I've survived much worse than this. *(Straightens out his appearance)* There. Let's go find us a boat. *(As he turns to exit, Death rises from on top of Stan and starts flitting around him. Robert swats at it as he exits.)*

Henslowe's Rose

Characters

Jack Henslowe, owner of the Rose Café in the British occupation zone of Germany
Captain Douglas, local British commander
Major Patterson, American badass on a mission
Hanks, American spy
Corporal Carmel, black American soldier, serving duty as Patterson's driver
Rudolf Kammler, German rocket scientist
Chantal Fournier, his French-born wife
Offy, former street whore, now moving Jack's merchandise
Horst, ex-Wehrmacht handyman
Waiters, assorted German civilians

Act I

Scene one
A dark, misty airfield at night, with the sound of an airplane propeller in the background. In the foreground lies a wooden coffin. Horst, a limping former Wehrmacht soldier, is exhorting two lackeys, appearing out of the night, to grab the coffin and load it onto the waiting plane. Captain Douglas is waiting in the shadows

Horst Schnell, schnell. (*The two lackeys pick up the coffin, Douglas steps in to impede them*)

Douglas Halt right there. Put down that coffin. (*The lackeys look at Horst, who signals them to put the coffin back on the ground.*)

Horst What is the problem, Captain? We have the papers here. (*He hands Douglas sheaves of paper, who looks at them suspiciously*)

Douglas Igor Tomvonovich, eh?

Horst No, Igor is already in the plane. This one is Alexander Ivanov.

Douglas You amaze me, Horst, with your knowledge of Russian names.

Horst I had a lot of contact with them on the eastern front.

Douglas Open the coffin. I want to make sure that's really Alexander in there.

Horst But, Captain, he is dead long time. He will not look like same Alexander.

Douglas Certainly not if he looks like contraband.

Horst I don't understand.

Douglas Oh, I think you do. Open the coffin.

Horst But, Captain, Russians are waiting. They have military band, guard of honor, many high people waiting for these heroes to come home.

Douglas Yes, in the middle of the night, I'm sure. Open it. (*Horst reluctantly signals the two lackeys to open the coffin. Douglas steps forward and, with a smirk on his face, bends over and pulls out a bottle of whiskey.*) Is this what killed Alexander, you think? (*Horst merely shrugs. Douglas pulls out several cartons of cigarettes.*) Maybe these?

Horst Look, Captain, war is over, but people are hungry. No job, no food, only whiskey and cigarettes is economy. Please, Russians are waiting.

Douglas Let them wait. In case you Germans haven't heard, they are officially the enemy now and smuggling with them is a crime. Now, what do the Russians give you in return for this contraband?

Horst Contra...?

Douglas Contraband! The goods! What do you get in return?

Horst I get only job. I do not know what they send over.

Douglas Don't make a fool out of me, Horst. Rommel couldn't do it and you're no Rommel.

Horst Of course. Rommel is dead.

Douglas A weak argument. (*The plane engine is switched off*) It sounds like your pilot realizes he's been grounded. I'm hereby confiscating all this contraband. Have your men put it in that storage locker over there. I'll send a unit by to pick it up in the morning. (*Jack enters, going up to Horst without realizing Douglas is standing there*)

Jack Horst, what's the hold up here? You think I've got fuel to run that engine all night? (*Horst gestures to Douglas*) Douglas? What are you doing here?

Douglas My men have uncovered this smuggling operation going on between the Germans and Russians and I'm putting a stop to it.

Jack What are you talking about?

Douglas That coffin is loaded with whiskey and cigarettes, not the remains of some missing Russian soldier.

Jack What of it? What the hell's going on here?

Douglas Horst, I advise you and your men to leave this scene immediately. We'll discuss your role in this operation later. (*Jack gestures that they should stand aside and they do*)

Jack All right, would you mind telling me what's going on?

Douglas I told you, we're putting a stop to this smuggling going on between the Germans and Russians.

Jack Stop it! My window for that plane to land in the Russian sector is getting smaller by the minute. There had better be a good reason for this little police action of yours.

Douglas A very good reason, I'm afraid. Let's take a seat. (*They sit on the coffin*) My commanders in Bad Oeynhausen have ordered it.

Jack But why? I thought it was clear to them that this operation was the only thing keeping the local economy alive. Without this traffic, the people here would starve. Not that it would bother the Allies any.

Douglas I quite agree with you and that's why we have tolerated it for this long. But a matter has come up that changes everything.

Jack What, the Allies are allies again?

Douglas No, if anything the situation is getting worse. You see, there is a man on his way here who will pay a fortune to reach the Soviet side.

Jack Yeah, what's his name?

Douglas Rudolf Kammler.

Jack Never heard of him. German, I presume.

Douglas Yes, a rocket scientist.

Jack A rocket scientist?

Douglas It would seem that in the run-up to the surrender, the Russians and the Americans were making a wild scramble to acquire all the German scientists they could get their hands on. Those working on the rocket program were naturally at the top of the list. This Kammler was in Bavaria the last anyone heard but unlike von Braun and the other geniuses he has refused to give himself up to the Americans. They've been looking for him ever since.

Jack What's he got against the Americans? They bomb his house or something?

Douglas It seems it's more political than that. The man is determined to make it over to the Russian sector because he's married to a communist. Apparently she is behind his decision to flee the Americans.

Jack Communist, huh? I've had a few love affairs with communist women, all of them came to grief in the end.

Douglas That's where you come in now. If anyone can smuggle a rocket scientist over to the Soviets, it's you.

Jack Hey, I don't traffic in people, all right? Only contraband.

Douglas It doesn't matter. You have connections on the other side, you've got that plane, that's all anyone's worried about.

Jack How many times do I have to tell you? All the connections I made fighting in Spain disappeared the minute they went back to the Soviet Union. They were tossed into Stalin's broth for all I know.

Douglas You really expect people to believe this story about you loading up a plane with contraband one day, sending it over to the Russian sector, and it comes flying back full of other types of contraband?

Jack Yes, I do. Of course we have established some guidelines since that first flight, in particular flight windows, and this one is about to close.

Douglas I'm afraid it's already closed, my friend. (*Rises*) My commanders want it to stop immediately.

Jack (*Also rises*) How soon is immediately?

Douglas Immediately. Now.

Jack Look, Douglas, at least let this flight go. Horst, Offy, my whole crew will be on the streets again within days without a return flight.

Douglas They'll be on the streets anyway, hawking that German loot you're importing to my boys.

Jack You know what I mean. Let this one flight go.

Douglas I can't, Jack. I have my orders. (*Jack reaches into the coffin and pulls out a bottle of whiskey*)

Jack This on top of that one you already got there for evidence.

Douglas Don't make this any harder than it already is, Jack.

Jack (*Handing Douglas two cartons of cigarettes*) For all your commanders know, this flight left before you got your orders. (*Pause*) Come on, Douglas, I've been good to you. Free drinks, girl when you need one.

Douglas (*Other pause*) All right. But I want the return flight unloaded and the plane locked up in the hangar by morning.

Jack Done. (*Whistling off stage*) Horst, get in here. (*Horst and the lackeys enter*) Get that coffin on the plane. Quickly. (*Horst gestures to the lackeys to grab the coffin*)

Horst Schnell, schnell. (*They leave with the coffin*)

Jack Go tell the pilot we're taking off. (*Horst leaves*) Thanks, Douglas.

Douglas Better be careful, Jack. I fear this is only the beginning. Kammler is not the only person on his way here. The Americans are sending a certain Major Patterson as well. It will be his job to see to it that Kammler doesn't reach the Russians.

Jack Why do you people care so much about what the Americans think? You're a free and independent zone of occupation.

Douglas Yes, but the British Empire is broke. We can barely feed our own subjects, much less the Germans under our rule. We would all but collapse without American charity at the moment. (*The plane's engine can be heard starting*)

Jack From what I understand, the Americans are also having a hard time feeding their Germans.

Douglas Hard time nothing. It's their policy, a way of making the Germans think long and hard about their concentration camps. Our policy is to be a bit more humane and understanding.

Jack That's easy to do when your country invented the whole concept of concentration camps in the first place. (*Douglas stops, obviously insulted by the remark. Jack keeps going, a wry smile on his face as the plane can be heard taking off in the background.*)

Scene two
The same airfield, the afternoon of the following day. The sound of a jeep pulling up can be heard. Hanks, a tall, gangly sneak with pointed features, enters from the left. Major Patterson, short and pudgy with a cropped moustache, enters from the right.

Hanks Major Patterson?

Patterson Hanks?

Hanks Pleased to meet you. (*They shake hands*)

Patterson Likewise I'm sure.

Hanks (*Looking over Patterson's shoulder*) Who's he?

Patterson My driver. Don't worry about him. Let's get down to the facts here: What exactly is your station here?

Hanks I work for the OSS. Their station chief here, you might say.

Patterson Don't get cute with me. You're a spy, right?

Hanks Of course.

Patterson Then what in the hell are we doing meeting in the middle of an airfield in the middle of the day?

Hanks I wanted to show you the place where Kammler would be departing from.

Patterson What's to show me about it? He isn't going anywhere.

Hanks I know, but if is what I'm saying.

Patterson There's no ifs ands and buts about it, Hanks. Kammler is coming back with me to Nuremberg one way or the other. Now, what can you tell me about his movements so far? Is he already in the vicinity?

Hanks No, but the British have every reason to suspect that he soon will be.

Patterson I know that, Hanks. That's why I'm here. What I want to know is why the British suspect it.

Hanks They think the one man who can help him is an American by the name of Jack Henslowe. He runs a local café here called the Rose, which in fact is little more than a front for a smuggling operation he has going on with the Russians.

Patterson The Rose? A smuggling operation with the Russians? I'd like to drag his ass back to Nuremberg too.

Hanks From what I've gathered, the operation works like this: The Russians send him valuable heirlooms that they've looted from the Germans. He gives these heirlooms to an army of street whores who pass them on to British soldiers, who then exchange them with American soldiers for whiskey and cigarettes. After everyone takes their respective cut, the whiskey and cigarettes are flown across the border to the Russian side.

Patterson Giving away our good whiskey and cigarettes to those heathens! Is this Henslowe a commie or what?

Hanks Apparently not, at least we haven't been able to find a red organization that has a membership card filled out by him. But he did fight on the Loyalist side in Spain in 1936.

Patterson That says it all. A commie.

Hanks In fact, he seems to be something of an apolitical type. More of an opportunist than anything. There's one report that he helped the Russians remove the Spanish gold reserves before Franco marched in and walked away with a hefty cut.

Patterson Petty thievery doesn't make one a capitalist. What did he do with the gold?

Hanks Took it to Paris, where he invested it in art works. All kinds of modern shit. You know, where the figures have huge deformed heads and feet.

Patterson Degenerate stuff, you mean.

Hanks That's not all. While there he hooked up with a woman whose parents were leading members of the Paris intellectual community. Short for active communists.

Patterson Paris and intellectual says it all.

Hanks He fled to North Africa when the Germans rolled in, set up some gin joint in Tangier, then came here right after the war was over. Again, to take advantage of an opportunity.

Patterson Trading with his commie buddies, the bastard. What about the woman? Is she still with him?

Hanks She didn't make the trip to North Africa. Near as we can tell, she and her parents ended up in a concentration camp.

Patterson And the commies wonder why we starve these Germans. We're doing it for them too.

Hanks My advice, Major, is to tread lightly here. Henslowe's operation has made him very popular among the locals. They won't take kindly to a foreign power coming in and putting a stop to it.

Patterson I don't care what the locals here think. They are just as guilty as the Germans we got in our zone. They all deserve to starve a little. What about the British command here? Will they take it too hard if I hit Kammler over the head and stuff him in the back of my jeep.

Hanks No problem. The commander is a Captain Douglas. Fought in North Africa against Rommel, but missed El Alamein because of illness. Didn't rejoin his unit until they had chased the krauts clear back to Tunisia.

Patterson Illness? Sounds like a case of malingering to me.

Hanks That doesn't stop him from talking about Rommel all the time. Usually does it in Henslowe's café, where he spends most of his nights.

Patterson A drunkard too. Good, so all we have to do is wait for Kammler to show up and he's ours.

Hanks Yes, but again, I must advise you, Major, to tread lightly here. This place is like a powder keg at times.

Patterson No offense, Hanks, but I don't appreciate advice given to me by draft dodgers.

Hanks Hey, I'm not a draft dodger. I'm 4F, okay? I have a busted ear drum.

Patterson Busted ear drum? Shit, that's a plus during warfare. You know how much racket a machine gun makes?

Hanks Look, Major, I did my part for the war too. I spent the whole time down in Mobile working in the shipyards.

Patterson Alabama, huh? (*Casting a glance over his shoulder towards his jeep*) Now I have a little advice for you: I noticed that sneaky look you were giving my driver a moment ago. I don't want any trouble between you two while we're here. Understand?

Hanks As long as he knows his place, there won't be.

Patterson That's not what I want to hear, Hanks. We've got to stay focused here. You can give him shit all you want back home, but here our target is this German asshole. Got it?

Hanks Got it. By the way, Major. Were you in D-Day?

Patterson Why are you asking?

Hanks I don't know. I mean, D-Day is D-Day. I'd like to hear about it.

Patterson Well, you'll have to wait for the movie, I'm afraid. I was in D-Day plus four.

Hanks What does that mean?

Patterson It means I landed four days after. There was no way you can put a million men on a beach at the same time. Some of us had to wait for our chance. Understand? (*Starts walking away towards the jeep*)

Hanks Sure.

Patterson (*Stopping and glaring back at Hanks*) Don't even think of drawing a comparison with El Alamein.

Scene three
The Rose Café, evening. There are several tables and chairs full of patrons, mostly German civilians and British soldiers. To the right is a piano, to the left off stage is a band playing orchestral music, and next to it is a bar. At the back of the stage sits Jack at a table, alone and playing solitaire. Offy, a former whore now running Jack's street operation, enters and sits down at his table. She hands Jack a piece of paper. He looks at it, then stuffs it in his shirt pocket.

Jack Fine time to shut me down, just when business is booming.

Offy Is it true, Jack?

Jack I'm afraid so, darling. For all intents and purposes, the British zone of occupation is controlled by the Americans now.

Offy What about my girls, Jack? Without this business they will have to go back to whoring again. Sleeping with dirty British soldiers just for a few cigarettes. You can't let that happen.

Jack There's nothing I can do about it.

Offy But why do the Americans hate us so? We never bombed them, never invaded their country like we did the others. Why?

Jack It's all in the pictures, darling, the ones from the concentration camps. It really did a number on a lot of people.

Offy But I swear, Jack, I didn't know anything about them, nor did my friends and family.

Jack Spare me, all right? The fact remains is you allowed those assholes to come to power in the first place, now somebody has to pay for their crimes. Better it be the whole population anyway, that way they can't put all of you to the sword.

Offy The sword? But we heard about some horrible new bomb they have that can destroy whole cities.

Jack Yeah, I heard about it too. Another reason why they're free to call the shots wherever they want to right now.

Offy But what about you, Jack? You're not like the other Americans. You got over it. You don't hold it against us.

Jack Don't make me out to be such an angel, darling. With me, business always comes first. But I also saw enough horror and savagery during the civil war in Spain to last me a lifetime. If you ask me, what happened in those concentration camps can happen anywhere. (*Douglas walks in and notices Jack. He approaches his table.*)

Offy You see? We Germans aren't the only barbarians. And remember, we also gave the world Goethe and Beethoven.

Jack It's too late to hide behind the giants now. But don't worry, if something comes up, I'll let you know.

Offy Thank you, Jack. And please can you... (*She notices Douglas standing there. She stands up.*) Excuse me. (*She leaves for the bar, Douglas sits down*)

Douglas Did you give Offy the bad news?

Jack I didn't have to. Word spreads like wildfire among people who live in rubble and eats rats every day.

Douglas They have nobody but themselves to blame for their problems.

Jack Like we haven't heard that a thousand times already. Say what you want, Douglas, but that cemetery out there isn't home to just Wehrmacht soldiers anymore. Quite a few children are making the trip there these days.

Douglas What do you want me to do about it? I'm no career soldier. I was happy plying my trade in dear old England before these Germans got uppity and decided they could take on the world. Believe me, I was missing English weather every second of the day I had to spend in the scorching heat of North Africa.

Jack I know, I know, fighting Rommel.

Douglas That's right, fighting Rommel. At least it's something I can hang my hat on when I finally get home. Of course you don't understand that because you have no home to go too.

Jack What makes you say that?

Douglas The Americans have been feeding us quite a bit of information about you, Jack, in the run up to Major Patterson's visit.

Jack You mean that sneaky Hanks. What's he saying about me?

Douglas Nothing we don't already know about what you've been doing since coming to Europe. But he did tell us something about your life in America before.

Jack Yeah? Let's hear it. I might learn something about myself myself.

Douglas Apparently you had to leave New York after absconding with the church funds. You made your way to Washington, where you ran off with a senator's wife. When the senator sent a member of his staff to fetch her back, you hit the poor bloke over the head with a poker, landing him in a hospital where he died some years later. Civil war had broken out in Spain in the meantime, so you fled there to fight for the Loyalists both to seek your fortune and repair your reputation with the authorities back home. Unfortunately sympathy for communist causes has waned since your president died and that same senator is now part of a new red scare faction in Washington, guaranteeing you will wind up behind bars if you try to go back.

Jack That's very thorough, only you left out the most important part.

Douglas Which is?

Jack Whatever became of his wife? She promised to join me in Spain, but I waited and waited. Maybe I wouldn't have taken up with so many communist women if she had fulfilled her promise.

Douglas I doubt it will help you at your trial. (*Hanks and Patterson enter and go to sit at a table at the right*)

Jack Your resident sneak has arrived with, I presume, this Major Patterson. If you find out anything about her, let me know.

Douglas With pleasure. (*He rises and goes to join Hanks and Patterson*) Good evening, gentlemen. (*Hanks and Patterson rise*)

Hanks Good evening, Captain. May I introduce Major Patterson of the Fourth Regular Armored Cavalry Unit. Major Patterson, this is Captain Douglas, the local British commander.

Patterson How do you do.

Douglas How do you do. (*They all sit*) Armored cavalry, eh? I was in the First Royal Armored Cavalry in North Africa.

Patterson Yes, I heard. That must have been some incredible fighting you saw around El Alamein.

Douglas (*Glaring at Hanks*) Quite. What about you? I'm sure you were at D-Day. Also some incredible fighting?

Patterson (*Glaring at Hanks*) Quite as well. But I haven't come all this way to trade war stories. Captain Douglas, you have been informed about the purpose of my visit, I take it?

Douglas Quite, Major. But if this Rudolf Kammler does indeed come within the confines of my authority, he will be subject to British administration, you are aware.

Patterson Of course. We're still loyal Allies. My mission here is purely an advisory one.

Douglas In what capacity, may I ask?

Patterson Our information suggests that Rudolf Kammler is being forced to undertake this foolish adventure.

Douglas At whose behest?

Patterson His wife's. She's the real communist. She's the one who wants to get to the Soviet Union. It's absurd to think this guy has any such inclination. The Nazis would've dumped his ass in a concentration camp if he were the real thing.

Douglas And you think if you talk to him, put some sense into his head as it were, he'll go back with you to the American sector just like that? Are you married, Major?

Patterson Yes, I am, but I wear the boots in my family. The point is, Captain, this marriage is a sham. They met in Paris when he was on holiday. Of course he fell in love with her. Lonely scientist living for his work suddenly meets a beautiful girl who speaks French, cooks French, kisses French. She naturally can't stand him, but he has influence and power and she eventually marries him to save her family from being shipped to the camps. Worked for a while, until the Germans started losing the war and took it out on defenseless civilians. In the end he couldn't save them, but because she had married a kraut, she found herself persona non grata in her own country. And being a communist, she was branded a traitor. So she had to join him in Bavaria. But instead of taking our offer to let bygones be bygones and hop the next flight to Florida, she comes up with this harebrained scheme to flee to the Soviet Union. If I could just get a few minutes alone with this guy, without this bitch hanging around him, I'm sure I could talk some sense into him.

Douglas You mean by way of comparing Florida to the Soviet Union?

Hanks Major, have you thoroughly thought through the Florida approach? Coming from the South, I can tell you that the humidity and mosquitoes there are murder.

Patterson If you don't mind, Hanks, military men are speaking here. (*Hanks starts to get huffy, then notices Carmel, a black soldier and Patterson's driver, walk in and approach the bar. He grows even more uncomfortable after Carmel strikes up a conversation with Offy.*) This is not about Florida, Captain. This is about the future of the world. Right now the only thing keeping the Russians in check is our atomic bomb. All that could change if they get their hands on German rocket technology and are able to threaten us directly.

Douglas You mean America getting a taste of what England got during the war?

Patterson For god's sake, Captain, don't start whining to me about all your people have suffered. You and the French had a chance to stop that goon back in '38, but you let him take this piece of land and that piece of land, all because he promised you peace. Right, some lunatic wearing a military uniform and shouting about enemies all around him is going to keep a promise about peace! (*Hanks rises and saunters over to the bar, where the focus eventually shifts. Carmel and Offy are standing there laughing, having an obvious good time.*)

Douglas Maybe if America hadn't played the neutrality card so long, we could've formed a united front and forced that goon to back down. It's always easy to sit back and look on when you've got a large body of water separating you from all the trouble that's brewing.

Hanks What's so funny?

Carmel Excuse me?

Hanks I asked what's so funny?

Carmel I don't see what business it is of yours.

Hanks I'm making it my business.

Offy Get out of here! Nobody wants you here!

Carmel Wait a minute. Now I get it. Where you from, Slick? Mississippi, Alabama?

Hanks Alabama, not that it should make any difference to you.

Carmel That explains everything then. You rednecks think you can come over here and push around black folk just like back home, is that it?

Hanks Just like you black folk think you can come over here and help yourselves to all these white whores just because you're wearing that uniform.

Offy How dare you call me a whore, you pig!

Hanks Ooh, looks like we got two uppity sorts here tonight.

Carmel Uppity? Slick, I think it's time someone put you in your place.

Hanks Now that's what I call some nerve. The likes of you putting me in my place. You're the one who needs to learn his place. So let me tell you about it now. Drive just beyond the city limits there (*pointing*), you'll come across the former ghetto where these krauts kept the Jews corralled before shipping them off to Auschwitz. All ready for your use, Corporal.

Carmel I can't believe this redneck. All right, homeboy, let's have it. (*As the two Americans square off, Jack bolts from his table and pushes them apart*)

Jack This ain't no saloon here, gentlemen. You feel like brawling, take it outside.

Carmel No problem, champ. Let's go, redneck. (*Carmel walks outside, followed by all the German patrons. Hanks follows, somewhat reluctantly. Douglas stands up.*)

Douglas Jack, if you please. (*Jack walks over*) Jack Henslowe, allow me to introduce you to Major Patterson. Major Patterson, Jack Henslowe.

Patterson (*Standing and shaking hands*) Good evening.

Jack Good evening.

Patterson (*Sitting*) Won't you join us? (*Jack and Douglas sit down*) What's going on over there between Hanks and my driver?

Jack It seems they didn't hit it off, so now they're going outside to hit each another.

Douglas Really? I'd better go and keep an eye on things. Pardon me. (*He rises and leaves*)

Patterson Good. It gives me chance to ask you something, just between us.

Jack What's that?

Patterson Why did you choose a faggoty name like "Rose" for this place?

Jack It was a business decision.

Patterson How so?

Jack When I came here after the war, the entire landscape was desolation. Everything was rubble, the people were dirty and miserable. The only bright spot was this young woman on the street selling roses. Sold out her entire stock every morning.

Patterson For what? There's no viable currency here.

Jack For barter. Heirlooms mostly, those that had escaped the grasp of the British. So I built this place and called it the Rose because it already had brand name recognition.

Patterson Why the symbol of a red rose out front? Why not a white rose?

Jack Red sells better.

Patterson I bet it does, especially when you're doing business with commies.

Jack There's something on your mind, Major, why don't you spit it out.

Patterson I'm sure you already know the particulars behind my presence here, Henslowe. All I'll say is that if you cooperate in this matter, we'll let bygones be bygones.

Jack What bygones are those?

Patterson Don't make a fool out of me, Henslowe. We know all about what you did in America, what you did in Spain and France, and what you're doing here. In none of these cases was any of your actions beneficial to America. Now you have a chance to finally prove yourself to be a proud and honorable American.

Jack Really? Maybe even become senator some day?

Patterson The fact is this Kammler is a scumbag. He and his group were using slave labor to make their rockets under conditions that were not much better than in the concentration camps. That's why he's trying to get over to the Soviets now. Slave labor is their normal economy so he should feel quite at home there. My duty, your duty too though you won't admit it, is to bring this bastard to justice.

Jack To justice? I thought you wanted to set him up in your own rocket program.

Patterson If a military court deems it a suitable punishment for him, then so be it. But first he must answer for his crimes.

Jack Spare me the melodrama, Major. You're not interested in bringing Kammler and his group to justice. You just want to beat the Russians in the rocket race. Göring and all those other Nazis wouldn't be sitting in the dock in Nuremberg right now if they were rocket scientists too.

Patterson You're very perceptive, Henslowe. My appeal to whatever is left of your good nature was only a mere formality. I didn't expect you to be moved because I know you're just a lowlife black marketeer trading on other people's misery. So now I would like to get to the real offer on the table. Kammler will likely give you a lot of money to help him get to the Soviet sector. We'll top whatever offer he makes if you help us get him back to the American sector instead.

Jack On top of making me a proud and honorable American.

Patterson Save the sarcasm, Henslowe. Now is the time for all Americans to stick together. (*Cheering is heard from outside, followed by Carmel leading the German patrons back into the café and to the bar after knocking out Hanks*)

Jack Try telling that to those two guys outside. (*Douglas comes in and walks up to the table*)

Patterson Simple sideshow, no more. A race war at home will be nothing compared to a nuclear war if the Russians ever catch up to us.

Douglas I haven't seen this much excitement here since we came rumbling into town with our tanks. Your driver has an incredible left hook, Major. Hanks fell like a sack of potatoes.

Jack Sounds like everyone deserves a round on the house. Excuse me. (*Jack rises and goes to the bar*)

Douglas You can be proud of your driver, Major. The whole crowd was rooting for him and he didn't let them down.

Patterson He's going to get himself into a whole lot of trouble with antics like that. He should know better.

Douglas But everyone said Hanks started it.

Patterson Doesn't matter. The racial situation in our country is too explosive at the moment. We brought in all of these black troops much the way the Russians brought in their Asians. But at the end of the war they told their Asians to go back to their hard life in Siberia and they did. Had no choice but to. I fear black soldiers like Carmel there will no longer be happy with their former station in life. They fought the war and now they're going to expect something in return. There's already talk about carrying out full integration of the armed forces.

Douglas Our victory was pyrrhic as well, I'm afraid. We're experiencing a severe shortage of manpower on account of this war. Two wars really, because we never quite recovered from the first one. Now with so many of us dead and maimed and doing occupation duty, there's no one left to man the factories and provide basic services. So the government is thinking about allowing immigration from the colonies. India, Africa and the West Indies. Sure, in America you enslaved your black people and kept them on the lower fringes of society, but at least they were always a fixture there. We have no such tradition with fixtures. The idea of someday meeting a black chap on the street speaking cockney absolutely boggles the imagination.

Patterson There you go again with that whining, Captain.

Douglas I'm not whining, Major, I'm lamenting, something you

Americans, with your brashness and total lack of inhibition, know nothing about.

Patterson Lament, whine, it all sounds like the same old song. We're soldiers, Captain. We should be swapping stories about our glory years in the military leading up to this point. Go on, tell me something about the Battle of El Alamein.

Douglas You first. I came up to Germany through Italy, so I had to miss D-Day. I'm dying to hear all about it.

Scene four
The Rose Café, late the following afternoon. The place is practically empty. Jack is sitting by himself drinking brandy and playing solitaire. Douglas enters and goes up to him.

Douglas Rather quiet here today. Nothing like the excitement we had last night.

Jack What do you expect after your boys came in here snooping around. All the Germans thought you were after them and ran for cover. What were you looking for anyway?

Douglas Nothing in particular. My superiors ordered me to put on some display of cooperation while Patterson was in town and this was the best I could come up with. The most harmless too, I might add.

Jack Oh yeah? One of your boys swiped a silver tea set from my office.

Douglas Part of the display, my dear Jack. Don't worry, I'll see you get it back, even if it is part of the silver horde you're taking from the east. (*A pause*) It is, isn't it?

Jack Douglas, you take cream or milk in your tea?

Douglas (*Chuckles*) Very good, Jack. Make it a brandy. (*Jack pours him a glass*) It may interest you to know that Kammler has arrived in town. He'll no doubt be calling on you soon.

Jack Old news, Douglas. He already called to reserve a table.

Douglas What? His first duty here, like all Germans on the move, is to report to my constabulary. Failure to do that would alone give me the right to deport him back to the American sector.

Jack Now's your chance, because that fellow walking in here looks like a rocket scientist if I ever saw one. (*Douglas turns and sees Kammler making his entrance, with a large painting wrapped in brown paper tucked underneath his arm. A waiter walks up to him.*)

Kammler Ich habe eine reservation. Rudolf Kammler.

Waiter Ja wohl, Herr Kammler. Bitte. (*Gesturing for Kammler to follow him to an empty table on the right. Jack and Douglas follow their movements. Kammler sits down.*)

Kammler Cognac. (*The waiter gestures and leaves. Douglas rises and approaches him.*)

Douglas Excuse me? Are you Rudolf Kammler?

Kammler Yes.

Douglas Allow me to introduce myself. I'm Captain Douglas, head of the British military garrison in this town.

Kammler Yes, what is it that you want?

Douglas Merely to welcome you and remind you that your first order of business here is to report to my office.

Kammler I wasn't aware of that order.

Douglas Please, Herr Kammler. All German nationals within the occupied territories are required to register their movements. Unfamiliarity with the law is no excuse. (*The waiter brings Kammler his cognac*)

Kammler Pardon me, Captain. I promise to make immediate amends. Could I at least enjoy my cognac first?

Douglas By all means. I'm going back to my office now. I will expect to see you there in, oh, half an hour?

Kammler Of course. Where will I find it?

Douglas Follow the street straight on after you leave this place. It's the first intact building you see on your right.

Kammler Very well. See you then.

Douglas Goodbye. (*Turns, gestures to Jack and leaves*)

Jack You Kammler?

Kammler Excuse me?

Jack I said are you Kammler?

Kammler It depends on who wants to know.

Jack The only person who can help you right now.

Kammler Are you the owner of this place?

Jack Yes. (*Kammler rises and goes to his table, carrying his glass and painting with him*)

Kammler May I?

Jack Help yourself. (*Kammler sits down*)

Kammler You are the man who has contacts in the Soviet sector?

Jack No. I'm the man who runs a smuggling operation with the Soviet sector.

Kammler Smuggling? (*Disappointed*) Perhaps I was misinformed. I'm looking for a man here with contacts in the Politburo, who can help me escape from the Americans.

Jack The Politburo? Nothing like rumor to raise a person's profile. No, Kammler, I'm a simple smuggler, that's all. I'm also fully abreast of your situation. You are on the run from the Americans and you've come here because my operation, call it smuggling or otherwise, is your best chance to get across to the Soviet occupation zone.

Kammler Then you have contacts? (*Finishes his cognac, Jack fills his glass*)

Jack I used to have contacts, made them while I was fighting alongside the Russians in Spain. Only they all seemed to have disappeared since returning home.

Kammler Maybe they died on the eastern front.

Jack Certainly in the east, I'll grant you that. Now, Kammler, let's get down to business. Do you want my help or not?

Kammler If you can provide it, yes.

Jack It's something of a problem now, I have to admit. You see, the Americans got wind of the fact that you were coming here and so asked the British to close down my operation.

Kammler Oh.

Jack But I'm willing to risk opening it up one more time just to accommodate you.

Kammler That's very kind of you.

Jack It's not out of kindness, I assure you, rather that thing you have in your hand there.

Kammler You mean this? How do you know what it is?

Jack I was told you were going to offer me a substantial sum to help you get over. Since the only currency in Germany these days is cigarettes, and since I've already got enough of those, I figure you came here to make some kind of swap. That looks like a painting you've got under that brown wrapping.

Kammler So it is. Could I have your name before we go any further? You know me but I don't know you.

Jack The name's Jack Henslowe.

Kammler Are you an American?

Jack I was born in New York City.

Kammler Your parents were American?

Jack My father was a drunkard. We don't need to go any further than that.

Kammler Well, pleased to meet you, Herr Henslowe. Now, about this painting: I don't know if you are a collector of art...

Jack I'm not.

Kammler ...or even if you appreciate art...

Jack I don't.

Kammler (*Slight pause and smirk on Kammler's face, as if to say, "That figures."*) I don't expect you to assume risks in this case without some kind of reward. Unfortunately this painting is the only thing I have to offer you.

Jack Let's have a look at it and we'll see if it's worth the risk. (*Kammler unwraps the painting and hands it to Jack*) Huh! *The lady with a big nose.*

Kammler You know this painting? But you just said...

Jack I know this painting very well. You see, Kammler, I lived in Paris before the Germans marched in. The value of the franc was in a free fall at that time, so I decided to invest my money in something more lasting, like art. When I saw this painting in one of the galleries I was affiliated with, I thought it was crap. I still think it's crap. But I remember there were a lot of collectors willing to pay through the nose for it.

Kammler So it would seem to be worth the risk.

Jack Not so fast. How did you get your hands on it?

Kammler It was given to me for safekeeping, to keep it out of the hands of people like Göring and other Nazis.

Jack Well, the war's over. Why not give it back to them?

Kammler I'm afraid the owners were deported to concentration camps and never came back.

Jack And their children?

Kammler Look, Herr Henslowe. I did not come here to discuss property rights. The painting is yours if you help me get across into the Soviet sector.

Jack Sure, and you leave me with a stolen piece of artwork? How gullible do you think I am?

Kammler I'm sure a man like you has the connections to unload it before somebody comes along to claim it.

Jack I do, that's true, but before we agree to anything, I'm going to have to get an appraisal of this work. There's an art historian who lives up the road. I'll swing by his place now, drop off a side of smoked ham for him and his family. He'll be only too happy to put a figure on this painting for me.

Kammler You know it's worth a lot of money. Why do you need to have an exact figure?

Jack Because the American military has officially offered to top any price you offer if I help them take you back to the American lines.

Kammler You are considering their offer?

Jack Of course. I'm a businessman, Kammler.

Kammler Then permit be in this instance to appeal to your humanity.

Jack Go for it, though somebody tried it last night and it didn't work.

Kammler I realize that you are an American, but do you know what it will mean to the world if your countrymen get their hands on me?

Jack Yeah, they'll have one more rocket scientist than the Russians.

Kammler It's more than just about rockets, Herr Henslowe. It's about the balance of power in the world. The Americans are now in possession of a horrible weapon that can destroy whole cities, whole civilizations. If they are allowed to deliver this weapon by rocket, the whole world will be at the mercy of the politicians in Washington. Nobody is strong enough to confront them anymore. Not the British, certainly not the French. Only the Russians can but we have to help them make use of their advantages first. If the Soviet Union can develop rockets that can reach the United States, then the Americans will be more humble, more willing to talk about peace and prosperity for the world. Now they only go around telling people what to do. Bullying, if you will. Imagine, a country with no history or culture!

Jack Or concentration camps.

Kammler Hah, my sources tell me America is full of them. The day after Pearl Harbor, your president ordered anyone who looked Japanese to be thrown into prison. Not because they were dangerous, but because it was the easiest way to steal their land and money.

Jack I wouldn't put that past Roosevelt and his cronies.

Kammler The same thing happened here in Germany, is still happening today. The American soldiers come in and they steal everything, valuable items that have been in families for years. They even steal bibles. Such hypocrisy!

Jack A Gutenberg bible probably fetches quite a sum these days.

Kammler This is serious business, Herr Henslowe. The Americans have to be stopped.

Jack So you decided to go to the Soviet Union.

Kammler Yes, together with my wife.

Jack Your wife? How does she feel about going to live in the Soviet Union? I hear Russians like to rape German women.

Kammler Yes, yes, we heard that too. Frankly I don't know if it's true or if it was just more Nazi propaganda. But the Americans robbing us blind I saw with my own eyes. In any case my wife is not German. She's French.

Jack French? I got to know a few French ladies during my time in Paris. Wonderful breed but fickle as hell. You never know where they stand one day to the next.

Kammler My wife is totally committed to our mission to the Soviet Union. She in fact is a communist party member and it was through her that I got to learn so much about the politics of the world.

Jack And now everything is riding on this painting, it seems. Come to my place tonight, Kammler, and I will let you know if we got a deal or not.

Kammler May I bring my wife?

Jack Sure. (*Kammler bows and starts to leave*) So long as she doesn't have a big nose. (*Kammler scowls, shakes his head and continues on his way*)

Act II

Scene one
The Rose Café that evening. The place is fuller, with Major Patterson and Captain Douglas sitting at the table in front of the piano. Hanks enters and sits down.

Hanks Gentlemen, it may interest you to know that Kammler is in town.

Patterson Old news, Hanks.

Hanks He's accompanied by his wife.

Patterson Old too.

Hanks He's already made contact with Henslowe?

Patterson Christ, Hanks, haven't you got anything useful to give us? What do you do around here all day long?

Douglas Sleep mostly, from what I gather.

Hanks That's not true, Captain. I lay low because I'm a spy.

Patterson Why don't you say it a little louder so everyone in here can hear you, Hanks.

Douglas Look, gentlemen. The British military authority is more than willing to cooperate with our American allies in this matter. But I must warn you that we will not tolerate any violations of our rule of law. Whatever your intercourse with Kammler, it will be handled strictly through my office. Is that clear?

Patterson Now I've got some news for you, Captain. The sun has finally set on the British Empire. The only thing keeping it together right now is inertia and that ain't gonna last for too long. Your day has come and you know it. America is the power on this continent now, the only thing keeping you and the rest of your ungrateful Europe from going red. If you ask me, it was a joke letting you guys have an occupation zone in

Germany. Okay, maybe not quite so funny as letting the French have one, but a joke just the same. You have it at our leisure, so don't be go putting on any airs about it. (*Jack enters*)

Douglas I think I'll go out for some air. The stuff at this table has become rather stuffy all of a sudden. (*Leaves in a huff*)

Hanks That's telling him, Major.

Patterson Settle down, Hanks.

Douglas (*Passing Jack*) It's finally dawned on me why you prefer our zone to theirs. (*Jack approaches Patterson*)

Hanks You missed it, Henslowe. The major here really told off the captain.

Jack Hanks, why don't you make yourself scarce.

Hanks Hah, I don't have to take orders from a saloonkeeper.

Patterson Hanks, get lost. (*Hanks rises and leaves in a huff*) Have a seat, Henslowe. (*Jack sits*) What's the good word?

Jack A hundred thousand.

Patterson A hundred thousand what?

Jack Dollars. That's what it will cost you for my help keeping Kammler way from the Soviets.

Patterson He offered you that much? I knew the swine was sitting on top of a treasure trove. All those Nazis were. Spent the whole war hoarding while their soldiers were freezing to death in Russia.

Jack That's not my concern. You said you were willing to top his offer. There it is.

Patterson Did he actually show you the money?

Jack He offered me a painting. But I have it on good authority it's worth that much.

Patterson Don't be a fool, Henslowe. It's stolen property, plain and simple. Somebody's gonna come along and claim it before long.

Jack It'll be out of my hands well before then, Major.

Patterson Look, Henslowe. I tried to appeal to your sense of honor and patriotism and that got me nowhere. Then I tried the better half of your nature and found there wasn't one.

Jack But you struck gold the minute you probed my mercenary side.

Patterson That's right. But you're still out of your mind if you think the United States government is going to pay you $100,000 for another war criminal. That isn't going to happen, not with so many starving people around.

Jack Then I guess we don't have a deal.

Patterson We're going to have a deal one way or the other. But before I start issuing threats, I'm going to take one more chance here and appeal to your sense of dignity.

Jack I hope it won't take long. I have a saloon to run here.

Patterson I'll give it to you short and sweet. I used to be on the krauts' side, you might say. My grandfather came from Germany, I still remember my great-grandmother speaking to us in German because she couldn't say a word of English. I would have preferred they sent me to the Pacific to fight, but these were the cards I drew. Finally the war was over and, despite the nasty looks from these civilians, I wanted to be a kind conqueror. Then one day we were trucked out to this camp, Dachau was the name, and it changed me forever. Walking through that hellhole, looking at the faces of those poor, frightened people on the wall, then looking at what remained of them. Bundles of hair, spectacles and gold teeth. But the worst, the absolute worst, were the baby shoes. The sight of those shoes filled me with such fury that I felt like taking a tank and finishing off what was left of Munich. Horrible, Henslowe, horrible.

Jack I have a similar story to tell from my service in Spain, Major. We all have these stories. Okay, maybe the Spanish lack the organizational skill of the Germans, but the end result was just as horrible I can assure you.

Patterson When we're in Spain, I'll be glad hear all about what Franco and his fascists did there. Now we're in Germany. Understand? Our prime mission here is to make sure what happened in those camps never happens again. The only way we can do that is by de-nazifying the population. That's going to take a lot of time and a lot of effort, especially when you're dealing with intellectuals. Maybe these rocket scientists weren't members of the Nazi party, but that's pointless. They put their special skills to their use, so that makes them corrupted. We have to purify them of ideology like all the others, otherwise we risk more senseless massacres in the future. If you let Kammler go over to the Soviets before he's been purified, in effect allow him to receive another dose of ideology, you'll leave the rest of us at the mercy of the secrets inside that man's head. And I ain't gonna allow that to happen.

Jack This is where the threat part comes in, right? (*Douglas enters and approaches*)

Patterson That's right, because I'm warning you here and now...what is it, Captain?

Douglas Just to inform you that the object of your mutual interest has arrived. (*He gestures towards the door, where Kammler and Chantal appear. Kammler notices Douglas and leads Chantal to the table. Patterson rises, followed by Jack whose back is still turned to the couple.*) Major Patterson, allow me to introduce you to Rudolf Kammler and his wife... (*Jack turns, notices Chantal and goes wide-eyed*) I'm sorry, my dear, I didn't get your name.

Jack Chantal Fournier.

Chantal Hello, Jack.

Douglas (*Surprised, as are the other two gentlemen*) Oh, you've already met. I flattered myself into thinking I was privy to the honor first.

Kammler May we join you?

Jack Certainly. (*They all sit*) I must congratulate you, Kammler.

Kammler On what?

Jack (*Gesturing to Chantal*) Your wife.

Kammler My wife?

Jack I told you not to bring a lady with a big nose and you kept your end of the bargain. (*Chantal looks at him suspiciously*)

Kammler I don't understand. I brought you *The lady with a big nose*. She's in your possession. (*Douglas and Patterson look confused*)

Jack Not that woman. This one here. (*Chantal looks hurt, the others embarrassed*) I'm happy to see she doesn't have big feet either. (*Chantal stands up and slaps him. She runs from the room crying.*)

Douglas What on earth was that all about?

Kammler I don't know, but I have to ask you, Herr Henslowe: Did you just insult my wife?

Jack I said she doesn't have a big nose or big feet. How can that be an insult?

Kammler Then why did she slap you?

Jack I don't know. She's your wife.

Douglas Maybe she was just tired after the journey. A bit cranky, perhaps.

Kammler Perhaps. We should retire early tonight.

Patterson I hope not until we discuss some business together, Herr Kammler.

Kammler Forgive me, Major, but I make it my policy not to do business with the United States Army.

Patterson Unfortunately I have to make it my policy to do business with Germans wanted for war crimes.

Kammler Are you suggesting that I'm a war criminal?

Patterson You and all the other scientists who employed slave labor in the making of your rockets.

Kammler I did not know those people were forced to work there, Major.

Patterson (*Laughing*) Did you at least notice they came from countries enslaved by your own?

Kammler Major, this is the British occupation zone. I am under no obligation to answer your questions. Isn't that right, Captain? (*He and Patterson look at Douglas*)

Douglas I suggest we all have a drink and then we can start this conversation over again on a more polite note.

Kammler I'm sorry, Captain, but you can see my wife isn't feeling well. I should go to her.

Jack (*Rising*) I'll go to her since I'm obviously the one who upset her. You sit and become further acquainted.

Kammler (*Rising*) I'm acquainted enough, thank you. Herr Henslowe, I take it from the major's attitude here that we have a deal?

Jack Not so fast, Kammler. The fact is the major is right. You trafficked in slave labor and now you're trafficking in stolen artwork. (*Douglas and Patterson look surprised*) I'll have to give it more thought before I deal with the likes of you. In the meantime maybe you and the major can come to an agreement without my help.

Kammler This is outrageous and I will not stand for it.

Jack Then sit for it, but like the good captain said, make some polite conversation while I go and fetch your wife back. (*Jack intercepts a waiter, whispers something to him, and exits at the back of the stage, presumably to his office. The waiter goes outside.*)

Kammler Captain Douglas, today I swore out a form in your office which stated my rights would be protected under your administration. I demand you enforce them this very instant.

Douglas Nobody is stopping you from leaving, Herr Kammler. I'm only suggesting we have a drink and start things off on the right foot.

Patterson Yes, Kammler, don't be such a stick in the mud. Nobody wants to get nasty here. Sit down and just talk with us. (*Chantal enters behind the waiter and goes up to the table. Douglas and Patterson rise.*)

Kammler Are you all right, my dear?

Chantal Yes. I must apologize for my behavior, gentlemen. The stress over the last few months has been severe. It got the best of me, I'm afraid, in your presence.

Douglas Nothing to apologize for.

Patterson That's right. Things like that can even happen to hardened men under battle. Please, have a seat and join us.

Chantal First, I would like to apologize to Mr. Henslowe. You see, I knew him in Paris, in the art world to be exact, and, well, we had some problems about a particular painting, which my husband here will tell you about. I will come back, I promise. (*She leaves at the back of the stage, the men sit down*)

Patterson Fine lady you got there, Kammler. She deserves a home and family.

Kammler That's what I plan to give her once you stop chasing us.

Patterson That's what we're planning to give you once you stop running from us. In sunny Florida.

Kammler Yalta is sunny too, Major.

Douglas I don't mean to rain on your parade, gentlemen, but if it's sunshine you're looking for, then nothing beats North Africa.

Scene two
Jack's office in the back of the café. He's standing there pretending to look through papers as Chantal enters. She looks at him angry.

Chantal How could you, Jack? How could you say those horrible things about me in front of the others?

Jack For god's sake, I complimented you on not having a big nose or big feet. What don't you people understand?

Chantal That's all you have to say after all these years?

Jack Let's get something straight here, darling. You ran out on me, left me standing at a train station looking like the biggest chump in the world. Be happy I kept the anatomy to your nose and feet.

Chantal (*Conciliatory*) You have every right to be angry at me. What I did was unforgivable.

Jack Unforgivable I can live with, but not unforgettable. You know what the worst part of it was? I still don't even know why you left me.

Chantal But I sent you a note at the station.

Jack Sure, but it was pouring rain outside and the stupid porter that handed me the note didn't bother to cover it up first. All the ink had run by the time I got it.

Chantal You can't be serious.

Jack Very serious, doll. (*He goes to a drawer, opens it and takes out a note. He hands it to her.*) There you go. You mind telling me what that's supposed to say?

Chantal Oh, Jack, let's not go into it again.

Jack Again? I've been waiting these five years to find out what was in that note. The least you can do is oblige me.

Chantal All it said was that I could not go with you. I hoped you would understand and never forget that I love you. That's all.

Jack Yeah, that's all. The perfect ending to the perfect love affair.

Chantal Jack, if only you knew what I was going through then.

Jack Tell me now. Your husband has made some new friends out there. Let them get to know each other better.

Chantal Would it do any good?

Jack Yes, no, I don't know, but there's only one way to find out. Would you care for a drink?

Chantal Yes, please.

Jack Whisky?

Chantal Anything. (*Jack makes her a drink*)

Jack I'm listening.

Chantal You remember my parents?

Jack Sure. Communists, influential in the art community. I met you through them.

Chantal You know then that their lives were at risk under the German occupation.

Jack So was yours and mine. That's why we planned to make the trip to North Africa together, remember?

Chantal Yes, but what I didn't tell you at the time was that I was planning to take my parents with us.

Jack Your mother too?

Chantal Yes, Jack, my mother! I couldn't leave them behind at the mercy of the Nazis.

Jack No problem. I still question some of those art deals they set up for me but otherwise we got along okay.

Chantal Important here, Jack, is at the last minute they changed their minds. They said they could not run away from France in her hour of need.

Jack That's the only reason?

Chantal There was also the very big fear that their communist friends wouldn't look kindly on it. Communism, as an ideology, can be very intolerant at times, I'm afraid.

Jack Is that why you ran out on me then? Because you were afraid of what the communists would do to you if you ever returned?

Chantal Yes. Communism, Nazism, it's all the same when it comes to vendettas. They surely would have made my parents answer for me running away.

Jack It's hard for me to believe all of this occurred to you after we already made our plans.

Chantal Oh, Jack, there were other things too, of course. The Germans were on the verge of marching into our city. Maybe being an American, it was easy for you to think about running away so easily. But for somebody like me, born and raised in Paris? My beloved Paris?

Jack Well, your beloved Paris is free again. Why not go back?

Chantal Because of him. (*Pointing towards the audience*)

Jack Kammler?

Chantal He came to Paris during the occupation as a tourist. Imagine that, a tourist in time of war! We met in the marketplace where I was working as a fish-wife.

Jack Fish-wife?

Chantal Yes. The Nazis allowed the art galleries to stay open, but to work in them was the same as collaboration to most people. So I had to work in the marketplace.

Jack Couldn't you sell fruit or vegetables instead of fish?

Chantal I didn't ask for this fate, Jack! It was handed to me. The same with Rudolf. He came to my stand one day and since he studied in England before the war like me, we could communicate in a common language. He seemed to fall in love with me there on the spot. He was not a soldier but a German just the same, so I kept my distance. Then one day the first orders of deportation came. My parents, because of their high profile in communist circles, were on the list. I was desperate, so I turned to the only person I knew who could help me.

Jack Kammler.

Chantal Yes. He was back in Paris again, still madly in love with me. He said he would fix things in return for me marrying him.

Jack That bastard.

Chantal Yes, total bastard. But everyone around me was a bastard, so he was just one more in the crowd.

Jack So you married him?

Chantal Yes, to save my parents' lives!

Jack And did he?

Chantal Yes, they were taken off the list. But then, as the Allies were approaching Paris, a new order came, this time with my name also on the list. Being the wife of a rocket scientist spared me the concentration camps, but it couldn't save my parents any more. (*Sobbing*)

Jack (*Going up to her and putting his arm around her*) Sorry about that, darling. I know how much they meant to you.

Chantal Yes, but try telling that to the French people, who finally discovered their courage in the form of revenge. They started rounding up any one who had anything to do with the Germans, and if it was a physical relationship, they shaved your head and locked you in the zoo along with the animals, so the people, the brave French people, could walk by and shout and laugh at you and enjoy your humiliation.

Jack Did those bastards lock you up in a zoo?

Chantal I fled to Rudolf before Paris was liberated. I had more to worry about than the zoo, Jack. The communists would have shot me if they found out I had been branded a collaborator.

Jack So like me, you can never go home again.

Chantal Yes, and I can't stay in this country either. To live alongside the people who killed my parents disgusts me.

Jack Kammler included?

Chantal Him most of all. I still haven't let that bastard sleep with me. Just to have him close is more than I can bear. It's not the fact that he basically blackmailed me into marrying him. He couldn't save my parents in the end. He is just another weak, impotent German like all the rest.

Jack The guy must have a lot of fortitude to put up with a wife with an attitude like yours.

Chantal Of course I don't tell him to his face what a bastard he is, even though it might turn him on. I'm only using him now, using him to get to the Soviet Union, where I can start life anew.

Jack So you are the driving force behind this little mission. What do you need Kammler for then? Germans are fleeing west every day, the Soviets might appreciate some people coming over to their side once in a while.

Chantal I need him because I don't want to start at the bottom of the refugee heap. With my parents' reputation in communist circles, and me bringing over a rocket scientist, a husband at that, the Soviets will be sure to reward me.

Jack What does his being your husband have to do with it?

Chantal My parents told me the Russians are terribly bourgeois, Jack. They frown upon the idea of men and women living together in sin.

Jack It's a wonder the Soviet Union and America don't get along any better. But if that's truly the case, you'll have to stay married to the guy.

Chantal No problem. The Russians will lock him away in a laboratory somewhere and hopefully I will never see him again.

Jack There is one more option available.

Chantal What?

Jack Forget this great escape and stay with me.

Chantal With you? But surely you hate me as much as I hate him.

Jack I have to admit you really worked me over there for a time. After making my way to North Africa, I was totally at a loss what to do next. My first thought was to head to Casablanca, where there was a thriving black market. But then this wild idea occurred to me. I would go to

Tangier and set up some base of operations for smuggling into Spain. It would be dangerous as hell but the rewards immense. I figured that would be enough to take my mind off you. Yet when I got there, all I did was bury my sorrows in cheap Berber moonshine.

Chantal No women, Jack?

Jack Sure, loads of them. All whorish and Moorish. But during the day I would plod along the beach wondering what in the hell was in that note you left me. (*Chantal puts her arm around him*)

Chantal Poor Jack. I'm so terribly sorry about that.

Jack (*Standing up*) Well, don't be. I eventually got over it, came out stronger you might say, and did in fact finally get something going in Spain. But when the war ended and it was clear the Allies were no longer on speaking terms, I saw a new opportunity arose and came here. The British have been very accommodating, if only because I'm the only economy the Germans got here. But I'm settled. In a saloon, it's true, working with smugglers, but there are worse fates in this world, I guess.

Chantal And you want me to join you here?

Jack Why not? Look, baby, we were truly in love if I'm not mistaken. It doesn't matter to me anymore all that's gone on in between. The fact is we're together again as it was meant to be.

Chantal Of course I love you, Jack, I will always love you. But now I feel it's necessary to have some purpose in my life. I was born and bred on ideology, I want to somehow carry on my parents' tradition. It wouldn't be saying much if I simply became a saloonkeeper's wife.

Jack Too bourgeois, you mean.

Chantal It's not that, Jack. It's just...I don't know. I have to get rid of him, that's the most important part. Then I can think straight.

Jack This will help. (*He takes Chantal in his arms and kisses her. She kisses him back, long and passionately, then pulls back.*)

Chantal No more funny stuff about my nose and feet. Okay? (*They smile, kiss again, the scene closes, intermission*)

Scene three
Outside the Rose. Lights can been seen coming out of the café, as well as music heard. Carmel is making out with Offy.

Carmel Come on, baby. Let me show you my jeep.

Offy What's so special about your jeep?

Carmel It's got a gun mounted in the rear.

Offy Aha. And you want to mount your gun in my rear, is that it?

Carmel Your rear? Damn, baby, let's take it slowly first. Come on now, (*tugging on her*) it's just around the corner here.

Offy Promise to take me to America?

Carmel Take you to America?

Offy Yes, I want to leave this terrible place. Here there is only dirt and rubble, all the men have some part of their bodies missing, the only job a woman can find is as a prostitute. I want to go somewhere nice.

Carmel America ain't quite the paradise you think it is, baby, at least not for black folk.

Offy Yes, I know they are racist pigs but I don't care what they think. We will have each other.

Carmel But I'm afraid it's a big deal what they think. A black man coming home from Europe with a white woman, especially the former enemy? Man, that spells all kinds of trouble.

Offy Is America really so intolerant?

Carmel Intolerant and ungrateful. Me and my troop fight our way across the Rhine up until the surrender, but you know what the first order they gave us after setting up occupation duty? No fraternization. No mixing with the locals. All because they knew prostitution would be rampant and they couldn't stand the thought of all these black men sleeping with white women.

Offy Good for them. I'm sorry, Carmel, I think a black man should be able to sleep with whoever he wants, but something has to be done about prostitution. Look at me. My father was a professor in Gymnasium before the war. He taught English and Shakespeare, made sure we knew English and Shakespeare too. But then one by one all the boys in his school were called to the front until finally the professors were too. He survived but came back a broken man with no one to teach. For my family to survive I had to become a street whore myself. Disgusting it was, laying down with these British soldiers and their dirty fingernails. After ten minutes they grunt, get up, hand you ten cigarettes, and walk out like life just couldn't be better.

Carmel Ten cigarettes? Shit!

Offy Yes, ten cigarettes, twenty if the girl is young enough to look like a virgin, thirty if she actually is one. But that's not even the top price. Imagine, there are some men who pay fifty cigarettes for a grandmother.

Carmel Grandmother!

Offy Yes, they enjoy the idea of saying "Oma" when they fuck her.

Carmel You mean "Oh my"?

Offy No, oma! Oma! It's German for grandmother.

Carmel Man, those Brits are some sick sonofabitches.

Offy Yes, and they only do it because they like to humiliate us. Humiliate us like they humiliated every population they occupied. That was their imperialist philosophy. Break the spirit of the people you occupy, that way everything is cheaper for them.

Carmel Ten cigarettes is pretty cheap, let me tell you.

Offy Fortunately for me, Jack Henslowe came to town. He needed someone who could speak English so he gave me a job. As his operation grew, I was able to give jobs to other whores, take them off the streets.

Carmel You're talking about that café owner, the smuggler?

Offy Yes, he's a smuggler! Yes, our business is smuggling. But at least come the end of the day we have our dignity, and more than just a few cigarettes.

Carmel All right, all right, I ain't judging you. You don't have to tell me about humiliation. It's been most of my life, like every black man in America. No matter what you do, what talent you got, how good you are or how much money you have, the white man always looks down on you as just another Negro. You can't eat here, can't walk there, always got to sit at the back of the bus. And let's say you get off that bus and you really got to take a piss, but the sign on the door says "Whites only". If you go inside, they arrest you for violating their segregation laws. If you piss on the wall, they arrest you for violating everything else. So what else can you do except piss on yourself.

Offy That's terrible. I think America needs to have a war at home.

Carmel We had one, that's what freed us in the first place. But they obviously did a half-ass job because we're still waiting to be full citizens. Wearing this uniform back home won't save my ass if I go around with you in my arms. If I'm lucky, the sheriff will ride up and tell me I got five minutes to get out of town. If I'm not, he and his boys will drag me down to the river and lynch my ass from the nearest tree they find.

Offy Me too?

Carmel Nah, they'd just gang rape you and send you packing the next day.

Offy Terrible, terrible. Is there nowhere in this world that's safe anymore?

Carmel Why not we stay here for a while? I know it looks like shit now, but they got to start rebuilding soon.

Offy Here, among German people? Hah! Your Jesse Owens made fools of their Aryan superiority at the Olympics in Berlin, but that still didn't change their feelings about race. We would be safer here than in America, but ostracized, ignored. Our children would be too.

Carmel Ostracized? You mean those motherfuckers don't tell you their feelings to your face?

Offy No, they do everything behind your back.

Carmel Shit, I can't handle that. Segregate me all you want, but at least look me in the eye when you do it.

Offy Forget America, forget Europe. Let's go to North Africa. Jack tells me that Morocco is a beautiful place. Beautiful beaches, lots to eat.

Carmel I don't know. I never pictured myself wearing a turban and riding a camel.

Offy Come on, it will be fun. We can play like you're Othello and I'm Desdemona.

Carmel Didn't he kill her in the end?

Offy (*Flirtatiously*) I promise I won't make you jealous.

Carmel can stand for a little jealousy, baby. Gets his blood all boiling. (*Takes her into his arms*) Now I'm gonna drag your ass to that jeep. (*She pretends to struggle. Patterson enters.*)

Patterson Let go of that woman, Corporal.

Carmel Oh, shit. (*Releasing her*)

Patterson Is he assaulting you, Ma'am?

Carmel (*To Offy*) See what I mean?

Offy No! What's going on here is none of your business.

Patterson I happen to think it is. Corporal, what were you told about the rules against fraternization?

Carmel We're in the British sector, Major. They ain't got the same rules.

Patterson As long as you're wearing that uniform, you will conform to the rules of the United States military. Is that clear?

Carmel (*Sarcastically*) Yes, sir, Major. Anything else?

Patterson Yes. I'd like you to come inside and play some piano for us.

Carmel What makes you think I can play the piano?

Patterson Can't you?

Carmel I can, but the only reason you think I can is because I'm black. Ain't that it?

Patterson What of it?

Carmel Major, don't you think us black soldiers get tired of white officers only asking us questions with regards to music and dance?

Patterson I'm sure you do, and I'll be happy to take up the matter with Eisenhower when I see him.

Carmel (*Impressed*) You're gonna see Eisenhower?

Patterson Sure. Ain't you? (*Starts laughing*)

Carmel Man, can't get a break from these dudes.

Patterson Look, Corporal, I need someone in there to play piano. I'm fed up with all those sneering looks the Germans are giving me. I want to sing a good old patriotic American song to put them in their place.

Carmel (*Again to Offy*) You see that? White Americans always talking about putting people in their place.

Offy They are not sneering, Major. They are tired, miserable and depressed. That's what happens when you've got only one arm to go out and forage food from dead horses.

Patterson Spare me the sob tale, sister. You people put yourselves into this jam, now live with it. As for you, Corporal, I want you inside playing that piano. Don't make me have to make it a direct order.

Carmel Fine, Major, whatever you say. What song you planning on singing?

Patterson "When Johnny comes marching home".

Carmel Don't know that one.

Patterson Then let me hum it for you. (*Hums "When Johnny comes marching home"*)

Carmel That's a song of the Confederacy! You expect me to play that?

Patterson Yes, and I don't want any trouble about it. Hanks is in there and he'll be singing too. No trouble, understand?

Carmel Aye-aye, Major. (*Patterson goes inside*) You just got a good taste of why I ain't looking forward to going home again.

Offy So let's go to North Africa.

Carmel Othello and Desdemona? (*She nods excitedly, he looks resigned as they go inside the café*)

Scene four
Back in the café, Douglas and Kammler are sitting at a table in the

middle, while assorted Germans, most of them maimed, are standing at the bar to the left listening to the offstage band. Patterson is sitting at a table to the right with Hanks, whose shiner from the night before is clearly visible. Carmel enters, smiles broadly at Hanks, and sits down at the piano next to them. Offy goes to stand next to the Germans at the bar.

Carmel All right, Major, what key you want it in?

Patterson What do you mean what key?

Carmel Do you want it in A or C or D?

Patterson How the hell should I know? Just play it!

Carmel I'll say it before and I'll say it again. Can't get a break from these dudes. (*He turns to the piano and starts playing "When Johnny comes marching home".*)

Patterson and Hanks (*Singing in bombast style*) When Johnny comes marching home again, hurrah, hurrah! We'll give him a hearty welcome then, hurrah, hurrah! The men will cheer, the boys will shout, and the ladies they will all turn out, and we'll all be gay when Johnny comes marching home. (*They sing the refrain again, inviting even more dirty looks from the German patrons. Jack and Chantal are drawn into the scene from the back by the noise. Enraged, Kammler marches up to the orchestra offstage to the left.*)

Kammler Spielen Sie „Das Deutschlandlied". Sofort! (*It would seem as if the orchestra is looking to Jack for guidance but he merely shrugs. They start playing „Das Deutschlandlied" with Kammler leading.*) Deutschland, Deutschland über alles (*Offy fervently joins in*) über alles in der Welt. (*The crowd of German patrons – one-eyed, one-armed, one-legged – also join in*) Wenn es stets zu Schutz und Trutze, brüderlich zusammenhält. Von der Maas bis an die Memel (*As the music grows lower, Patterson and Hanks attempt to regain the upper hand with a couple of belting "hurrahs" but they are no match for the Germans and give up*) von der Etsch bis an den Belt. (*The crowd grows enthusiastic and patriotic*) Deutschland, Deutschland über alles, über alles in der

Welt! Deutschland, Deutschland über alles, über alles in der Welt! (*Sounds of "Deutschland! Deutschland!" are heard coming from the crowd as they gather around to congratulate Kammler. Patterson and Hanks continue to sit and sulk. Suddenly Carmel dashes for the middle of the stage.*)

Patterson Corporal, get back here!

Carmel This sounds like all taboos are off. (*Turning to the orchestra*) Hit it, boys! (*The orchestra starts playing some swing music, Carmel grabs Offy and together they start dancing in front of the crowd. Hanks can't believe it.*)

Hanks Of all the nerve. Do you believe this, Major?

Patterson Forget about him, Hanks. We've got a bigger problem here. These Germans are still a band of Nazis from what I just witnessed.

Hanks Yeah, but I don't have to live with them like I have to with this guy. He's got to be put in his place once and for all. (*Rising*)

Patterson Hanks, don't be stupid. Do you hear me? (*Hanks ignores Patterson and walks onto the dance floor*)

Hanks Quit dancing with that girl, boy.

Carmel (*Still dancing*) Boy, am I? Well, this boy done kicked your ass once and he's gonna kick it again if you don't take it out of my sight.

Hanks I ain't gonna warn you again.

Carmel Fuck off, Slick. This ain't no Alabama here. (*Hanks pulls out a pistol and shoots Carmel in the gut. General screaming ensues as Carmel sinks to his knees.*) I guess it is. (*Carmel slumps to the floor as Offy, screaming and crying, tends to him. Douglas marches up to Hanks and seizes his pistol.*)

Patterson Hanks, you idiot! How dare you make Americans look like a bunch of barbarians in front of these barbarians.

Douglas Hanks, you're under arrest. Kindly come with me.

Hanks I'm sorry, Major. I couldn't help myself.

Patterson Well, I sure as hell am not going to help you now.

Douglas Come along. (*Douglas escorts Hanks out the door*)

Jack Folks, I'm gonna have to ask all of you to leave. The café will be closed until further notice. (*Patterson notices Kammler ushering Chantal through the departing crowd and approaches them*)

Patterson It would seem, Herr Kammler, that your shameless display has resulted in the death of one of my men.

Kammler My shameless display? You started it, Major, with that ridiculous song of yours. You couldn't even sing it in the right key.

Patterson I have some news for you, Mr. Rocket Scientist. The Allied Control Council has declared the public playing of your ridiculous song a crime. Now, either you come back with me willingly to the American sector or I'll make sure the British authorities clamp you in irons. That is, until we eventually get our hands on you, which we will. You've got just one night to sleep on it. (*Patterson leaves*)

Scene five
A dingy hotel room. Kammler and Chantal are mulling around inside, visibly upset over the evening's events.

Kammler Never! Never will I let the Americans get a hold of me. Shooting that poor soldier just for dancing with a white woman. They are totally uncivilized, I tell you.

Chantal Stop it, Rudolf. Maybe if you hadn't made such a spectacle out there, he might still be alive.

Kammler Oh, so it's my fault.

Chantal Yes, it is. How dare you sing such a song like that after what Germany did to the peoples of the world.

Kammler They started it, my dear, with their childish "When Johnny comes marching home".

Chantal I don't care who started it or what they sang. You still had no right to sing that song.

Kammler The people inside thought I did. Didn't you see how inspired they were by it?

Chantal Great, so we can all look forward to another world war from the German folk someday.

Kammler Now you're being childish, my dear. It doesn't matter what song it was, just something to finally put some hope back into these people. My people. Okay, yes, we started the war, yes, we did some terrible things, but look at those people, with their one arms and one eyes and god knows what else with only one of it. They need inspiration if they're ever going to be able to pick up the pieces of their lives again.

Chantal And what about that soldier lying on the floor back there? He can't even pick himself up any more.

Kammler I will not be held responsible for that tragedy.

Chantal Oh, Rudolf, I'm not blaming you for his death. It's just, I feel, death all around me. Wherever we go, death is stalking. I'm tired of it. I want peace in my life.

Kammler We shall have it once we make it over to the Russians.

Chantal And how now? That major said you would be under arrest for singing that song.

Kammler He's bluffing. The idea of a soldier knowing the law is simply too absurd to take seriously. Everything now depends on this Henslowe fellow. What was that all about between you two?

Chantal I thought we agreed no questions about our pasts.

Kammler That was four years ago, when I didn't care about your past. But now it seems to need an explanation.

Chantal I'm tired, worn out by the day's events. Let's go to sleep.

Kammler I wish you would quit taking me for such a fool. Now I want to know what is between you and Henslowe.

Chantal (*Angrily*) What do you want me to say? Okay, we knew each other in Paris, before you came into my life.

Kammler And?

Chantal And what? Did we sleep together?

Kammler Yes.

Chantal Yes, we did. We were lovers, all right! Two crazy people carrying out a passionate romance with the world falling apart around them.

Kammler Passionate?

Chantal Yes, passionate. Full of tenderness, soft caresses, looking into one another's eyes. Is that enough or shall I give you more details, my husband?

Kammler I might wish you could have chosen a better sort of man. This Henslowe strikes me as just another American boor who found the mercenary life more profitable than a hard day's work.

Chantal For your information, I met him through the art world in Paris.

Kammler Of course. Americans always try to conceal their lack of culture and refinement by pretending to be collectors. Only I will give your Mr. Henslowe one thing. He at least had the honesty to tell me he knows nothing about art, only about its value.

Chantal He told you that?

Kammler And proved it. He couldn't see any beauty or elegance in *The lady with a big nose*. Nor did he say anything that remotely suggested he is a man for the underdog, a man who fights for the good cause.

Chantal He fought for the Loyalists in Spain.

Kammler I've heard that story a thousand times already. For all we know he was only there to pillage and plunder.

Chantal There you are wrong. When I first met Jack, he didn't want to tell me anything about his past either. Then, in one of our more tender moments together, he finally opened a little window into his life. Literally. He told me the story of how, when he was a boy, he had to work in a factory to help support his family. He and many other children in New York. One day he looks out the window and he sees a bird building a nest. With a child's curiosity and delight, he calls the other children over to look at it. The manager comes by, notices that the children are not working but he doesn't get angry at them, doesn't beat them, merely agrees that it is a beautiful sight but asks them to kindly go on with their work. They do and the next day they are all so eager to come to work, the first time in their lives that they are looking forward to coming to the sweatshop, just to see the bird. Only when they get there, they find that the management had frosted over the windows so they could never look out them again. Never see a bird building a nest again. From that day forward he swore to always be on the side of people who value the little things in life, and not just power and money.

Kammler Quaint story, my dear. I've also heard that one a thousand times or more.

Chantal Ach, you disgust me.

Kammler I disgust you, eh? Remember who it was that got your parents off the proscription list. Where was Henslowe then?

Chantal He had to flee. He was also on the proscription list.

Kammler So he says. He's probably the type who always plays the big man until he starts to feel the heat.

Chantal You can't even begin to measure up to him as a man.

Kammler What is wrong with you? I am a rocket scientist, a connoisseur of art and fine Rhine wine. I am the complete man, not your mercenary birdwatcher!

Chantal Hah, complete man! You spent the war sitting in a laboratory, working poor prisoners to death, just so you could build rockets to spread even more death around.

Kammler I was in the service of technology. Only with technology can we make the lives of people better.

Chantal How can rockets make the lives of people better? You're a fool!

Kammler Yes, you're right. I am a fool, a fool for letting you treat me like a fool all these years. I loved you, Chantal, loved you like no other woman in my life and all I earned for it was your scorn and contempt.

Chantal It was all you deserved for forcing me to marry you like that, taking advantage of my vulnerability.

Kammler I didn't want it to happen that way. I tried to court you with chocolate and flowers and devoted attention but you spurned my every advance.

Chantal Because I didn't love you! Can't you understand that?

Kammler Maybe now, after all these fruitless years of trying, I can. But I still don't accept it. I've been more than patient with you, my dear, waiting for the moment when you would finally come around, finally see that I deserve better than I'm getting.

Chantal Go on being patient, because believe me, this is as good as it's going to get between us.

Kammler I beg to disagree. You can go on loving your birdwatcher for all I care, but for once you're going to make love to me whether you like it or not.

Chantal You can't be serious.

Kammler I just watched a man get killed tonight in cold blood. Strangely enough, it has seemed to arouse me, that and listening to your stories about another man. It makes for the perfect opportunity to finally enjoy you myself. Take off your clothes.

Chantal I swore on our wedding night you would never see me without my clothes on and that's one oath I intend to keep.

Kammler I won't tell you again. Take your clothes off, else I will rip them off.

Chantal You wouldn't dare!

Kammler Wouldn't I? (*Advancing on Chantal and grabbing her*)

Chantal Take your hands off me, you German pig!

Kammler Not until you've finally had your fill of me, you little French slut. (*He pushes her to the bed and jumps on top of her. She continues to struggle violently.*) Oh, so your breasts are firm, my dear. (*There's a knock at the door. He quickly places a pillow over her head, not to smother her but to keep her quiet.*) Who is it?

Douglas (*From off-stage at the left*) Captain Douglas, Herr Kammler.

Kammler Yes, what do you want?

Douglas I have some matters of business to discuss with you.

Kammler Now is hardly the time or place.

Douglas I'm afraid it can't wait. Please open the door. (*Grunting, Kammler leaves the bed and goes to unlock and open the door. Chantal* *escapes to the bathroom.*)

Kammler Yes?

Douglas Let me in, Herr Kammler. (*Kammler grudgingly opens the door and lets Douglas in. He warily notices Chantal's disappearance.*) I'm sorry to disturb you and Frau Kammler but I'm afraid you will have to come with me.

Kammler What for?

Douglas To put it bluntly, you're under arrest.

Kammler On what charge?

Douglas On incitement to play a song that has been outlawed by the Allied Control Council.

Kammler Did Major Patterson send you here to tell me that?

Douglas Major Patterson is not the authority here. I am.

Kammler And you know what song it was we were singing?

Douglas Yes, the one that was outlawed by the Allied Control Council.

Kammler Wrong, Captain. It was a beautiful tune written by Hayden 150 years ago, one that every German knows.

Douglas I'm positive I heard that song in the Nazi newsreels we used to see.

Kammler Forgive me, Captain, but Germany was a complete culture before the Nazis hijacked it. You simply can't throw away Hayden and Beethoven and Goethe simply because gangsters are running the show.

Douglas I don't know, Herr Kammler. A man was murdered tonight after you played that song.

Kammler Again, forgive me, Captain, but connecting the death of that young man to Hayden is utterly absurd. It's late now. I will be happy to come down to your office tomorrow to discuss this matter further if you like.

Douglas But I have a warrant for your arrest.

Kammler Please, Captain. Let us discuss this matter tomorrow and if you indeed see a cause for my arrest then, you will already have me there at the station. Otherwise to take me in now, under so flimsy a charge, will only make you look like a stooge for the Americans.

Douglas I am nobody's stooge, Herr Kammler.

Kammler Exactly. So let us do it tomorrow under your own authority.

Douglas (*After a heavy pause*) I will concede to your wish only because it's late. But tomorrow, Herr Kammler, in my office at ten o'clock and not a minute later. Understand?

Kammler Completely.

Douglas Good night then. Sorry to disturb you. (*He leaves*)

Kammler Good night. (*Closes the door*) The fool. How we ever lost the war to this group I'll never understand. (*Calling to the bathroom*) All right, my dear, your respite is over. Time for our long-awaited honeymoon. (*The bathroom door opens and Chantal comes out in a negligee making sultry moves, with one hand behind her back*) Well, I'm glad to see someone has finally come to her senses.

Chantal Yes, well before I married you, you can be sure. I'm not wearing this for you, darling. Rather I wanted you to see what another man is going to see tonight.

Kammler Over my dead body. (*Advancing towards her, she pulls a gun on him*)

Chantal Gladly if you take one step closer.

Kammler Don't be a fool, Chantal. We've come too far for you to throw it all away now for some old fling.

Chantal Fling? It was no fling, my husband. It was rapturous lovemaking in the moonlight as you can only dream about. So get ready to dream some more tonight. (*She grabs her coat and heads for the door*)

Kammler Wait, Chantal. What about our commitment? All right, so you don't love me, don't want to sleep with me ever, but we're still united in our cause against the Americans. We have a mission to fulfill. Tomorrow I may be behind bars. Let us go away tonight, make our way on foot towards the Soviet sector. Leave all this pestilence behind.

Chantal Pestilence? You whose rockets rained destruction on London, the London where you lived and went to school once. You talk about pestilence!

Kammler All right, maybe I could choose my words better. The point is we have come too far not to finish. Please, Chantal. Don't throw it away now.

Chantal I'm going to Jack, Rudolf. Maybe he will still have me, maybe he will throw me in the gutter for the way I treated him. Either way it will be better than spending one more night near you. (*She storms out the door*)

Kammler Hah! Go to your birdwatcher then! American mercenary and French slut. You're made for each other. But you haven't heard the last of Rudolf Kammler. I'll make it to the Soviet Union all right. They know how to treat their scientists. Delicious caviar and simple peasant girl for the night, one who knows how to wash her feet before getting into bed. You, you lost your ideology. You don't wash your feet anymore. That I know. That I've seen. Wait till Mr. Birdwatcher finds out too. You'll be in the gutter all right. Then you'll come crawling back to me. Me, Rudolf Kammler, rocket scientist.

Act III

Scene one
Same night, Jack's office in the back of the café. He sitting looking glum while Offy displays a mixture of tears and fury over the killing of Carmel.

Offy He shot him. Shot him! That poor, sweet boy. Now he'll never get to see his mother again.

Jack Yeah.

Offy But why? Because he was dancing with a white girl? What kind of silly reason is that? Can Americans be so bitter?

Jack Don't start asking me about Americans. I haven't lived there for ten years now.

Offy But how to understand something like this?

Jack What do you care about understanding it? He's dead, nothing else matters.

Offy You know, we were talking outside right before. He was telling me how dangerous it would be to be seen with a white woman. But here, he thought he was safe.

Jack Yeah, millions of men walking around in this country with guns in their hands and he thought he was safe.

Offy We talked about going away together, to some place like North Africa. You know, all those stories you told me about Tangier. We were going to play Othello and Desdemona by the sea.

Jack I don't understand what you were doing getting involved with him anyway. He was here on a mission, a mission that could well shut down our business. You've got to keep your eyes on the prize, baby, else we're out of business for good and your girls will have to go back to whoring again.

Offy I know, Jack. It just seemed like such a wonderful dream. To finally get out of this miserable place and go to an exotic land, a land where orange trees grow and dates fall off the tree by the hour.

Jack I hate to spoil your dream, baby, but Spain was such a place and the people there couldn't get enough out of flaying and torturing each other with delight.

Offy I don't want to hear about it. I will go to North Africa, I don't care what will happen to me there!

Jack Fine, go to Tangier, but until that time comes you've got responsibilities here. (*There's a knock at the door. Horst comes in with his two lackeys.*) He's in the back. (*Horst and the lackeys go behind Jack to an offstage room*) If the Americans succeed in shutting us down, I'll see to it that you get your dream. (*Offy comes up to him and drops on her knees, taking his hand and crying*)

Offy Oh, Jack, you are so good to me. (*Horst and the lackeys reappear carrying Carmel's body*)

Jack (*Getting her to stop*) All right, all right.

Horst (*Sneering*) Hure. (*The lackeys laugh*)

Offy Du Missgeburt, geh auf Scheisshaus!

Jack All right, all right, knock it off. It's bad enough the Americans are at each other's throat. (*Horst and the lackeys leave with Carmel*)

Offy It's terrible to watch those lowlifes carrying his body.

Jack Do you want to carry it? I'm telling you, baby, get your focus back here.

Offy Yes, yes. I'm sorry. (*There's another knock at the door. Chantal comes in.*)

Chantal Am I disturbing something?

Jack No, no, come in. Offy here was just about to leave. (*To Offy*) Go on, baby, bright and early in the morning.

Offy (*Sobbing*) Yes. (*Gives a wary glance at Chantal as she passes her and leaves*)

Chantal Is she your girl?

Jack She was the girl of the soldier who got killed tonight.

Chantal Oh, I'm sorry.

Jack Yeah, everybody is.

Chantal Rudolf isn't. All it made him do was start preaching again.

Jack Is that why you're here now? Tired of his preaching?

Chantal That and I've changed my mind. I will stay here and become a saloonkeeper's wife.

Jack What about your ideology?

Chantal Let's say I'm no longer wed to it. Kammler destroyed all vestiges of it in me.

Jack Surprising how you could survive with that prick for so long.

Chantal But there's one thing I ask of you. Help him get over to the Russians.

Jack What? Why?

Chantal It will be a final gesture to my parents. They would appreciate it if I performed some act in service of the cause, like giving the Russians German rocket technology. If they decide they have enough scientists and choose to put him in the gulag instead, too bad, but I did my duty.

Jack I don't know, baby. The Brits have closed down my operation in anticipation of me trying to help Kammler. They especially won't go for it now in light of recent events.

Chantal Well, I tried. Let him stew on his own.

Jack It might be better for us all if he stewed in American hands. That way we're rid of him and Patterson and life will go back to normal here. Just another watering hole in the midst of this wasteland.

Chantal You won't mind if I have no part in it. For my parents.

Jack No problem, baby. I'll work out the details with Douglas tomorrow. Now, where you spending the night tonight? (*Chantal takes a step back and opens her coat to reveal her negligee*) Good choice. (*He picks her up in his arms and carries her into the back room. A moment later a knock is heard at the door. Nobody answers it. A knock again, followed by Douglas opening the door and walking in.*)

Douglas Jack, you here? Jack? (*Jack emerges from the back room*)

Jack What is it, Douglas? It's late.

Douglas Sorry to bother you, old boy, but we have big problems. I was just on the phone with my superiors. A military contingent from the American sector will arrive here, to take Carmel home and Hanks into custody.

Jack Hanks? He shot him here, under British jurisdiction. He should be tried here.

Douglas I have my orders, Jack.

Jack You know what they're going to do? They'll let Hanks off with a slap on the wrist, whitewash the case.

Douglas It's a dirty business, Jack.

Jack So? You're the commander here, do something about it.

Douglas Don't you think I would if I could?

Jack For god's sake, Douglas, you're not up against a field marshal here. Just an arrogant, nasty army major.

Douglas But this is not about warfare, Jack. It's about politics. Far worse, if you ask me.

Jack And this contingent will be taking Kammler back with them as well?

Douglas Probably. I'm supposed to arrest him on the charge of playing that silly song, that way I will be free to deport him to Bavaria, where he's originally from. I just feel so ridiculous using that as an excuse. My fellow officers will make a laughingstock out of me for kowtowing to the Americans so.

Jack Maybe I can help you?

Douglas How?

Jack Chantal, come on out here. (*Chantal emerges from the back room still in her negligee*)

Douglas Frau Kammler?

Chantal Please don't call me that.

Jack Douglas, there's something you ought to know. Chantal and I were lovers during my time in Paris before the occupation. For reasons we won't go into here, we were separated. There's only one thing keeping us from getting back together again. Her husband. We would like to see him safely locked away somewhere.

Douglas So you're for this plan to charge him with playing that song?

Jack Hardly. I need to get my operation up and running again and for that I need you. But if you buckle down to the Americans, even on orders, you could well find yourself on your way to India the next day. What you need is something heavier to stick it to Kammler.

Douglas Like what?

Jack This. (*Jack goes over to his desk and pulls out a packet of papers from a drawer*) These are maps of this entire area leading up to the Soviet sector. Whoever is on the end of my operations over there requested them, saying he would pay a mighty high price for them.

Douglas You were going to sell secrets to the Soviets? I should arrest you here and now!

Jack Take it easy. You can see for yourself I never sent them. But what we can do is this. Chantal will go to her husband and tell him that I have agreed to fly him over the border in return for the painting. She will give him these maps, adding that if something came up and he has to flee on foot, these maps will direct him to the border. They will then make their way to the airfield, where you will already be waiting with Major Patterson. Once you see him, you come in out of the shadows, discover the maps on him, arrest him for espionage, and hand him over to Major Patterson for deportation to Bavaria.

Chantal That means I have to go back to him tonight?

Jack We all got to make sacrifices here, baby.

Douglas Isn't Patterson's involvement only going to complicate things?

Jack He witnesses you carrying out your job like a real soldier and will be only too happy to commend you to your superiors afterwards.

Douglas How can you be sure Kammler will agree?

Jack Because I've got his painting, his wife, and his escape route. He has nothing left to bargain with.

Douglas Do you agree, Madame?

Chantal I'm not looking forward to going back to him but if it's only for a few hours.

Douglas A few hours? You mean tonight?

Jack Yes. It's got to be. I've got a window open to the Soviet sector till six in the morning. After that the American contingent will arrive and will no doubt start bossing people around. Here, Chantal, (*handing her the packet*) make sure he takes this after you pack and before you take a taxi to the airfield. Douglas, escort her to the hotel, then go find Major Patterson and explain our plan to him. I will go to the airfield to get everything ready and meet you all there in two hours' time. Clear?

Douglas Clear. I'm proud of you, Jack. You're a born leader.

Chantal But, Jack, what about...(*gesturing to the back room*) Couldn't we at least have a few minutes alone first?

Jack She's right, Douglas. It's been over five years.

Douglas But I'm supposed to escort her to the hotel.

Jack Yes. You don't mind waiting, do you?

Douglas Well...in view of your service in resolving this difficult situation, I agree.

Jack Thanks.

Chantal Thank you, Captain. (*They start to leave for the back room*)

Douglas Should I wait here or in the hallway?

Jack Whatever you wish. (*They disappear into the back room, Douglas smugly makes himself comfortable at Jack's desk, then grows noticeably uncomfortable as the sounds of passionate romance emanate from the room. Finally he can't take it anymore and slips away to wait out in the hallway.*)

Scene two
The hotel room, with Kammler working at a drawing board with a sketch of a primitive rocket on it. There's a knock at the door. He approaches the door suspiciously.

Kammler Yes, who is it?

Patterson Major Patterson.

Kammler If you've come to arrest me, Major, you will have no more chance at succeeding than Captain Douglas did.

Patterson I'm not here to arrest you, Kammler. I have no authority here. I just want to talk to you, man to man. (*Kammler opens the door*) You see, just me by myself.

Kammler Come in, Major, though I have no idea what we could possibly talk about. (*Patterson enters, Kammler closes the door*)

Patterson I don't know about that, Kammler. In many ways we're alike. We're both men very much committed to our causes, and even if our causes are not the same, we still have a latent amount of respect for each other, I'm sure. At least I have more for you than I do for Captain Douglas and the rest of the Brits. I have no use whatsoever for men like that. It strains me to even call them men.

Kammler If you've come here to flatter me, Major, I'm afraid it won't work either. I have no intention of coming over to the American side. (*Patterson notices the drawing of the rocket*)

Patterson This your work? Pretty primitive stuff, if you ask me.

Kammler I wouldn't expect a man like you to understand it.

Patterson What's not to understand? It's just the outline of a rocket, nothing more. I don't see any gadgets, any hydraulics, no gyros systems, nothing. (*Kammler shakes his head*) So tell me then. What the hell is in this drawing that's making a lot of people go through a lot of trouble to get your ass?

Kammler Like I said, Major, you could not possibly understand.

Patterson Right, so you're not even going to try. Not waste any time trying to educate us poor, stupid Americans.

Kammler I would prefer to use the word cultivate.

Patterson (*Starting to seethe*) Yeah, you Germans like to use that word a lot. Makes you think you're superior to everyone else. Well, you're right in one sense. The work you did in the concentration camps, that was pure cultivation. Other nations just let the corpses of their enemies lie around rotting in the sun, with crows picking at them and ants wiping the bones clean. But you guys make them disappear into thin air.

Kammler Do we have to hear this story again? (*Patterson loses his temper and grabs Kammler by the collar*)

Patterson You listen to me, you smug rocket scientist. I've had enough of your aloof behavior. If I had my way, you would be walking up the gallows along with those other Nazis. But as it is, my superiors want you for whatever it is in your head and I hope to dear god it's something more cultivated than that shit I see on that piece of paper over there.

Kammler Take your hands off me or else I will pull the full weight of the Geneva convention on you. (*Reluctantly releasing his grip*)

Patterson I changed my mind. Douglas may be weak, but he would never go running to the Geneva convention like a little girl. You're pathetic, Kammler.

Kammler Is that all, Major? I have work to do.

Patterson Well, if your work is truly that child's toy over there, I think the Russians should get you after all.

Kammler You can leave any time now, Major.

Patterson Not hardly, Kammler. I also came to tell you that a squad of my men are on their way here now. Officially they're here to pick up

Carmel but you're going back with us too, any way it takes.

Kammler And what are these ways, may I inquire?

Patterson You go willingly is one. Captain Douglas arrests you on some charge and orders you deported to your native Bavaria is another. And the final way is I hit you over the head with a rubber hose and my men bundle you into the back of a jeep.

Kammler Gangster-style, you mean?

Patterson Yes. I was planning to do that tonight, but was counting on Carmel and Hanks helping me. I had to change my plans after one shot the other and ended up in custody.

Kammler I'm surprised you're not planning to pin that murder on me too.

Patterson The night is still young, Kammler. (*There's a knock at the door*) See what I mean? (*Patterson goes to open it. Douglas and Chantal are standing there.*)

Douglas Major Patterson, what a surprise to find you here. I was just about to go looking for you.

Patterson I was just about to go looking for you. Why isn't this man under arrest?

Douglas It's a complicated situation, Major. I will explain it to you in my office.

Patterson There's nothing to explain. Arrest him!

Douglas Please, Major.

Patterson What are you doing with his wife anyway? What's going on here, Douglas?

Douglas Major, now is not the time or place. Come with me and everything will be settled to your satisfaction.

Patterson All right, but I'm warning all of you here – British, French, German. There's a new player in town and you had better all start cooperating. (*Leaves with Douglas*)

Kammler I thought you left to spend the night with your birdwatcher. Couldn't find him?

Chantal I was picked up by Captain Douglas. Apparently there's a curfew in this town.

Kammler Too bad for you, my dear.

Chantal Please, Rudolf, let's forget about all that. You said we are united in one cause, let us keep that the focus of our mission. Let's get to Russia and try to make a start of it again.

Kammler You must certainly take me for a fool if you expect me to believe you had such a change of heart so fast.

Chantal I haven't had a change of heart. I still have no intention of sleeping with you. But there are more important things in this world to worry about right now.

Kammler Well, even if you're serious about getting over to the Russians, I'm afraid the Americans have the upper hand. Their soldiers are on their way here now to take me back in the morning. I don't see how I can possibly escape any more. But you are free to go, free to enjoy life with your birdwatcher.

Chantal Ach, I wish you would quit calling him that. Makes you sound like a child.

Kammler If it makes me feel any better.

Chantal Look, Rudolf, the game isn't over yet. Captain Douglas, you may have noticed, is no more happy with Major Patterson than the rest of us. He informed me now that Jack wants to keep *The lady with a big* *nose* and being an honorable businessman, he feels it's necessary to keep his end of the bargain with you. So together they have devised a scheme for you to escape.

Kammler What scheme? (*She takes out the packet and hands it to him*)

Chantal These are maps covering this area to the Russian border. Jack is at the airfield now getting his plane ready to take you across, only he's worried that Patterson might get wind of it and try to head you off. We will go to the airfield. If something comes up, take off on foot into the night and use these maps to take you to the border.

Kammler But the border must be hundreds of miles from here.

Chantal It's only just in case. That's why Douglas is taking Patterson to his office now. To keep him there while we go to the airfield. Of course, Patterson is suspicious and may think something is up, so you have to be prepared to run at any moment.

Kammler But I don't know how to survive by myself, alone in the wilderness.

Chantal For god's sake, Rudolf, millions of Germans are surviving right now in the wilderness. Women, children, old people. If they can do it, so can you. Besides, the only other alternative is to go back and be a slave for America.

Kammler And what about you, my dear? You don't want to come with me, help me to survive in the wilderness if necessary?

Chantal Oh, Rudolf, why do you even still want me? I treat you with total contempt. Why not go to Russia where you will be honored, where so many other young communist women will be only too happy to share your bed at night.

Kammler But I hear they have bad teeth.

Chantal Oh, for god's sake, quit complaining. But if it makes you feel any better, I promise to sleep with you at least once if for some reason I also make it over there one of these days.

Kammler You mean you get tired of your birdwatcher.

Chantal Perhaps.

Kammler Or he gets tired of you.

Chantal Oh, god, shut up and start packing, will you? (*She turns, only to stop dead in her tracks when she sees the drawing*) What is this?

Kammler What do you think it is? My work.

Chantal This?! It looks like a toy.

Kammler I wouldn't expect you to understand. (*Goes to take it down. She continues to look at him suspiciously.*) Yes, yes, the gadgets, hydraulics, gyros, all of it will come later. (*He takes the drawing to the bathroom and closes the door*)

Scene three
The airfield, sometime after midnight. The scene opens with Major Patterson and Captain Douglas after arriving in Patterson's jeep, stationed on the right and outfitted with a mounted 50 caliber machine gun in the rear. Jack approaches them from the left.

Jack What took you so long? Kammler and his wife will be here any minute.

Douglas Major Patterson here needed extra convincing as to the merits of our plan.

Patterson That's right, Henslowe. You're the last person in the world I would expect to rally to the red, white and blue. But then I remembered that you're essentially a mercenary at heart, so it all came together in the end. We pull this off and I'll see the two of you get decorated.

Jack Don't press your luck, Major.

Douglas So, Jack, how do you suggest we nab him?

Jack Easy. He comes and Douglas, you arrest him. (*Easing alongside Patterson*)

Douglas What about the major here?

Jack Easy. He'll be on the ground. (*Jack lifts his hand and hits Patterson over the back of the head with a revolver. Patterson falls unconscious.*)

Douglas What in blazes? Have you taken leave of your senses?

Jack I have. (*Douglas moves towards Jack, who points the gun at him*) Stay where you are.

Douglas Put that gun down. (*Taking another step*)

Jack I'm warning you, Douglas. One more step and you'll be joining Carmel in the meat locker.

Douglas What's the meaning of this?

Jack Simple. Kammler is getting on that flight.

Douglas I knew it. You're a communist sympathizer, just like I always suspected. Do you really think you can get away with this?

Jack We won't find out until the plane is airborne. (*The sound of the taxi can be heard off to the left, followed by the opening and closing of car doors*)

Douglas Listen, Jack. It's not too late to forget this crazy scheme. I'm sure Patterson will forgive you for the knot on the head if Kammler still winds up in his custody.

Jack Sorry, Douglas. But I'll be sure to mention at my trial that I kept you at gunpoint the whole time.

Douglas Great. Another trophy to hang on my mantle of service in occupied Germany. (*Kammler and Chantal enter. They immediately notice the unconscious form of Major Patterson.*)

Kammler Is everything all right here?

Jack Perfect.

Douglas I should think not.

Jack All right, Kammler, here's the deal. You walk that way there (*pointing to the back of the stage*) to the waiting plane. Three of my men will be there standing next to a coffin. You get in that coffin and they will load you up onto the plane. Under no circumstances get out of that coffin by yourself. Wait till somebody on the other side opens it up.

Kammler You've got to be joking.

Jack At a time like this? You're not very smart, are you, rocket scientist?

Kammler I'm afraid I have too much dignity to allow myself to be transported in a coffin. Alive anyway.

Jack Would you prefer dead instead?! Listen, Kammler, this is a smuggling operation, in case you didn't get the word. Whatever goes to the other side, goes in a coffin. Isn't that right, Douglas?

Douglas Oh, now you want my cooperation. Sorry, Jack, you're on your own with this one.

Chantal Rudolf, do as he says. There isn't much time.

Jack She's right, Kammler. If Patterson here wakes up and sees you, the game's up.

Kammler Yes, but a coffin?

Chantal Rudy!

Jack All right, Kammler, I've had enough of your glorified opinion about yourself. (*Turning the gun on him*) Walk to that plane, get in the coffin, or Douglas and I will put you in it ourselves.

Douglas I told you, Jack. Leave me out of it.

Kammler You're going to shoot me, Herr Henslowe?

Jack Ach, this is hopeless. Come on, Chantal. Douglas, he's all yours. (*Turning to leave*)

Kammler Wait. All right, I'll go. But on one condition. Chantal must join me.

Chantal Rudy, we've already been over this.

Kammler I'm sorry, my dear. I can't make the trip there in a coffin alone.

Jack No problem. There are two coffins there. (*Chantal jerks her head towards him*)

Chantal Jack!

Jack But since they can load only one coffin at a time, go get into yours while I say goodbye to your wife here.

Kammler How can I be sure she'll follow me?

Jack I'm a man who always keeps his word. Isn't that right, Douglas?

Douglas All right, Jack, I've had enough of this buffoonery! Give me that gun. (*Stepping towards Jack*)

Jack Douglas, what Rommel couldn't do, I will if you get any closer. Let's just get this over with. (*Turning to Kammler*) So what's it gonna be, Kammler?

Kammler All right. But first, for what it is worth, thank you, Mr.

Henslowe. I secretly suspected you were with the cause all along, that all this mercenary behavior was just a cover for a true compatriot. I can see now that you're in possession of a heart after all.

Jack No, Kammler. I'm in possession of *The lady with a big nose*. Now get going and don't ever come back.

Kammler Captain. My dear, see you on the other side. (*Slowly leaves for the plane and disappears*)

Jack All right, Chantal, now it's your turn.

Chantal But, Jack, I thought we agreed. I'm staying with you.

Jack Sorry, darling. It looks like you're not going to be a saloonkeeper's wife after all.

Chantal Why? What happened?

Jack What happened is they're never going to let me get away with this. Isn't that right, Douglas?

Douglas You can be very sure of that.

Jack It'll be jail if I stay here, the likes of Patterson on my ass if I leave. There'll be no peace, only hardship ahead for us.

Chantal I don't care. As long as we have each other.

Jack You say that now, but after one or two years of life on the run, you're going to wish you had been on that plane.

Chantal But Jack...

Jack Listen, Chantal. I'm no good at being funny, but it doesn't take a rocket scientist to figure out we're not talking about a hill of beans here.

Chantal Hill of beans? I don't understand.

Jack It means you're getting on that plane.

Chantal (*Snarling*) So you're just giving me to Kammler, is that it? Revenge for all the pain and hurt I caused you?

Jack No, I'm giving you to the Soviet Union. You see, my contacts tell me that the Russians really aren't interested in Kammler. They have plenty of German rocket scientists already and those of them who know Kammler have indicated that he's pretty second rate when it comes to the actual science. Apparently he would make a better political officer instead, but the Russians have enough of those.

Chantal What will they do with him then?

Jack Who knows? Use him as a propaganda tool, maybe dump his ass in the gulag. But you, darling, you're another story.

Chantal Me?

Jack Yes. Your parents are communist martyrs. The Russians will only be too happy to have you there, telling the story of their lives to young pioneers, propping them up as an example for future leaders of the cause. (*A light starts to shine in her eyes*)

Chantal My parents?

Jack Yes, dear. Your parents. They'll finally be getting their due. But it means you've got to join Kammler in the next coffin.

Chantal But, Jack, I promised him I would finally sleep with him if I ever made it over to the Soviet Union.

Jack Well, darling. You are his wife.

Chantal (*As if in a daze*) His wife. Yes, I will have to make the ultimate sacrifice. (*The sound of the plane engine can be heard starting in the distance*)

Jack That's your cue.

Chantal (*Hugging him*) Oh, Jack, will we ever see each other again?

Jack Now, now, don't talk like that.

Chantal But what about Tangier?

Jack We'll always have Paris.

Douglas (*Cynically*) And last night.

Chantal (*Softly*) Yes. Last night. We'll always have...what is the name of this city anyway?

Jack Hamm.

Chantal (*Disbelief*) Hamm?

Jack Goodbye, dear. (*She briefly nods to Captain Douglas, takes one more teary look at Jack, then heads off into the darkness*)

Douglas This is just perfect, Jack. Do you realize how much trouble you're in, how much trouble I'm going to be in?

Jack Sorry, Douglas, but this is the way it had to be.

Douglas Had to be? Who gains anything from this except Kammler? Even Chantal loses. I can't believe she fell for that fairy tale you told her.

Jack What fairy tale?

Douglas That nonsense about her becoming a pioneer booster. You yourself said you don't have any contacts over there. Why make up all that stuff to send her along?

Jack Because, for better or worse, it's the fate she deserves.

Douglas Let's hope it's nothing like the fate you're about to receive. Do you realize Kammler walked away with those maps? If the Americans get a hold of you, they will execute you for treason.

Jack Relax, Douglas. Those were geological maps of the Sahara. I picked them up while in Morocco, to use in case the authorities decided to crack down on my operations there. I didn't expect a genius like Kammler to figure out their real nature.

Douglas (*Indignantly*) Lucky for you I didn't have a look at them back in the hotel.

Jack Yes, I know. You and North Africa.

Douglas Well, what do you plan to do now?

Jack I actually didn't give that much thought. But I would like to see the look on Patterson's face as the plane takes off. (*Shakes Patterson awake with his foot*) Hey, get up there. Final boarding call. (*Patterson groggily comes to and stands up*)

Patterson What happened? With going on? Where's Kammler? (*Silence*) Well!?

Douglas (*Pointing to the darkness*) Kammler, I'm afraid, is on that plane.

Patterson What!? Why do you stand here? Stop him!

Douglas Tell that to Mr. Henslowe here. (*Patterson turns to see Jack pointing the gun at him*)

Jack Take it easy, Major. I'll be glad to answer all of your questions as soon as the plane takes off.

Patterson I knew it along. You are a communist sympathizer!

Jack I thought I was a mercenary, Major.

Patterson Whatever you are, you will get yours in good time. (*Patterson hops up onto the back of his jeep, swings his machine gun around towards the darkness and prepares it for firing*)

Jack Don't be an idiot, Major! I was willing to shoot Captain Douglas and I'll be even more willing to shoot you. Get down off of that jeep!

Douglas Please, Major, what's one rocket scientist more or less? Come to your senses.

Jack I mean it, Major. Get down now or I'll shoot!

Patterson Listen to me, Henslowe. Whatever you are now, somewhere in that soul of yours must be some good memories of America. Think of those now and it will remind you what it means to be a proud, honorable American. Think of the blue skies as far as the eye can see, the beautiful red rock of the canyons and the snow-tipped peaks above them. The glorious amber waves of grain and... (*He suddenly swings his machine gun around to take aim at Jack but Jack is quicker. Patterson clutches his abdomen, struggles to get his final words out*) By the dawn's early light... (*Falls out of the jeep dead.*)

Douglas That's it! Give me that gun! (*He goes up and takes it out of Jack's hand*) What's with all you Americans shooting each other?

Jack He was a fool thinking he could sway me like that. I never saw any of that stuff in America. Spent all my life on the East Coast.

Douglas Try using that as a defense at your trial.

Jack You're going to arrest me, Douglas?

Douglas How else should I explain this to my men? (*Pointing to Patterson's body*) Tell them to round up the usual suspects!?

Jack It's worked before. (*The plane can be heard taking off overhead. The sound of the engine eventually fades away.*)

Douglas My advice, Jack, is for you to lay low for a good long while.

Jack Already taken care of, Douglas. I knew from the moment I saw Chantal that my time here was up, so I made a deal with Horst. He and his boys will get The Rose in return for giving you a twenty-five percent cut.

Douglas Please, Jack. I can't be involved in the local economy. (*Jack looks at him in silence*) What I mean to say is... Did you say twenty-five percent?

Jack Yes.

Douglas What about you?

Jack I'm going back to Morocco and taking Offy with me.

Douglas Offy?

Jack Yes. We will hang out there for a while, wait for the French to finish their vendettas against each other and straighten out their currency market, then settle down in Paris.

Douglas Sounds like another fairy tale of yours.

Jack Let's hope this one has a happier ending.

Douglas But if I may, Jack, you could have gone to Tangier with Chantal, a beautiful woman. That's not to say Offy isn't beautiful, but is there really any comparison between them?

Jack Yes. Chantal ran out on me the first time I went to Tangier. There was no way of guaranteeing she wouldn't do it to me again. And Offy is nothing if not loyal.

Douglas I guess you know what you're doing.

Jack Goodbye, Douglas. It's been a real pleasure.

Douglas You mean you're going now? This instant?

Jack Have to, before the American military arrives.

Douglas But what do I say about this? (*Pointing again to Patterson*)

Jack All you know is Patterson's dead and Kammler's gone. Patterson will be taken back to the States for a hero's funeral and Kammler will make the FBI's most wanted list.

Douglas Most wanted list? But that means we'll have more agents snooping around here before long. Looking for you, I might add.

Jack I'll be sure to leave them a note in my apartment. Otherwise just tell them I've moved on.

Douglas Moved on. How I would love to be able to say those words about myself now.

Jack Some day you will, Douglas. Maybe I'll even see you in Tangier.

Douglas North Africa? You've got to be joking.

Jack Goodbye, Douglas. (*Jack slowly disappears into the night. End.*)

Locked Down

Characters

Irving, *an unassuming office worker*
Judy, *his co-worker*
Emma, *another co-worker, Judy's live-in*
Gracie, *a third co-worker, moonlights as a waitress*
Guard, *building security*
Alison, *Irving's fiancée*
Tim, *a single guy, hits on Alison*
Mr. and Mrs. Waters, *Irving's parents*
Psychiatrist
Dream girl
Waitress

The set design consists of a white wall standing 250 m high, divided into two sections. Directly behind the seam where the sections meet in the middle of the stage is a box standing 200 cm tall, 200 cm wide, open at the front and top and painted to look like an elevator on the inside, with a control panel on one wall and a code of regulations on the other.

Scene one

The two sections of the wall are opened to line up with each front corner of the box. The theater is dark with the exception of one high-wattage light beaming directly inside the box. Dull elevator music permeates the auditorium. Irving is standing there, clearly annoyed by the light and music, annoyed because he's trapped in this elevator and nobody seems to notice.

Irving Hey, come on. The elevator's stuck. Let's go, fix it. Get this thing moving. I'm in here. Hey! (*He bends low and pushes the intercom button*) Hello, is anyone there? I'm stuck in here, all right? Hello? Jesus Christ! (*Checks his pockets, pulls out a calculator*). Oh no! Goddamn calculator? Hey! Open up, dammit! (*Thinking*) Wait a minute. (*Pulls out* *his pack of cigarettes and lighter. Looks at the code of regulations mounted at the side of the elevator opposite to the control panel.*) Let's see...no leering, no jumping, no kicking... yeah, yeah. Finally! No smoking. (*Reading*) "This elevator is equipped with a smoke alarm. Anyone caught smoking will be prosecuted to the fullest extent of the law." Yeah, well come and get me. (*Looks in his cigarette pack*) Hah, last one. I'm sure going to enjoy this. (*He goes to light it, but can't get the lighter to work*) Come on, not now. (*He tries and tries but gets no flame*) Jesus Christ, doesn't anything work around here anymore? (*He slowly, carefully flicks the lighter, but to no avail*) Goddammit! (*In a fury he threatens to chuck the lighter, but not quite knowing where*) Fuck, let me out of here! (*Banging on the door*) Let me out! Let me out! (*A pause*) At least stop this shitty music!! (*The theater goes dark, the music stops*)

Scene two

The walls are slid closed, the stage is set up to look like an office with a table and chairs in the front center of the stage. Emma, Judy and Gracie are sitting with their laptops open. On the left wall section facing the audience, 130 cm from the floor, is a square painted to look like a hand scanner. On the right wall section hangs a picture of Lenin.

Gracie (*Closing her laptop*) That should do it! You ready, Judy?

Judy Sure am. (*Closing her laptop*) Emma? What about you?

Emma Wait a minute. (*Working the mouse and keyboard*) I just have to save this bit here. There, that should do it. Now I'll put this over here and...that should do it. Move this window over here and...that should do it...and now...

Judy And now *what*? Are you finished or not?

Emma Yes. I just have to...

Gracie What about Irving? Where'd he take off to?

Judy He went down for a cigarette break.

Gracie What? He couldn't wait till we left?

Judy He says he's meeting his girlfriend after work and didn't want to smell like smoke.

Gracie Oh, so he can smell like smoke for us, but not for her. (*Picks up her cell phone, rises from her chair*) I'll call him and tell him to get his ass in gear. (*She pushes some buttons, then presses it to her ear*)

Emma There, that should do it. Now I will just...

Judy Close your computer, Emma, and let's get out of here. I'm starving. (*A phone rings from underneath the papers on the table. She rummages through them and retrieves Irving's phone*) Looking for this, Gracie? (*Gracie is not amused*)

Emma Finished! (*Starts to close her laptop*) Wait a minute. I will just...

Judy (*Closes it for her, just missing her fingers*) Just nothing! We're out of here. (*The guard enters from the left*)

Guard I'll say you are. You're the last ones in the building.

Gracie We're done. We're just waiting for one of our colleagues to come back from his smoking break.

Guard Ain't nobody behind the building on a smoking break. I just swept the place clean.

Gracie Maybe he's on his way up now.

Guard No chance. I swept the whole building. Like I said, you're the last people here.

Gracie How do you like that? Irving just took off.

Judy Why would he go and leave his cell phone behind?

Emma (*Looking around the table*) Hm, I don't see his calculator. Maybe he took it by mistake.

Guard Look, people, we can't argue about this all day. It's 5:00, time to lock down the building.

Gracie Lock down the building? You mean there's no coming to work here this weekend?

Guard That's right. Unless you want to be locked up here the whole weekend. (*Judy and Emma stand to leave*)

Gracie What about Irving's phone? (*Picking it up*) We can't just leave it here. He probably needs it.

Judy I know I need mine. I can't imagine surviving a weekend without it.

Emma Neither can I. (*She sneers at her*)

Gracie Will you take it to him then?

Judy Forget it. If I take his phone, he can tell the boss on Monday that I rang up a bunch of calls on his account.

Gracie Irving wouldn't do that.

Judy Irving also wouldn't take off without finishing his work for today, but he did. We should give his phone and laptop to Security here.

Guard So I get stuck with his phone bill? No way.

Judy Then lock them away in the safe. He can come claim them on Monday morning. (*Picking up the gear and handing them to the guard*)

Guard (*Sighing*) Anything to get you people out of here. I'm supposed to have lights out here by 5:15.

Emma Wait a minute. I just remembered. Irving's got office security this week. We need him to lock up.

Guard Are you telling me this guy's got hand duty and he just took off. He should be reported.

Gracie Look, he probably forgot, that's all. We'll just use the backup system.

Guard I don't know anything about a backup system.

Emma It's new technology. It hasn't been approved by the board yet, but it's as smooth as clockwork.

Guard Whatever, people. It's now 5:03. (*Emma takes a cleaning glove from her pocket and puts it on. She walks up to the open notebook, taps some keys, and then places her hand against the screen. An alarm goes off. She pulls her hand away, rubs the gloved hand on a trouser leg and tries again. Still the alarm.*)

Emma Sorry. Like I said, new technology. (*Inspired*) Maybe the problem is a smudgy glass.

Judy Jesus, Emma, we don't need a play-by-play. (*Emma exhales on the screen and wipes it with her forearm*)

Gracie Especially with Security looking on. (*Innocently looks at the guard*) Right?

Guard I don't see nothing.

Emma (*Trying the gloved hand again. The alarm stops.*) That's it. Like I said: clockwork. (*Removes the glove from her hand*)

Guard Make sure you got all your belongings, because once I lock the front door, that's it. This place becomes a fortress. Part of the company's new ATAT measures.

Gracie ATAT?

Guard Anti-thief, anti-terrorist.

Judy Ah, yeah. I read about them on the internet yesterday. (*They pack up all their things and head for the door*)

Guard Follow me, please, to the north elevator. I've already locked down the south one and will do the same to the north one as soon as I get you people out of here.

Gracie What for, if nobody's going to be in here?

Guard There's always a chance that thieves and terrorists can get in, and if they do, (*sarcastically*) we don't want to make it easy for them to get around, now do we?

Emma Of course not. *Die Hard* would have been a boring movie otherwise. (*The girls giggle, Judy and Gracie exit, the guard stops Emma short*)

Guard (*Pointing to Lenin on the wall*) Who is this guy anyway?

Emma Just some crackpot who invented a program called "Worker's Paradise".

Guard Never heard of it.

Emma That's because he died before he finished it. Syphilis. (*Exits*)

Guard Just like my uncle Leroy. (*Takes one look around, exits, lights go off and the alarm sounds again. Lights go back on, the guard reenters and goes to the notebook. He taps some keys, looks around, and pounds the table. The alarm stops. He exits, lights off.*)

Scene three

The wall is again slid open to reveal Irving stuck in the elevator. He is sitting with his legs crossed, holding the lighter in both hands, totally focused on it. He slowly and carefully tries to light it but to no avail. Then, very carefully, he gives it one last go. Nothing. Chucks the lighter in rage.

Irving Goddammit, piece of shit! (*Standing up, banging on the walls*) Hey, let me out of here! Let me out, let me out!! I'm hungry, thirsty, I gotta piss! My girlfriend's gonna be pissed! Come on, doesn't anybody work in here? Hey, if don't start this thing right now, I'm gonna...gonna...ah, piss on it! (*He turns his back to the audience, unzips his pants, and starts relieving himself on the elevator wall.*). Piss on me, will you? (*Lights out*)

Scene four

The walls are slid shut. The set is now made up to look like a restaurant. Two tables are set up, one in the center, the other on the right side of the stage with a man and woman sitting at it. At the center table sits Alison. On the left side in front of the insert is a counter with two bar stools in front. The waitress stands behind it, Tim sits in front of it nursing a drink and casting glances at Alison. The waitress comes from behind the bar and approaches her from the back.

Waitress Are you ready to order?

Alison No, I'm still waiting for my fiancé but he's not answering his phone.

Waitress Would you like another gin-and-tonic while you wait?

Alison I don't know. That would make three already. (*Pause*) Okay, and could you please drop a couple of cherries in it?

Waitress Together with the lime?

Alison Yes, I'm getting hungry waiting here.

Waitress Shall I bring you some breadsticks? We have onion and garlic flavored. Very delicious.

Alison Onion and garlic? No, thank you. This is supposed to be a romantic dinner.

Waitress Just the cherries then?

Alison Please.

Waitress Fine. (*She goes back to the bar, Alison picks up her phone from the table and tries calling. No answer. She looks at the screen, then puts the phone back down, frustrated.*)

Alison Great. No answer, no messages, from Irving, from anyone. (*Tim leaves the bar with his drink in hand and heads for Alison. She doesn't see him coming.*) What am I supposed to do, just sit here and read the menu?

Tim You can talk to me.

Alison (*Startled*) Good lord, you frightened me.

Tim Oh, sorry. (*Turns to walk away*)

Alison No, it's okay.

Tim In that case, do you mind if I sit down?

Alison Well, I'm kind of waiting for somebody.

Tim Aren't we all. (*Starts to sit down*)

Alison I'm waiting for my fiancé.

Tim Oh, sorry. (*Gets up to walk away again*)

Alison But you might as well stay. It doesn't look like he's coming.

Tim (*Interested, sitting down*) Good lord, stood up by your fiancé?

Alison (*Defensive*) He hasn't stood me up! He's just…late.

Tim Has he ever stood you up before? (*An extra goes to sit on Tim's stool at the bar and starts to make small talk with the waitress*)

Alison (*Annoyed*) I told you he hasn't stood me up.

Tim (*Consoling tone*) Look, it's okay. We've all been stood up before.

Alison (*Pointing to the bar*) You can go back to the bar any time now.

Tim (*Looking over his shoulder*) Hm, somebody took my seat. Looks like you're stuck with me.

Alison (*Dismayed*) I don't believe this.

Tim (*Contrite*) Look, I didn't mean to come across as such a...

Alison (*Snarling*) Creep?

Tim I was going to say asshole, but okay. It's just whenever I see a nice girl sitting all alone, she's always taken. It's so frustrating. Makes me want to go back to internet dating.

Alison (*Calmly, after a slight pause*) I met my fiancé through the internet.

Tim (*Bored*) Interesting. (*Pause*) Well, I think I'll go back to the bar and stand. (*Starts to get up; back at the bar the waitress is handed Alison's drink loaded with cherries through the insert*)

Alison (*Gesturing to him*) No, wait. I'm sorry too. Let's start over. (*He sits back down, the waitress approaches and places Alison's drink on the table in front of her.*)

Waitress Would you like another drink, sir?

Tim Sure. This time the same thing that the lady's drinking.

Waitress (*Incredulous*) Gin-and-tonic with lime and cherries?

Tim (*Shocked*) Cherries? (*Notices them in Alison's glass*) Sure, why not. (*The waitress goes back to the bar and quietly announces the order through the insert*)

Alison (*Munching on a cherry*) You like cherries?

Tim No. They're for you.

Alison (*Sitting back, smiling*) Listen, uh...

Tim Tim.

Alison Tim. You're very sweet. But I am engaged.

Tim And apparently hungry.

Alison But you should know I'm familiar with all the guy things.

Tim What guy things?

Alison Like how a man orders the same drink that a woman does because he thinks she will think he understands her and therefore it will be easier to get her into bed. (*Munching on another cherry*)

Tim (*Pretending to be surprised*) That doesn't work?

Alison (*Surly*) No.

Tim (*Hollering over his shoulder*) Yo, waitress, make that a whisky and soda.

Waitress Coming right up. (*The waitress relays the order through the insert*)

Alison (*Again dismayed*) I don't believe this! So you really had thoughts about coming over here to try and get me into bed?

Tim I have thoughts about getting every girl into bed. Look, I'm not married, I'm not a programmer, I don't surf the web. What else is there to do?

Alison Well, I appreciate your honesty. (*Taking a sip from her drink*)

Tim What about you? No thoughts about sleeping with another man while you're engaged?

Alison I'm not sure if that's any of your business, Tim. We just met.

Tim Yeah, I don't even know your name. (*Silence*) Do I have to ask for it?

Alison It's Alison. And my fiancé's name is Irving.

Tim (*Tiresomely*) Interesting. (*Pause*) So no thoughts about cheating on Irving? (*The waitress is handed the whiskey and heads for Tim*)

Alison No. And if I did, it certainly wouldn't be with some guy here at the restaurant.

Tim (*Pointing to the man sitting with the woman at the other table*) You mean that guy there? (*Alison laughs, the waitress approaches and sets his whiskey on the table.*)

Waitress Here you are, sir.

Tim Thanks. (*The waitress goes back to the bar, Tim picks up the glass and gives the cherries a long, dismissive look.*) I can't believe this. She still put the cherries in it.

Alison You asked her to.

Tim But that was only because I was trying to make a move on you. She couldn't figure that out?

Alison You know, it feels nice having a guy hit on me again. Irving and I have been together so long I almost forgot what that feels like.

Tim So you're not worried that he's getting cold feet and is in the process of bailing out? (*Takes a drink after giving the cherries another dismissive look*)

Alison (*Adamantly*) No way. He knows I'm on to all the guy things and

232

wouldn't dare do something like that.

Tim (*Tiresomely*) And which guy thing is this one?

Alison When you act like jerks so we end the relationship ourselves. Of course, you are jerks, but no way would we ever let you off so easily.

Tim That's for sure. I tried it with this one girl and she clung to me like a baby koala bear, despite all the nasty things I did to her.

Alison Exactly. No fooling us. (*Pause as she munches on another cherry*) So what kind of nasty things did you do to her? Don't tell me you slept with another woman?

Tim (*Matter-of-factly*) That too, but probably the worst thing I did was ignore her. (*Takes another labored drink*)

Alison (*Wounded*) That is the worst.

Tim What do you say you take all these cherries off my hands? Cherry Coke I can live with, but no way cherry whiskey.

Alison Thanks. (*Reaching over, she holds her glass next to his with one hand and uses three fingers from her other hand to scoop his cherries into her glass. He's surprised and impressed.*) What's the matter, Tim? Afraid of women who go for it?

Tim No, not at all. I just thought a spoon might be easier. (*Picking up a table napkin*) Need one of these?

Alison For what? (*Suggestively licking her fingers clean*)

Tim (*Stunned, then snapping out of it*) So where the hell is Irving then?

Alison I have no idea. (*Pause, munches on another cherry*) But if he doesn't get here soon, he's going to find me drunk with another man.

Tim (*Puts his glasses on the table*) I'm sorry, Alison, but I have to say something that you're going to think is a real guy thing.

Alison What's that?

Tim I have the feeling you are one deep woman inside.

Alison (*Unsure*) Thanks, but how is that a guy thing?

Tim You know, complimenting a woman on what's inside her, not what's on the outside. That way she thinks he's a deep guy, ready for a serious relationship.

Alison (*Laughs*) Ah, the trouble you men go through. But, just for the sake of conversation, what do you think of my, you know, outside? (*Looking coyly as she takes a sip*)

Tim Would it be a total guy thing to say you look really elastic?

Alison (*Confused*) I'm not sure I know what that means.

Tim That you're very nimble. Know how to stretch. (*She's still confused*) A really athletic girl.

Alison (*Relieved, putting her drink down*) Ah. Well, I was a cheerleader in high school.

Tim You still look like one. (*Takes a sip*)

Alison (*Laughs*) Now that's a guy thing! (*Pause*) And I love it. Ah, Tim, thanks for keeping me company. It's too bad we can't have dinner here together. (*Another cherry*)

Tim Why not?

Alison Are you crazy? What if Irving walks in?

Tim You still think he's coming?

Alison (*Looking at her watch, then at her phone*) No.

Tim Great. (*Hollering over his shoulder*) Waitress!

Alison (*Nervously*) No. Maybe he's held up somewhere. He could be walking through that door any minute now.

Tim I know a nice place not too far from here.

Alison I don't know, Tim. I would feel guilty here or there.

Tim Then at least I can see to it that you get safely home.

Alison (*Meditatively*) Yes, that would be nice of you. And if I get hungry on the way, we can always stop somewhere.

Tim Sure. (*The waitress approaches*)

Waitress Yes, sir?

Tim (*To Alison*) Would it be a guy thing to offer to pay for your drinks?

Alison No, that would be a gentleman thing.

Tim Sounds good to me. (*Hands the waitresses some bills from his pocket*) There you go.

Waitress Thank you, sir. Have a good evening.

Tim You too. (*Leaves with Alison through the exit*)

Waitress (*Out loud*) Oh, Irving, you're in a fine fix now.

Scene five

The elevator again, the music again. Irving, looking really haggard, is sitting with his legs crossed and holding the calculator. He's doing arithmetic guessing, first calling out the numbers and then checking the results with the calculator. His whole demeanor suggests that of a man losing his mind.

Irving Hah, I knew it! Irving's got this down pat! Okay, let's try a real ball breaker: 4,127 times 391. (*Plugs the numbers into the calculator*) Hah, again! No fooling this boy! The screen ain't even big enough to hold my answers. Okay, let's work our way down. 6,124 times 819. (*Plugs the numbers into the calculator*) Of course, of course! He's the man, the man of the hour! No mistaking that! God, if only the rest of the world could see how good I really am! Okay, now it's double or nothing. Now it's time to really show who the master wizard here is. 12,500 divided by... what the hell, 75. And the answer is... (*Plugs the numbers into the calculator*) What?! That can't be right! It's not possible! (*Plugs the numbers into the calculator*) What!! It's not true! I'm the math wizard here, not you! You're no better than that piece of shit lighter. Well, I didn't take it from it and I'll be damned if I take it from you! (*He tosses the calculator violently against the wall, smashing it*) Oh no, what have I done? I didn't want to do that. I swear I didn't. It's just that...that... Oh no! (*Picking up the pieces of the calculator in his hands*) Forgive me! Please forgive me! Please, won't all of you forgive me!! (*He buries his head in his hands crying. Darkness on stage.*)

Scene six

The wall is again slid shut to make the scene resemble a restaurant different from the one in the second scene. A table is set up in the front center, another one at the back left with two different people sitting there, and this time the bar is on the right side. Judy and Emma sit at the bar while Gracie, dressed as a waitress, is clearing the center table.

Judy (*Looking at Gracie, frustrated*) Finally, I'm starved.

Emma Poor girl. Has to work a day job, night job and weekend job, all to pay for an apartment in mid-town.

Judy It's her choice. She could live in a dump like us too but she decided she wanted something more upscale.

Emma You know, I'm getting tired of you calling our home a dump. Do you wanna live in mid-town too? Do you wanna be waiting tables at night while I mop floors in the supermarket?

Judy Well, what else is there to do?

Emma (*Flustered*) What else? Gee, you know... (*Tim enters from the left, walks up to Gracie, whispers something into her ear and hands her some money. Gracie nods and Tim exits.*)

Judy What I know is this, Em. At home you spend all your time in front of the TV, the internet or the refrigerator.

Emma While you're on the phone talking or texting. In front of all three, I might add! (*Gracie finishes cleaning the table and walks behind the bar*)

Gracie Sorry, guys, I got some bad news: This fellow just walked in and booked the table.

Judy What?!

Emma But you're clearing it for us.

Gracie I know, but you don't have a reservation.

Judy Apparently this fellow didn't either if he just walked in.

Gracie But he greased me a ten. Sorry, but this is how I make most of my wages here.

Judy Fine, we'll grease you too. Em, give her a ten. (*Emma reaches into her back pocket*)

Gracie Come on, I can't take money from you guys. Look, I told you how it was here. But I swear, the next table is yours.

Judy At least give us something to snack on while we wait. Got any breadsticks?

Gracie (*Looking behind the bar*) Looks like we're all out. Here, have some cherries. (*Places a bowl of cherries in front of them. Sees Tim entering with Alison and goes to escort them to the table.*) Right this way if you please. (*Alison sits with her back to Judy and Emma, Tim sits down opposite her. Gracie hands them each a menu.*) Would you like to start with a drink?

Alison Gin and tonic.

Tim Whiskey and soda.

Alison Put lots of cherries in mine, please.

Gracie (*Surprised*) Wouldn't you rather have lime in that?

Tim (*Serious*) She said cherries.

Gracie Very well.

Tim And put lots of cherries in mine as well.

Gracie Wouldn't you rather have ice in that?

Tim I said cherries.

Gracie Very well. (*She goes back to behind the bar to start fixing the drinks. Tim and Alison make small talk.*)

Emma (*Looking behind him towards the table*) That's the guy who greased you a ten? Looks like a programmer.

Judy (*Craning her neck to look*) At least he knows how to treat a lady.

Emma Oh yeah? Well, I would also like to be the lady for once!

Gracie Come on, guys, don't fight. This is supposed to be a classy joint. (*Starts dishing all the cherries into the gin and tonic*)

Judy What are you doing?

Gracie The lady ordered cherries in her drink.

Judy That bitch! First she takes our table, now my cherries. (*Gracie dishes the rest of cherries into the whiskey*) Now what are you doing?

Gracie The guy with her ordered the same for his whiskey. Looks like they're in for something kinky tonight.

Emma (*Tiresomely*) Lucky couple.

Judy (*Sarcastically*) Hey, you were the one who ate all the ice cream, not me! (*The argument at the bar continues in quieter tones. Mr. and Mrs. Waters enter. Alison notices them and ducks her head down.*)

Alison (*Panicky*) Oh, no, it's Irving's parents.

Tim Where? Behind us? (*Starts to turn around*)

Alison Don't turn around! I can't let them see me with you, not until I've told Irving.

Tim Well, we can't sit here with our heads on the table. The waitress will stop bringing us drinks before we've even had the first ones.

Alison This is no time to be making jokes. (*Gracie comes from behind the bar with their drinks and places them before them. She gives Alison a quick curious look before approaching the Waterses.*) It looks pretty full here. She'll probably tell them they'll have to come back later.

Gracie Good evening. Do you have a reservation?

Mr. Waters Not exactly. I kept getting a busy signal every time I tried to call to make one.

Gracie I'm sorry about that, sir, but we're all full right now. It's about a 45-minute wait for a table, I'm afraid.

Mr. Waters I'm sure we can do better than that. (*He greases her a ten*)

Gracie I'm sure we can too. Now let's see...(*Scanning the restaurant*)

Alison Oh no, Mr. Waters just greased the waitress. God, I hate when people do that.

Emma Oh no, that old guy just greased Gracie. She's going to seat them before us.

Judy What? Go over there and stop her!

Emma How?

Judy I don't know, but if you do it, we'll talk kinky tonight.

Gracie Yes, sir, if you'll just follow me. (*He starts leading the Waterses across the stage. Mrs. Waters stops when she notices Alison crouching there.*)

Mrs. Waters Why, Alison. What an unexpected surprise.

Alison Oh, hello, Mrs. Waters. Mr. Waters. Fancy seeing you here?

Mrs. Waters I should say. (*Looking at Tim*) Aren't you going to introduce us to your friend here?

Alison (*Bucking up the courage*) With pleasure. (*Tim rises*) Mr. and Mrs. Waters, this is Tim. Tim, these are Irving's parents.

Tim Nice to meet you.

Mrs. Waters Nice to meet you.

Mr. Waters Young man. Darling, the waitress is waiting.

Mrs. Waters Yes. Well, Alison, have a nice meal. I guess we'll meet some time to pick out the floral arrangement. (*Mr. Waters ushers her behind Gracie*)

Alison (*Standing abruptly*) Mrs. Waters. There's something I have to tell you. You too, Mr. Waters.

Mr. Waters Yes?

Alison I'm afraid the engagement is off. Irving and I are not getting married.

Mrs. Waters (*Shocked*) What? This is sudden.

Alison I think you should hear it from Irving and me or at least from Irving, but circumstances have decided otherwise.

Mrs. Waters And how did this all come about?

Mr. Waters Dear, we're standing in the middle of a restaurant. We can discuss it later.

Alison I'm sorry it has to happen this way. I'm even sorrier I haven't told Irving yet.

Mrs. Waters You haven't told Irving yet? And you're already seeing another man? (*Indicating Tim*)

Alison Not exactly. Please, if you could sit with us for a moment, I'll explain everything.

Mrs. Waters (*To Gracie*) Thank you. We'll be having dinner here. (*She sits down*)

Mr. Waters Dear, we shouldn't intrude like this.

Mrs. Waters It's not an intrusion so long as it concerns our son. (*To Tim*) Isn't that right, young man?

Tim Well, actually...

Mrs. Waters Good lord, look at all those cherries in your drinks.

Gracie Can I get you a drink in the meantime?

Mr. Waters (*Waving her off. Gracie goes back behind the bar*) Dear, really...

Mrs. Waters Will you please sit down. (*To Tim*) You too young man. (*Mr. Waters and Tim grudgingly sit down*) Now, Alison, what's this all about? (*Small talk commences at the table between the two ladies*)

Emma What the hell is going on over there?

Gracie I don't know. Apparently the older couple found out that that woman there has been two-timing their son. (*Judy twists her body to look behind her*)

Judy I don't believe this! That's Alison, Irving's girl. And that sure as hell ain't Irving sitting with her.

Gracie That's Alison? I thought I had seen her somewhere before.

Emma Irving's girlfriend is named Alison?

Judy So Irving's parents stumbled in on an affair she's having behind their son's back?

Gracie Looks like it.

Emma I guess that means they'll all be having dinner together. You can give us the table you were going to give his parents for greasing you.

Judy Forget it, Em. I'm not missing this.

Alison So I wanted to tell Irving, was hoping to tell him, but he hasn't been answering his phone all weekend and I haven't got a clue where he is.

Mrs. Waters Be that as it may, dear, there is decorum to think about here. You just don't start up with another man until you've notified the first one. Otherwise, you're just cheating, plain and simple.

Alison Rest assured, Mrs. Waters, Tim and I haven't started anything up. We're, ah, old friends, that's all.

Mrs. Waters Mr. Waters here and I were also old friends and look how we ended up.

Mr. Waters Half-starved, for one thing.

Mrs. Waters Oh, stop it. Your son is about to get some terrible news and all you can think about is your stomach.

Mr. Waters If you get terrible news, it's because you deserve it.

Mrs. Waters Are you saying our son deserves to be treated this way?

Mr. Waters Yes, he does. Alison just told you that standing her up like this was the final straw. That boy has always been unreliable and undependable and we have you to thank for that.

Mrs. Waters So it's my fault?

Mr. Waters That's right, it is. Always waiting on him hand and foot, never letting him finish anything on his own. You made him into a mama's boy.

Mrs. Waters Well, maybe if you had shown him a little more attention.

Alison Look, Mr. and Mrs. Waters, it's really nobody's fault here. It's just the way things ended up.

Tim That's right. I'm sure your boy has some good qualities.

Mr. Waters How the hell would you know? You don't even know him.

Mrs. Waters You don't know him either.

Mr. Waters Like hell I don't! The boy is 30 years old and still living at home with us! How the hell could I not know him? (*The argument continues at the table*)

Judy Looks like things are getting out of hand over there. Do you think Irving's father and that guy will get into a slugging match?

Emma Hey, Gracie, maybe you'd better get over there and separate them.

Gracie (*Coming from behind the bar*) I have a better idea. You two come with me. I'll pretend I'm leading you to your table, you see Alison there, and say hello.

Judy (*Excitedly jumps to her feet*) Great, let's do it.

Emma (*Ironically*) Okay, but I get to be the lady this time. (*They follow Gracie to the table. As they pass by, Judy leans over to Alison.*)

Judy Alison, is that you?

Alison (*Unsurely*) Yes.

Judy It's me. Judy. I work with your fiancé, Irving. And this is my fiancée, Emma. She also works with Irving.

Emma (*Mumbling*) We're engaged? (*She pokes her. Tim and Mr. Waters cast observant looks at Judy and Emma.*)

Mrs. Waters Oh, great. So everybody will know that the engagement is off except for my son.

Alison I told you, Mrs. Waters. I've been trying to contact Irving to tell him, but he's not answering his cell phone.

Judy That's because he left it at the office.

Alison/Mrs. Waters At the office?

Judy Yeah, it was still on his desk when we left. So we gave it to the security guard for safekeeping until he gets back to work tomorrow.

Mrs. Waters Did he say anything about where he was going? Because he hasn't been home all weekend.

Judy No, he said he was going down for a cigarette break and never came back.

Alison/Mrs. Waters He smokes?

Gracie All we know is he left the office and never came back.

Mr. Waters How the hell would you know?

Gracie I'm sorry, I also work with your son at the firm. I do this job part time to pay for my apartment in mid-town.

Emma Look, people, this is all very interesting, but it doesn't answer the question where Irving is.

Mrs. Waters Good lord, you don't suppose something has happened to him?

Mr. Waters What could have happened to him? He's probably in some dive with his friends right now.

Mrs. Waters Irving doesn't have any friends. Only co-workers and ex-fiancées, it would seem.

Mr. Waters That's beside the point. Let's wait to see what happens tomorrow before we go off and panic.

Mrs. Waters That's just like you. Put everything off till Monday morning! Well, I'm going home right this instant and start making some phone calls. (*She rises*)

Mr. Waters At least wait until we've had supper.

Mrs. Waters (*Leaving*) Stuff your face for all I care. I'm going to look for my son. (*Exits*)

Mr. Waters (*Throwing a napkin on the table*) Perfect! I should have thrown that boy out of the house the minute he finished college. (*Rises and leaves, then turns around to Gracie*) Under the circumstances, young lady, I'm afraid I'll have to ask for my tip back. (*Gracie grudgingly* *reaches into her pocket and hands him the ten. Mr. Waters exits.)*

Alison Do you really think something could have happened to Irving? He never stood me up before. I wished you had taken his phone with you.

Emma (*Casting a snide look at Judy*) Yeah, whose idea was it to leave it with the security guard?

Judy (*Angrily*) I guess you can kiss kinky goodbye right now.

Alison Tim, I think under the circumstances, we can try this again another night.

Tim Yeah, sure. (*Rises, followed by Alison*)

Alison I think I will go to your office tomorrow to straighten this thing out personally with Irving. Please don't say anything to him if you see him before I do.

Emma Of course not.

Judy You can count on us. (*Gracie nods*)

Alison Well, goodbye. (*Leaving*)

Emma/Judy/Gracie Goodbye.

Tim Goodbye. It was nice to almost meet you. (*Starts to leave, then turns to Gracie*) Sorry, but I think under the circumstances... (*Gracie grudgingly digs into her pocket and hands him a ten. Alison and Tim exit.*)

Gracie Perfect! And nobody waiting to be seated either.

Judy Not entirely. (*She quickly sits down, followed by Emma*) Menus, please. (*Lights off*)

Scene seven

The tables, bar and all the chairs except one are removed. Irving is now hallucinating that he's in a psychiatrist's office. He's lying on the stage floor, the lone light fixed on him. The psychiatrist, wearing a white physician's coat and glasses with her hair tied up in the back, is hidden in the shadows.

Voice of the psychiatrist Irving? (*He doesn't respond*) Irving? (*She enters the pool of light carrying a chair and pen and notebook. She kicks him.*) Irving, pay attention! (*She sits down on the chair, crosses her legs, ready to jot down notes. She intermittently writes as he speaks.*)

Irving (*Startled*) I'm sorry. What did you say?

Psychiatrist I asked you to tell me about your parents.

Irving My parents? There's nothing to tell. They're just mom and dad.

Psychiatrist Do they get along?

Irving Hah, they never got along. Always fighting about stupid little things.

Psychiatrist Like what?

Irving Like what's for dinner, where's my newspaper, why don't you get off your ass...That kind of crap.

Psychiatrist Do they ever argue about you?

Irving Me?

Psychiatrist Yes, you. You still live at home, don't you?

Irving Yes, but I'm no trouble. I go to work, go home, I try to stay out of their hair. I sometimes buy groceries, help with the laundry.

Psychiatrist But you're 30 years old. Shouldn't you have left the nest a long time ago?

Irving I don't know. I'm happy where I am so...why bother?

Psychiatrist What do your colleagues think about that?

Irving I don't know. I work with a bunch of women. They only talk about themselves and their problems.

Psychiatrist And do you listen to them?

Irving No, because it's always the same old story. Gracie is constantly whining about having to pay for a new apartment, and Judy and Emma are always bringing their personal relationship into the office.

Psychiatrist What relationship is that?

Irving They're a couple. Lesbians. Always arguing over who gets to be the lady. Christ, get yourself a man, I say, and then it's simple. I mean they squabble all the time. I used to fantasize about being in a relationship with more than one woman, and then I met those two.

Psychiatrist Do you have any other fantasies, Irving?

Irving What do you mean?

Psychiatrist What about your girlfriend?

Irving My girlfriend? I don't know. We've been sleeping together for six years. What else is there to fantasize about?

Psychiatrist I'm not talking about sex, Irving? Do you ever fantasize about her being different in any other way?

Irving In any other way?

Psychiatrist Oh God, Irving, wake up! I'm talking about your girlfriend as a person, the one you're going to marry and spend the rest of your life with? Is there something you would like to change about her?

Irving Well, even if I could, it's too late now.

Psychiatrist Irving, I'm giving you the chance once and for all to come to terms with the woman you love. What's her name anyway?

Irving Alison.

Psychiatrist So, is there anything about Alison you would like to change?

Irving (*Hesitantly*) Well, sometimes she... I mean I wish... you know like... if she would only...

Psychiatrist Yes, Irving?

Irving If only she knew right now that I didn't stand her up, that I really do want to marry her, have kids with her. So what if she's not out looking for me right now? Nobody is. Important is we'll still have each other in the end.

Psychiatrist Good. Now let's talk about the sex. No problem there?

Irving Not really, but if only she would...

Psychiatrist Would what?

Irving I don't know how to say this but... You see, I would like to take her to some island for our honeymoon. I have all these fantasies about us kissing under a waterfall and rolling together in the waves.

Psychiatrist And you don't think she would like that?

Irving I'm sure she would, but when we get there, she'll start worrying about our passports, and getting to the hotel safely, and what time breakfast is. All that organizational crap. I want to let go. Have a woman to do all that island crap with instead.

Psychiatrist You're right. You're absolutely right and I, for one, think you deserve it, Irving.

Irving Thank you, but what good does it do me now?

Psychiatrist Oh, I think it can do you a lot of good. (*The psychiatrist stands up and snaps her fingers. A dream girl enters from the left.*) What do you think?

Irving (*Jumps up*) Oh, she's beautiful!

Psychiatrist Yes, and she's ready to go with you to the island.

Irving With me?

Psychiatrist That's right. You will relax, drink margaritas and have hot monkey sex on the beach. Sound good to you?

Irving What about Alison?

Psychiatrist Don't worry. You'll be back in time to help her clean the windows for Christmas. No problem.

Irving Is life really that simple?

Psychiatrist It is now. Ready to go?

Irving (*A moment's hesitation*) Sure! What do I gotta do?

Psychiatrist (*Pointing to the elevator*) Just step right in there.

Irving (*Also pointing*) In there? No way! That place is a hellhole. I'm never going back in there!

Psychiatrist Irving, you're hallucinating. It's a fantasy portal. All you have to do is follow her in.

Irving (*Unsure*) I don't know.

Psychiatrist Come on, Irving. Are you a man or not?

Irving Well...

Psychiatrist (*Enticingly*) Hot monkey sex.

Irving (*Pause*) All right! I'll do it. (*He points to the dream girl*) She'll still look like that on the island, right?

Psychiatrist Just like that.

Irving Oh, mother of Jesus! All right, let's do it. (*The dream girl steps into the elevator, followed by Irving. The stage goes dark.*) Hey, what happened? Where's the island? Where'd the girl go?

Psychiatrist (*Laughing*) Oh, Irving, you're so naïve.

Irving (*Banging on the door*) Hey, come on! You tricked me! Let me out! This isn't fair!

Psychiatrist Nothing in life is, Irving. But don't worry. I'm not going to leave you in there all alone. I have something else for you.

Irving (*Whimpering*) What? (*The psychiatrist snaps her fingers and the elevator music comes on.*) No, no, no!!!

Scene eight

The wall is slid shut and the stage set up to resemble the reception area of an office building, with the desk standing to the right, profile to the audience. The guard and Alison enter from the left.

Guard I told you, miss, I'm just opening the building up now. I don't know a thing about this guy.

Alison (*Showing him a picture*) At least look at his picture here.

Guard (*Takes the picture*) This guy?

Alison Yes.

Guard Did you say he was a designer?

Alison Yes.

Guard Looks like a programmer.

Alison But have you seen him?

Guard I don't know. I just got here. (*Handing her the picture back*) Look, I've got to open this place up before the employees start arriving. (*He goes to the reception desk*)

Alison (*Looking fearful*) Oh, dear. (*Emma, Judy, Gracie enter*)

Judy Alison, here quite early. Afraid we were going to tell Irving before you got here?

Alison No, I couldn't sleep all night. I'm really afraid something happened to him. I asked the guard there but he says he knows nothing.

Gracie Nothing new.

Guard I heard that. Look, folks, if you've got a missing person, I suggest you go down to the police station and file a report. Otherwise let me do my job here.

Emma But you did lock away his cell phone and laptop like we asked you to?

Guard Yes, the cell phone and laptop you gave me are nicely tucked away. But it's in the electronic safe and I can't retrieve them from there until power has been restored throughout the building.

Emma You mean power has been off in the building all weekend?

Guard Yes. We have a new lockdown policy to conserve power, cut costs and thwart terrorists. Only essentials like servers and elevators are still connected.

Gracie Why elevators if nobody's here?

Guard They're hooked up to the same power supply. Can't shut one down without shutting the other one down as well. That's why we have to personally lock them down.

Emma Is it possible, just possible, that Irving was still inside the building when you locked it up? That he has in fact been locked inside here all weekend?

Alison Dear god!

Guard No chance. I did an entire sweep of this building beforehand. If he was still in here, he had to be hiding on purpose and I won't be responsible for any foolhardy act like that.

Judy Why would he be hiding in here?

Guard How the hell should I know? I don't even know the man! (*Mr. and Mrs. Waters enter*)

Mrs. Waters All right, everyone, I've had enough of this. I want to know where my son is and I want to know now.

Guard Now who are these people?!

Alison We're sorry, Mrs. Waters, but he hasn't shown up for work yet. But maybe he will be in at any moment.

Mrs. Waters I'm not falling for this nonsense anymore. I want to know where he is right now!

Mr. Waters The boy's all right. Will you just let him be a man for a change?

Emma (*To the guard*) You said something about locking out the elevators.

Guard Yeah, to thwart burglars and terrorists. You got a problem with that?

Emma No, but did you sweep the elevators before you locked them out?

Guard If I'm not mistaken, you rode down with me in the elevator.

Gracie One elevator. What about the other one?

Guard The other one?

Emma/Gracie Yeah, there are two elevators in this building.

Guard (*Nervously*) Well, of course I swept it. But I can guarantee nobody was in it between that time and the time I threw the disable switch.

Gracie And when did you throw the switch?

Guard I don't know. Before we rode down in the other elevator. Five, maybe ten minutes.

Emma Good lord, Irving could be in that elevator right now. Locked in there the entire weekend!

Alison Oh my God!

Mrs. Waters What? My poor baby trapped in here this whole time. With no food or water?

Guard People, people, just relax. Now I don't know nothing about anybody being in no elevator, but the only way we're going to find out for sure is for me to start them again and then we'll know. Actually we would have known ten minutes ago if you would have let me come in and do my job.

Judy Will you just start the thing, for chrissakes!

Guard All right, all right. Tell you one thing, being a bus driver was a whole lot easier than this crap. (*The guard exits. The cast gathers around the entrance to the elevator waiting for it to descend. A ring is heard, Mrs. Waters and Alison scream, the cast part to show Irving looking* *dazed and out of his mind.*)

Mrs. Waters My poor baby!

Alison Irving, darling, you poor man!

Mr. Waters Son, what did they do to you? (*He, Mrs. Waters and Alison grab Irving and drag him out of the elevator to the side. He lies there flat as the three try to revive him.*)

Emma Irving, are you okay? (*The guard enters*)

Guard So everyone happy? (*He sees Irving lying there and jumps in shock*) Shit, he was in there?

Judy (*Pushing the guard*) You call that sweeping an elevator? You locked the poor man in there all weekend!

Guard How was I to know he was in there after I swept it? Is it my fault he gets in there before I have a chance to switch it off?

Gracie So why didn't you hang an "out of order sign" on the door?

Guard Where am I supposed to find an "out of order" sign at five o'clock on a Friday? You know you people are really starting to get on my nerves. (*Walks inside the elevator to check it out as the others put Irving in the sitting position*)

Mrs. Waters Irving, dear, are you all right? Can you speak? (*Irving tries to speak but can only mumble gibberish*)

Alison Oh, Irving, you poor, poor darling.

Mrs. Waters Ach, spare us your sympathy now. Go to your new man.

Alison Please, Mrs. Waters, we should be thinking about Irving now.

Irving (*Still dazed*) New man?

Mrs. Waters Maybe you should have been thinking about him all weekend.

Mr. Waters For god's sake, women, the poor boy must be hungry and thirsty. Let's get him to a restaurant where he can get washed up and have a healthy breakfast. How about that, son? Does that sound good? (*Lifting Irving to his feet*)

Irving New man?

Alison Nothing, darling. I'll explain everything to you later. Let's do as your father says.

Mrs. Waters As he says? Hah! He didn't even want to come here this morning.

Mr. Waters Will you just shut up for five minutes! Come on, son. (*He races Irving out the exit with Alison and Mrs. Waters following*)

Guard (*Emerging from the elevator*) Hold on there, people. (*Exhibiting a cigarette and lighter*) It looks like your Mr. Irving was smoking in the elevator. That's a violation of one of the most important safety rules in this building. I'm afraid we're going to have to take him downtown to the police.

Gracie Are you out of your mind? After what you just put that man through? You're the one they should take downtown!

Judy Yeah!

Emma (*Grabbing the guard by the arm and showing him the cigarette*) Yeah, and it's clear he wasn't even smoking.

Guard The rule says even the intent to smoke is a violation.

Emma Well, maybe, just maybe, he was hoping to do it in order to set off the fire alarm so somebody would come and rescue him from the elevator.

Guard So why didn't the fire alarm go off?

Emma I don't know. (*Taking the lighter from the guard*) Maybe the lighter wasn't working. (*Tries it. It works.*) Look, cut the guy some slack. How would you like to be stuck in there all weekend?

Guard I used to work in a coal mine, so I know all about being stuck in cramped places. Dark and wet too, without any nice music like this either.

Emma Come on. You saw how he looks. He must be practically out of his mind sitting in there with no food or drink.

Judy Or phone.

Gracie Or a bathroom, for chrissakes!

Guard All right. Go to your friend. Besides, I may need you people on my side when I have to go and explain this thing to the building supervisor.

Emma Thanks. (*Starts to leave with Judy and Gracie. The guard turns and goes back into the elevator doorway.*)

Judy What are you thanking that moron for?

Guard I heard that! (*They exit. The guard starts sniffing around in the elevator*) What is that... (*More sniffing*) That smells like...Why, that son of a bitch. He took a leak in the elevator! That's it! That boy's going downtown! (*The lights go off*) Hey! What happened? Who closed the doors? Come on, it's dark in here. Hey, open up. This isn't funny! Come on, open up... (*Curtain*).